Praise for
Anne Perry's Charlotte
and
Thomas Pitt mysteries

FARRIERS' LANE

"[A] devious affair of passion and political intrigue in Victorian London."
—*The New York Times Book Review*

BELGRAVE SQUARE

"So pulsates with the sights and sounds of Victorian London that the reader soon gets caught up in Anne Perry's picaresque story of life, love, and murder that involves both the upper and lower classes of that colorful era."
—*The Pittsburgh Press*

HIGHGATE RISE

"When it comes to the Victorian mystery, Anne Perry has proved that nobody does it better. Once again, her recreation of its manners and morality, fashions and foibles is masterful."
—*The San Diego Union-Tribune*

SILENCE IN HANOVER CLOSE

"[A] complex, gripping and highly satisfying mystery...An adroit blend of thick London atmosphere and a convincing cast...A totally surprising yet wonderfully plausible finale."
—*Publishers Weekly*

By Anne Perry
Published by Fawcett/Ivy Books:

Featuring Thomas and Charlotte Pitt:
THE CATER STREET HANGMAN
CALLANDER SQUARE
PARAGON WALK
RESURRECTION ROW
BLUEGATE FIELDS
RUTLAND PLACE
DEATH IN THE DEVIL'S ACRE
CARDINGTON CRESCENT
SILENCE IN HANOVER CLOSE
BETHLEHEM ROAD
HIGHGATE RISE
BELGRAVE SQUARE
FARRIERS' LANE
THE HYDE PARK HEADSMAN
TRAITORS GATE
PENTECOST ALLEY
ASHWORTH HALL
BRUNSWICK GARDENS

Featuring William Monk:
THE FACE OF A STRANGER
A DANGEROUS MOURNING
DEFEND AND BETRAY
A SUDDEN, FEARFUL DEATH
THE SINS OF THE WOLF
CAIN HIS BROTHER
WEIGHED IN THE BALANCE
THE SILENT CRY
A BREACH OF PROMISE

THE CATER STREET HANGMAN

Anne Perry

FAWCETT CREST • NEW YORK

A Fawcett Crest Book
Published by The Ballantine Publishing Group
Copyright © 1979 by Anne Perry

www.randomhouse.com/BB/

ISBN 0-449-20867-2

This edition published by arrangement with St. Martin's Press.

All the characters in this book are fictitious, and any resemblance to actual persons living or dead is purely coincidental.

Manufactured in the United States of America

First Fawcett Crest Edition: September 1980
First Ballantine Books Edition: December 1985

30 29 28 27 26 25 24

Charlotte Ellison stood in the centre of the withdrawing room, the newspaper in her hand. Her father had been very lax in leaving it on the side table. He disapproved of her reading such things, preferring to tell her such matters of interest as he felt suitable for young ladies to know. And this excluded all scandal, personal or political, all matters of a controversial nature, and naturally all crime of any sort: in fact just about everything that was interesting!

All of which meant that since Charlotte had to obtain her newspapers from the pantry where the butler, Maddock, put them for his own reading before throwing them out, she was always at least a day behind the rest of London.

However, this was today's paper, 20 April 1881, and the most arresting news was the death the day before of Mr. Disraeli. Her first thought was to wonder how Mr. Gladstone felt. Did he feel any sense of loss? Was a great enemy as much a part of a man's life as a great friend? Surely it must be. It must be the cross thread in the fabric of emotions.

There were footsteps in the hall and she put the paper away quickly. She had not forgotten her father's fury when he had found her reading an evening journal three years ago. Of course, then it had been about the libel case between Mr. Whistler and Mr. Ruskin, and that was a little different. But even last year when she had expressed interest in the news of the Zulu War, reported in person by those who had actually been in Africa, he had viewed that with equal disfavour. He had refused even to read them selected pieces such as he considered suitable. In the end it had been Dominic, her sister's husband, who had regaled her with all he could remember—but always at least one day late.

At the thought of Dominic, Mr. Disraeli and the whole matter of newspapers vanished. From the time Dominic had first presented himself six years ago when Sarah had been only twenty, Charlotte herself seventeen, and Emily only thirteen, she had been fascinated by him. Of course, it was Sarah he had called on; Charlotte was only permitted into the drawing room with her mother so that the occasions might be conducted with all the decorum suitable to a courtship. Dominic had barely seen her, his words polite nothings, his eyes somewhere over her left shoulder, seeing Sarah's fair hair, her delicately boned face. Charlotte, with her heavy, mahogany-coloured hair that was so difficult to keep tidy, her stronger face, was only an encumbrance to be endured with good manners.

A year later, of course, they had married, and Dominic no longer held quite the same mystery. He no longer moved in the magical world of someone else's romance. But even with five years of knowledge of each other, of living under the same spacious, well-ordered roof, he still exerted the original charm, the original fascination for her.

That had been his footstep in the hall. She knew it without conscious thought. It was there, part of her life: listening for him, seeing him first in a crowd, knowing where he was in the room, remembering whatever he said, even trivial things.

She had come to terms with it. Dominic had always been out of reach. It was not as if he had ever cared for her, or could have done. She had not expected it. One day perhaps she would meet someone she could like and respect, someone suitable, and Mother would speak with him, see that he was socially and personally acceptable; and of course Father would make the other arrangements, whatever they were, as he had done with Dominic and Sarah, and no doubt would do with Emily and someone, in due course. It was not something she wished to think about, but it remained permanently in the future. The present was Dominic, this house, her parents, Emily and Sarah, and Grandmama; the present was Aunt Susannah coming to tea in two hours' time and the fact that the footsteps in the hall had gone away again, leaving her free to take another quick look at the newspaper.

Her mother came in a few moments later, so quietly Charlotte did not hear her.

"Charlotte."

It was too late to hide what she was doing. She lowered the paper and looked into her mother's brown eyes.

"Yes, Mama." It was an admission.

"You know how your father feels about your looking at those things." She glanced at the folded paper in Charlotte's hand. "I can't imagine why you want to; there's very little in them that's pleasant, and your father will read those things out to us. But if you must look at it for yourself, at least do it discreetly, in Maddock's pantry, or get Dominic to tell you."

Charlotte felt the colour flood her face. She looked away. She had had no idea her mother knew about Maddock's pantry, even less about Dominic! Had Dominic told her? Why should that thought hurt, like a betrayal? That was ridiculous. She could have no secrets with Dominic. What had she let herself imagine?

7

"Yes, of course, Mama. I'm sorry." She dropped the paper behind her onto the table. "I shan't let Papa catch me."

"If you want to read, why don't you read books? There's something of Mr. Dickens' in the bookcase over there, and I'm sure you haven't read Mr. Disraeli's *Coningsby* yet?"

Funny how people always say they are sure when they mean they are not sure.

"Mr. Disraeli died yesterday," Charlotte replied. "I wouldn't enjoy it. Not just at the moment."

"Mr. Disraeli? Oh dear, I am sorry. I never cared for Mr. Gladstone, but don't tell your father. He always reminds me of the vicar."

Charlotte felt disposed to giggle.

"Don't you like the vicar, Mama?"

Her mother composed herself immediately.

"Yes, of course I do. Now please go and prepare yourself for tea. Have you forgotten Aunt Susannah is coming to call on us this afternoon?"

"But not for an hour and a half, at the soonest," Charlotte protested.

"Then do some embroidery, or add some more to that painting you were working on yesterday."

"It didn't go right—"

"Grammar, Charlotte. It didn't go *well*. I'm sorry. Perhaps you had better finish the comforters so you can take them to the vicar's wife tomorrow. I promised we would deliver them."

"Do you suppose they really comfort the poor?" It was a sincere question.

"I've no idea." Her mother's face relaxed slightly as the thought occurred to her, obviously for the first time. "I don't think I've ever known anyone really poor. But the vicar assures us they do, and we must presume he knows."

"Even if we don't like him very much."

"Charlotte, please don't be impertinent." But there was nothing harsh in her voice. She had been caught in an unintentional truth and she did not resent it. She was annoyed with herself, perhaps, but not with Charlotte.

Obediently, Charlotte left the room to go upstairs. She might as well finish the comforters; it would have to be done sometime.

Tea was served by Dora, the kitchen maid, in the withdrawing room. Tea was the most erratic affair. It was always at four o'clock, and always (when they were home) in this room with its pale green furniture and the big windows onto the lawn, closed now, even though the clear spring sun was slanting onto the grass and the last of the daffodils. It was a small garden, only a few yards of lawn, a patch of flowers, and the single delicate birch tree against the wall. Climbing the old brickwork were the roses Charlotte loved best. The whole summer from June till November was glorious with them, old roses, rambling undisciplined in showers and fronds, shedding carpets of petals.

It was the company that was erratic. Either they called on someone, perching on unfamiliar chairs in some other withdrawing room and making self-conscious conversation, or one of them received callers here. Sarah had young married friends whose conversations were indescribably boring to Charlotte. Emily's friends were little better; all romantic speculation, fashion, who was, or was about to be, courting whom. Most of Mama's friends were stiff, a little too consciously righteous, but there were at least two who were given to reminiscences which Charlotte loved to hear—memories of old admirers, perished long since in the Crimea, Sebastopol, Balaclava, and the Charge of the Light Brigade, and then memories of the few who came back. And there were stories told with mixed admiration and disapproval of Florence Nightingale, "so unfeminine, but you have to admire her courage, my dear! Not a lady, but an Englishwoman one might reasonably be proud of!"

And Grandmama's friends were even more interesting. Not that she liked them, not many of them; they were singularly disagreeable old ladies. But Mrs. Selby was over eighty, and she could remember the news of Trafalgar, and

9

the death of Lord Nelson, black ribbons in the streets, people weeping, black borders on the newspapers; at least she said she could. She spoke frequently of Waterloo, and the Great Duke, the scandals of the Empress Josephine, the return of Napoleon from Elba, and the hundred days. Most of it she herself had overheard in drawing rooms much like this one, perhaps a little more austere, with less furniture, lighter, neoclassic; it was nevertheless fascinating to Charlotte, a reality sharper than this.

But today was 1881, a world away from such things, with Mr. Disraeli dead, gaslights in the streets, women admitted to degrees in London University! The queen was empress of India and the empire itself stretched to every corner of the earth. Wolfe and the Heights of Abraham, Clive and Hastings in India, Livingstone in Africa, and the Zulu War were all history. The prince consort had been dead of typhus twenty years; Gilbert and Sullivan wrote operas like *H.M.S. Pinafore.* What would the Emperor Napoleon have made of that?

Today Mrs. Winchester was here to see Mama—which was a bore—and Aunt Susannah was here to see them all, which was excellent. She was Papa's younger sister; in fact she was only thirty-six, nineteen years younger than her brother and only ten years older than Sarah; she seemed more like a cousin. It was three months since they had seen her, three months too long. She had been away visiting in Yorkshire.

"You must tell me all about it, my dear." Mrs. Winchester leaned forward fractionally, curiosity burning in her face. "Who exactly are the Willises? I'm sure you must have told me"—sublime assurance that everybody told her everything!—"but I do find these days that my memory is not nearly as good as I should like." She waited expectantly, eyebrows raised. Susannah was a subject of permanent interest to her: her comings and goings, and above all any hint of a romance, or better still, of scandal. She possessed all the elements necessary. She had been married at twenty-one to a gentleman of good family, and the year after, in 1866, he had been killed in the Hyde Park Riots, leaving her comfortably provided for, in a well-run establishment of her own, still very young and enormously handsome. She had never married again, although no doubt there had been numerous offers. Opinion veered between the conclusion that she was still mourning her husband and, like the queen, could never recover from the grief, to the reverse conclusion that her marriage had been so acutely painful to her that she could not entertain the thought of a second such venture.

Charlotte believed that the truth lay between, that having satisfied the requirements of family in particular and society at large by marrying once, she now had no desire to commit herself again unless it were for genuine affection—which apparently had not yet occurred.

"Mrs. Willis is a cousin, on my mother's side," Susannah replied with a slight smile.

"Indeed, of course," Mrs. Winchester leaned back. "And what does Mr. Willis do, pray? I'm sure I should be most interested to know."

"He is a clergyman, in a small village," Susannah answered dutifully, although her eye caught Charlotte's momentarily in unspoken amusement.

"Oh." Mrs. Winchester struggled to hide a certain disappointment. "How very nice. I suppose you were able to be of much assistance in the parish? I expect our own dear vicar would be much encouraged to hear of your activities. And poor Mrs. Abernathy. I'm sure it would take her mind off things, to hear about the country, and the poor."

Charlotte wondered why either the country or the poor should comfort anyone, least of all Mrs. Abernathy.

"Oh, yes," her mother encouraged. "That would be an excellent idea."

"You might take her some preserves," Grandmama added, nodding her head. "Always nice to receive preserves. Shows people care. And people are not as considerate as they used to be, in my young days. Of course, it's all this violence, all this crime. It's bound to change people. And such immodesty: women behaving like men, and wanting all sorts of things

11

that aren't good for them. We'll have hens crowing in the farm yard next!"

"Poor Mrs. Abernathy," Mrs. Winchester agreed, shaking her head.

"Has Mrs. Abernathy been ill?" Susannah enquired.

"Of course!" Grandmama said sharply. "What would you expect, child? That's what I keep saying to Charlotte." She gave Charlotte a piercing glance. "You and Charlotte are alike, you know!" That was an accusation aimed at Susannah. "I used to blame Caroline for Charlotte." She dismissed her daughter-in-law with a wave of her fat little hand. "But I suppose I can hardly blame her for you. You must be the fault of the times. Your father was never strict enough with you, but at least you don't read those dreadful newspapers that come into this house. I had you too late in life. No good comes of it."

"I don't think Charlotte reads the newspapers as much as you fear, Mama," Susannah defended.

"How many times do you require to read a thing before the damage is done?" Grandmama demanded.

"They are all different, Mama."

"How do you know?" Grandmama was as quick as a terrier.

Susannah kept her composure with only the faintest colour coming to her face.

"They print the news, Mama; the news must be different from day to day."

"Nonsense! They print crimes and scandals. Sin has not changed since Our Lord permitted it in the Garden of Eden."

That seemed to close the conversation. There were several minutes' silence.

"Do tell us, Aunt Susannah," Sarah began at last, "is the country in Yorkshire very pretty? I have never been there. Perhaps the Willises would permit Dominic and me..." she left the suggestion delicately.

Susannah smiled. "I'm sure they would be delighted. But I hardly imagine Dominic enjoying such a very rural life. He always seemed to me a man of more—cultivated tastes than visiting the poor and attending tea parties."

"You make it sound terribly dull," Charlotte said without thinking.

She received a general stare of surprise and disapproval.

"Just the thing poor Mrs. Abernathy needs, I don't doubt," Mrs. Winchester said with a sage nod. "Do her the world of good, poor woman."

"Yorkshire can be uncommonly cold in April," Susannah said quietly, looking from one to the other of them. "If Mrs. Abernathy has been ill, don't you think perhaps June or July would be better?"

"Cold has nothing to do with it!" Grandmama snapped. "Bracing. Very healthy."

"Not if you've been ill—"

"Are you contradicting me, Susannah?"

"I am trying to point out, Mama, that Yorkshire in early spring is not an ideal place for someone in a delicate state of health. Far from bracing her, it might well give her pneumonia!"

"It will at least take her mind off things," Grandmama said firmly.

"Poor dear soul," Mrs. Winchester added. "To leave here, even for Yorkshire, would surely only be an improvement, change her spirits."

"What's wrong with here?" Susannah asked, looking at Mrs. Winchester, then at Charlotte. "I've always thought this an unusually pleasant place. We have all the advantages of the city without the oppression of its more crowded areas, or the expense of the most highly fashionable. Our streets are as clean as any, and we are within carriage distance of most that is of interest or enjoyment to see, not to mention our friends."

Mrs. Winchester swung round to her.

"Of course, you've been away!" she said accusingly.

"Only for two months! It surely cannot have changed so

much in that time?" The question was ironic, even a little sarcastic.

"How long does it take?" Mrs. Winchester gave a dramatic shudder and closed her eyes. "Oh! Poor Mrs. Abernathy. How can she bear to think of it? No wonder the poor soul is afraid to go to sleep."

Now Susannah was totally confounded. She looked at Charlotte for help.

Charlotte decided to give it, and bear the consequences.

"Do you remember Mrs. Abernathy's daughter, Chloe?" She did not wait for a reply. "She was murdered about six weeks ago, garotted, and her clothes ripped from her, her bosom wounded."

"Charlotte!" Caroline glared at her daughter. "We will not discuss it!"

"We have been discussing it one way or another all afternoon," Charlotte protested. Out of the corner of her vision she saw Emily stifle a giggle. "We have merely covered it in words."

"It is better covered."

Mrs. Winchester shuddered again.

"I can't bear to think of it, the very memory makes me quite ill. She was found in the street, all huddled up on the footpath like a bundle of laundry. Her face was terrible, blue as—as—I don't know what! And her eyes staring and her tongue poking out. Been lying in the rain for hours when they found her; all night, I shouldn't wonder."

"Don't disturb yourself!" Grandmama said tersely, looking at Mrs. Winchester's excited face.

Mrs. Winchester remembered quickly to be distressed.

"Oh, terrible!" she wailed, screwing up her features. "Please, my dear Mrs. Ellison, let us not speak of it again. The whole subject is quite unbearable. Poor dear Mrs. Abernathy. I just don't know how she bears it!"

"What else can she do but bear it?" Charlotte said quietly. "It has happened. There isn't anything anyone can do now."

"I suppose there never was," Susannah stared at the tea.

"Some madman, a robber no one could have foreseen." She looked up, frowning. "Surely she was not alone in the street after dark?"

"My dear Susannah," Caroline remonstrated, "it is dark from four o'clock on in the middle of winter, most especially on a wet day. How can one guarantee to be indoors by four o'clock? That would mean one could not even visit neighbours for tea!"

"Is that where she was?"

"She was setting out to take some old clothes to the vicar, for the poor." Caroline's face pinched with a sudden very real sorrow. "Poor child, she was barely eighteen."

Without warning it became real, no longer a scandal to be toyed with, a titillation, but the real death of a woman like themselves: footsteps behind, sudden agony in the throat, terror, the struggle for breath, bursting lungs, and darkness.

No one spoke.

It was Dora coming in from the hallway who broke the silence.

Charlotte was still feeling depressed when her father returned to the house a little after six. The sky had darkened outside and now it was spattering the first heavy drops of rain on the roadway as the carriage drew up. Edward Ellison worked with a merchant banking house in the city, which provided him with a very satisfactory income and a social standing of at least acceptable middle class. Charlotte had been brought up to think perhaps rather more.

Edward came in now, brushing the raindrops off his coat in the few seconds before Maddock came to relieve him of it, and put his top hat gently in its place.

"Good evening, Charlotte," he said pleasantly.

"Good evening, Papa."

"I trust you have had a profitable day?" he enquired, rubbing his hands together. "I fear the weather is distressingly seasonal. We may well be in for a storm. The air has that oppressive feeling."

"Mrs. Winchester came to tea." She answered his question about the afternoon by implication. He knew she disliked her.

"Oh dear," he smiled faintly. There was some understanding between them, even though it did not show itself as often as she would have liked. "I thought Susannah was expected?"

"Oh, she came too, but Mrs. Winchester spent the entire time either questioning her about the Willises, or talking about Chloe Abernathy."

Edward's face darkened. Charlotte realized that she had inadvertently betrayed her mother. Papa would expect her to control such talk in her own drawing room. It would meet with his considerable displeasure that she had not.

At that moment Sarah came out of the sitting room into the hall, the light behind her creating a halo around her fair hair. She was a pretty woman, more like Grandmama than Caroline, with the same porcelain skin and neat mouth, the same soft chin.

"Hello, Sarah, my dear," Edward gave her a little pat on the shoulder. "Waiting for Dominic?"

"I thought you might have been he," Sarah answered, the faintest flicker of disappointment in her voice. "I hope he arrives before the storm. I thought I heard thunder a few minutes ago."

She stood back and Edward went into the sitting room, crossing immediately to the fire and standing with his back to it, blocking most of its heat from everyone else. Emily was sitting at the piano, flipping pages of music over idly. He surveyed his daughters with satisfaction.

There was another low rumble of thunder and the door closed sharply. All of them turned to the sitting room door automatically. There was a shuffle outside, the sound of Maddock's voice, and then Dominic came in.

Charlotte felt her throat tighten. Really, she ought to be over this by now; it was ridiculous! He was slim and strong, smiling a little, his dark eyes first on Edward, as manners and breeding required in the patriarchal house, and then on Sarah.

"Hope you had a pleasant day," Edward said, still standing by the fire. "As well you made it home before the storm. I think it might become quite violent within a quarter of an hour or less. Always afraid the horses will take fright and cause an accident. Becket lost his leg that way, you know?"

The conversation washed over Charlotte's head; it was the usual comfortable family exchange, more or less meaningless, one of the small rituals of the day that established a pattern of life. Would it always be like this? Endless days of needlework, painting, house chores and skills, teas, Papa and Dominic coming home? What did other people do? They married and raised children, ran houses. Of course the poor worked, and society went to parties, rode in the park or in coaches, and presumably had families as well?

She had never met anyone round whom she could imagine centering her life—anyone except Dominic. Perhaps she should copy Emily and cultivate a few more friends like Lucy Sandelson, or the Hayward sisters. They always seemed to be beginning or ending a romance. But they all seemed so incredibly silly! Poor Papa. It was hard for him to have had three daughters, and no son.

"... could, couldn't you, Charlotte?"

Dominic was looking at her, his eyebrows raised, amusement in his elegant face.

"Daydreaming," Edward commented.

Dominic smiled broadly.

"You could take on old Mrs. Winchester at her own game, couldn't you, Charlotte?" he repeated.

Charlotte had no idea what he was talking about. The loss must have been obvious.

"Be just as inquisitive as she is," Dominic explained patiently. "Answer all her questions with another question. There must be something she would rather not discuss!"

Charlotte was honest, as she always was with him. Perhaps that was why he loved Sarah?

"You don't know Mrs. Winchester," she said straight away. "If she doesn't want to discuss a subject she will simply ignore you. There is no reason in her mind why her reply should be related to your question. She will say whatever she is thinking of."

"Which today was poor Susannah?"

"Not really, it was *poor* Mrs. Abernathy. Susannah was only a side adventure, leading up to how much good it would do *poor* Mrs. Abernathy to go to Yorkshire."

"In April?" Dominic was incredulous. "The wretched woman would freeze, and be bored stiff."

Edward's face darkened. Unfortunately at that moment Caroline came in.

"Caroline," he said stiffly. "Charlotte tells me you have been discussing Chloe Abernathy this afternoon. I thought I had made myself plain, but perhaps I did not, so I will do so now. The death of that unfortunate girl is not to be a subject for gossip and speculation in this house. If you can be of some assistance to Mrs. Abernathy in her bereavement, then by all means do so; otherwise the matter is closed. I trust there can be no misunderstanding as to my wishes in this regard now?"

"No, Edward, of course not. I'm afraid I am not able to control Mrs. Winchester. She seems..." she trailed off, knowing it would serve no purpose. Edward had expressed his feelings and was already thinking of something else.

Maddock came in and informed them dinner was served.

The following day the storm had passed and the street was clean in the white April light, the sky bleached blue, and the garden tremulous with dew, every grass blade bright. Charlotte and Emily spent the morning occupied with the usual household duties, while Sarah went to visit the dressmaker. Caroline was closeted with Mrs. Dunphy, the cook, going over kitchen accounts.

In the afternoon Charlotte went alone to deliver the mufflers to the vicar's wife. It was a duty she disliked, especially since it was a day on which the vicar himself was highly likely to be at home, and he was a man who always produced in her a profound depression. Still, there was no avoiding it this time. It was her turn, and neither Sarah nor Emily had seemed in the least likely to relieve her of it.

She arrived at the vicarage a little before half past three. It was mild after the storm and it had been a pleasant walk, something under two miles, but she was used to exercise, and the mufflers were not heavy.

The maid opened the door almost immediately. She was a severe, angular woman of indeterminate age, and Charlotte could never remember her name.

"Thank you," she said politely, stepping in. "I believe Mrs. Prebble is expecting me."

"Yes, ma'am. If you'll come this way."

The vicar's wife was sitting in the smaller back parlour and the vicar himself standing with his back to the black, smoking fire. Charlotte's heart sank as soon as she saw him.

"Good afternoon to you, Miss Ellison," he said with a very slight bow, more a bending of his back. "How pleasant to see you spending your time in small duties for others."

"A very small thing, vicar." She instinctively wanted to deny it. "Only a few mufflers my mother and sisters have made. I hope they will be..." she trailed off, realizing she did not really mean anything, uttering empty words, noises to fill the silence.

Mrs. Prebble reached for the bag and took it. She was a handsome woman, broad-busted, strong, with fine, strong hands.

"I'm sure next winter there will be those who will be most grateful for them. I have frequently noticed that if your hands are cold, your whole body is chilled, haven't you?"

"Yes, yes, I suppose I have."

The vicar was staring at her and she looked away quickly from his cold eyes.

"You seem a little chilled now, Miss Ellison," he said very clearly. "I'm sure Mrs. Prebble would be happy to offer you

19

a dish of hot tea." It was a statement. There was no avoiding it without discourtesy.

"Thank you," she said, without feeling.

Martha Prebble rang the little bell on the mantel and when the maid came back a moment later she requested the tea.

"And how is your mother, Miss Ellison?" the vicar enquired, still standing with his back to the fire, shielding them all from its heat. "Such a good woman."

"Well, thank you, vicar," Charlotte answered. "I'll tell her you were asking after her."

Martha Prebble looked up from the sewing she was doing. "I hear your Aunt Susannah has returned from Yorkshire. I hope the change of air has done her good?"

Mrs. Winchester had lost no time!

"I believe so, but she was not ill, you know."

"Things must be hard for her, at times," Martha said thoughtfully. "Alone."

"I don't think Aunt Susannah minds," Charlotte spoke before thinking. "I think she prefers it."

The vicar frowned. The tea arrived. Obviously it had been already prepared and only awaited the signal.

"It is not good for a woman to be alone," the vicar said grimly. He had a large, squarish face with a strong, thin mouth and heavy nose. He must have been quite fine as a young man. Charlotte was ashamed of how deeply she disliked him. One should not feel that way about a man of the Church. "It leaves her vulnerable to all kinds of dangers," he went on.

"Susannah is perfectly safe," Charlotte replied firmly. "She has adequate means, and she certainly doesn't venture out alone except in the daytime. And at night, of course, the house is quite secure. I believe her manservant is very proficient, even in the use of firearms."

"I was not thinking of violence, Miss Ellison, but of temptation. A woman alone is subject to temptations of the flesh, to lightmindedness and entertainments that by their very shallowness tend to pervert the nature. A good woman is about the tasks of her house. Consider your Bible, Miss Ellison. I recommend you read the Book of Proverbs."

"Susannah keeps a very good house," Charlotte felt impelled to defend her. "And she doesn't occupy herself in—in lightminded amusements."

"You really are a most argumentative young woman," the vicar smiled at her stiffly. "It is unbecoming. You must learn to control it."

"She is only being loyal to her cousin, my dear," Martha said quickly, seeing Charlotte's face colour in quick anger.

"Loyalty is not a virtue, Martha, when it misguidedly praises that which is evil and dangerous. You have only to look at Chloe Abernathy, unfortunate child. And Susannah is her aunt, not her cousin."

Charlotte could still feel the heat under her skin.

"What has Chloe Abernathy to do with Susannah?" she demanded.

"Bad comapny, Miss Ellison, bad company. We are all weak vessels, and in bad company women, especially young women, are easily led to become subject to vices, even to fall under the influence of evil men and end their lives in destitution and abandonment on the streets."

"Chloe wasn't anything like that!"

"You are soft-hearted, Miss Ellison, and so a woman should be. You should not know of such things and it does your mother credit that you do not see them. But great evils begin in small ways. That is why even the most innocent of women need the protection of men, who see the seeds of sin in time to guard against them. And bad company is the seed of sin, child; there can be no doubt of it. Poor Chloe was much taken with the company of the Madison daughters lately, before her death. And perhaps you did not fully appreciate their lightmindedness, the frivolous painting of their faces, the wearing of clothes intended to attract the attention of men, and the lingering about without chaperones indulged in by the Misses Madison. But I am sure your father was aware, and would not have let you associate with such people. You may thank his wisdom that you are not also lying murdered in the street."

"I know they giggled rather a lot," Charlotte said slowly; she tried to recall the Misses Madison, to see in them any of the beginnings of sin the vicar spoke of. Her memory produced nothing more than a lot of romantic nonsense and very little harm. Empty, certainly, but not wicked, even in embryo. "But I don't remember anything spiteful in them."

"Not spiteful." The vicar gave a faintly patronizing smile. "Sin is not spite, my dear child; sin is the beginning of the road to damnation, to indulgence of the flesh, to fornication and the worship of the Golden Calf!" His voice rose, and Charlotte knew instinctively it was the beginning of a sermon. She clutched desperately.

"Mrs. Prebble," she leaned forward in total hypocrisy. "Please tell me what else you would like us to do, what next we may make to contribute to the relief of the poor? I'm sure both my mother and my sisters would be most grateful to know!"

Martha Prebble was a little startled by the vehemence in her voice, but she too seemed more than happy to leave the subject of sin.

"Oh, I'm sure any blankets, or especially clothes for children. The poor always seem to have so many children, you know. They seem to have more than those of us who are more comfortably suited."

"Naturally." The vicar was not to be left out. His face was massive, resting on his broad shoulders like a monument. "It is precisely because they indulge themselves and give birth to more children than they can support that they are poor, and the rest of us inherit the obligation to care for their needs. I suppose it is productive of patience in affliction for them, and of Christian charity and virtue in us."

Charlotte had no answer for that. She drank the last of her tea and stood up.

"Thank you for the tea. I'm quite warm and refreshed now.

I must return home before the evening begins to chill. I shall inform my mother of your satisfaction with the mufflers, and I'm sure she will be most grateful that there is more we can do. Children's clothes. I shall begin tomorrow. I expect we shall do well."

Martha Prebble came to the front with her. She put her hand on Charlotte's arm in the hallway.

"My dear Charlotte, don't mind the vicar; he is solicitous for our well-being, and doesn't mean to sound so harsh. I'm sure he was as distressed as anyone that—that tragedies should happen."

"Of course. I understand." Charlotte loosened herself. She did not understand at all. She thought nothing but ill of the vicar, but she was sorry for Martha. She could not imagine living with such a man. Although he was perhaps not so different from many men. They all tended to be pretty severe with girls like the Misses Madison, and in truth they were more than a little tedious. But not sinful —just incredibly silly.

Martha smiled.

"You are very gentle, my dear. I knew you would." And she stood on the doorstep watching Charlotte down the path.

Two days later they were all sitting in the withdrawing room sewing the children's clothes Martha Prebble had requested, when Edward returned home as usual.

They heard the front door close. There was a murmur of voices as Maddock took his coat and hat, but a moment later, instead of Edward, it was Maddock whose face showed at the door.

"Madame," he looked at Caroline, his face flushed.

"Yes, Maddock?" Caroline was surprised, not yet aware of anything wrong. "What is it? Was that not Mr. Ellison?"

"Yes, Madame. Would you be so good as to come into the hall?"

Now Charlotte, Emily, and Sarah all stared at him. Caroline stood up.

"Of course."

As soon as she was gone they turned to look at one another.

"What's happened?" Emily said immediately, excitement in her voice. "Do you suppose Papa has brought company? I wonder who it is, and if he is wealthy—a man from the city perhaps?"

"Then why doesn't he bring him in?" Charlotte asked.

Sarah frowned and looked at the ceiling in exasperation.

"Really, Charlotte, he would naturally consult Mama first, and introduce him. Maybe he is not suitable for us to meet. Perhaps he is only someone in trouble, someone who needs help."

"What a bore," Emily sighed. "You mean a beggar, someone in reduced circumstances?"

"I don't know. Papa may be having Maddock take care of him, but he would naturally tell Mama about it."

Emily stood up and went to the door.

"Emily! You aren't going to listen?"

Emily held her finger to her lips, smiling.

"Don't you want to know?" she asked.

Charlotte got to her feet quickly and went over to Emily, standing almost on top of her.

"Well, I certainly do," she joined in. "Open the door, just a crack."

Emily had already done so. They crouched over it together, and a moment later Charlotte felt the warmth of Sarah right behind her, her taffeta afternoon dress rustling a little.

"Edward, you must destroy the newspapers," Caroline was saying. "Say that you lost them."

"We don't know that it will be in the newspapers."

"Of course it will!" Caroline was angry, upset. Her voice quavered. "And you know that—"

Charlotte drew in her breath sharply; her mother was about to betray her.

"—that it might get left where one of the girls could see it." Caroline went on. "And I won't have the servants read it either. Poor Mrs. Dunphy sometimes uses newspapers to

24

wrap kitchen refuse, or Lily might use them in cleaning. It would frighten the poor things out of their wits."

"Yes," Edward agreed. "Yes, my dear, you are quite right. I shall read it and destroy it before returning home. It would be wise if we could keep Mama from hearing about it. It is bound to distress her."

Caroline's agreement lacked any conviction. Charlotte smiled, hiding her face in Emily's silk back. It was her private opinion that Grandmama was tougher than a Turkish soldier in the Crimea she was always talking about. Apparently Caroline thought so, too. But what was it that had happened? Her curiosity was boiling over.

"Was the poor girl—" Caroline swallowed; they could hear it from behind the door—"garotted, like Chloe Abernathy?"

"Hardly like Chloe Abernathy," Edward corrected, but there was a catch in his voice too, as if reality had just overtaken him. "Chloe was a...a respectable girl. This maid of the Hiltons' was—well, it seems regrettable to speak ill of the dead, especially dead in such a terrible way, but she was a girl of dubious reputation. She had more followers than any decent girl would. I dare say that was what brought about her terrible death."

"You said she was found in the street, Edward?"

"Yes, in Cater Street, not half a mile from the vicar's."

"Well, don't the Hiltons live in Russmore Street? That leads off Cater Street at the far end. I suppose she went out to meet someone and it...it happened."

"Hush, my dear. It was quite horrible, obscene. We won't speak of it any more. We had better go into the withdrawing room or they will begin to wonder what is keeping us. I just hope the whole neighbourhood won't be buzzing with it. I imagine Dominic will have the sense not to speak of it, at least of the more...bestial aspects of it?"

"Well, *you* only heard by chance, because you were in Cater Street at just the moment when the police were there; otherwise in the dark you would have known nothing."

"I must warn him to be discreet. We don't want the girls

upset, or the servants either. But I had better have a word with Maddock, and see that neither Dora nor Lily goes out walking alone until this wretched man is caught." There was a sound of footsteps as he moved.

Charlotte felt Emily's elbow in her ribs as a sharp warning and they all collapsed backwards and fled to their respective seats. They were sitting awkwardly, skirts crumpled, when the door opened.

Edward's face was pale, but he was perfectly composed.

"Good evening, my dears. I hope you had a pleasant day?"

"Yes, thank you, Papa," Charlotte said breathlessly. "Quite pleasant. Thank you."

But her mind was out in a shadowed street in some unimaginable horror of dark shapes, sudden pain, choking—and death.

Chapter Two

Emily was excited. This was the kind of day she loved, even more than the day after. Today was the day of dreams, of preparations, of last-minute stitching, of laying out every detail of clean underwear, of washing hair and brushing, of curling irons, and then at the very last minute of all, the delicate, infinitely discreet touches to the face.

Tonight they were going to a formal ball at the house of one Colonel Decker and his wife, and far more to the point, his son and his daughter. Emily had seen them only twice, but had heard delicious stories from Lucy Sandelson as to their dashing style, their elegance, the flair with which they wore the latest fashions; and yet more intoxicating, the abundance and intimacy of their acquaintances among the wealthy and the aristocratic. Truly this ball gave promise of endless doors which, with a little luck and a little skill, might open onto worlds heretofore only dreamed of.

Anne Perry

Sarah was going to wear blue, a soft baby blue which was extremely becoming to her. It flattered her skin, highlighting its delicacy, and caught the colour of her eyes. It was a colour that suited Emily's warmer tone very well also, complementing her cheeks, darker eyes, and brownish hair with its hazel and gold lights. Still, it would flatter neither of them to wear the same; indeed it would make them look ridiculous and Sarah naturally had first choice.

Charlotte had decided upon a rich, wine pink, another shade which would have suited Emily. But to be honest, it suited Charlotte, with the redwood colour of her hair and her honey-toned skin even better. No one could call her eyes blue; they were gray in any light.

Which left only yellow or green for Emily. Yellow always made her look sallow. It looked dreadful on Sarah too; only Charlotte was flattered by it. So, with a touch of ill humour, Emily had settled for green, a soft, lighter than apple green. Now, holding it up in front of her, she had to admit that chance had favoured her. It really was most excellently becoming. She looked all delicacy and spring, like some flower in its self-chosen setting, as if she owed nothing to artifice. Indeed, if dressed in this she could not attract the admiration, and thus of course the attention, of one of the Decker family's friends, she did not deserve to succeed. Sarah was not in the field, being married; the Madison sisters were unattractively dark, and let us be honest, much thicker round the waist than was desirable, both of them! Perhaps they overate?

Lucy was handsome enough, but so clumsy! And Charlotte, she knew, would be no rival, because Charlotte always spoilt any visual effect she might have made as soon as she opened her mouth! Why did Charlotte always have to say what she thought, instead of what she certainly had enough wit to know people wished?

This green really was excellent. She must get another gown in the same shade for daytime. And where was Lily? She was supposed to be coming with the curling irons!

She went to the door.

"Lily?"

"Coming, Miss Emily. One moment, and I'm coming right now!"

"What are you doing?"

"Just the last touches to Miss Charlotte's dress, Miss Emily."

"The irons will get cold!" Really Lily was stupid at times! Didn't the girl ever think?

"They're still too hot, Miss Emily. I'm coming right now!"

This time she fulfilled her promise, and half an hour later Emily was totally satisfied. She turned slowly in front of the mirror. The reflection was dazzling; she could think of nothing to add or alter. This was the best image she was able to present; young yet not totally unsophisticated, ethereal without being quite out of reach.

Caroline came into the room behind her.

"You've been standing in front of that mirror too long, Emily. You must know every fold of your dress by now." Her reflection was smiling, meeting Emily's eyes. "Vanity in a woman is not an attractive quality, my dear. However beautiful you are—and you are pretty enough, but not beautiful— it becomes you to pretend indifference to it."

Emily stifled a laugh. She was far too excited to be offended.

"I don't intend anyone else to be indifferent to it. Are you ready, Mama?"

"Do you feel there is something I have yet to do?" Caroline's mouth twisted a little.

Emily swung round, flouncing her skirt. She regarded her mother in mock consideration. On anyone else the brown-gold dress would have been sombre, but against Caroline's rich skin and mahogany hair it was very handsome indeed. Emily had too much honesty to do anything but approve.

"Thank you," Caroline said with some acerbity. "Are you ready to come down? Everyone else is prepared to leave."

Emily came down the stairs carefully, holding her dress, and was the first into the carriage. All the way there she was

29

silent, her mind whirling faster and faster through dreams, picturing handsome men, faces as yet indistinct, all turned towards her as she danced, music in her ears, in her body and in her feet, barely touching the ground. One vision melted into another. She progressed to the next day, to admirers calling, to letters, then to rivalry for her attention. A pity gentlemen did not duel any more. Of course, it would all be very proper. Perhaps one of them would be titled. Would she marry him? Become Lady something? There would be a long, passionate courtship first—his family would have chosen someone else for him. Someone of his own social standing, an heiress. But he would be prepared to risk everything! The dream was delicious. It was almost an anticlimax when they arrived. But she knew the difference between dream and reality.

They had judged it perfectly—probably Mama's doing. The ball was already in progress; they heard the music even as they mounted the steps to the great doors. Emily caught her breath and swallowed hard in the excitement. There were more than fifty people, swirling gently like flowers in a breeze, colours blending and drifting one into another, interspersed with the dark, stiffer forms of the men. The music was like summer and wine and laughter.

They were announced. Mama and Papa went down the steps slowly, then Dominic and Sarah, then Charlotte. Emily hesitated as long as she dared. Were all those faces looking at her? Oh, yes, please let it be that they were? She picked up her skirt just an inch or two in her hand, delicately, and began to descend the stair. It was a moment to be savoured, like the exquisite first strawberry of the year, at once sweet and tart, drawing the mouth.

They were formally introduced, but most of it passed over her head. She was aware only of the son of the family. He was a bitter disappointment. Reality shattered the remnant of the dream. He was ruddy-faced, short-nosed, and definitely too stout for a man of his youth.

Emily curtsied, as habit dictated, and when he asked her

for the honour of the dance she accepted. There was no other civil way to behave, and she was duly led away. He danced badly.

Afterwards Emily found herself deposited among a group of other young women, most of whom she knew, at least by sight. Conversation was minimal and extremely silly, as everyone's mind was on the men now congregating at the far side or dancing with others. Such remarks as were made were not listened to, either by those who made them or by those to whom they were addressed.

Emily saw Dominic and Sarah together, and Mama dancing with Colonel Decker. Charlotte was talking, with an attempt at interest, to a young man with an elegant and weary air.

It was half an hour, and several dances later, before young Decker returned—much to Emily's dismay, until she saw that he brought with him quite the handsomest man she had seen in a year. He was of no more than average height, but his brown hair curled richly to his head, his colour was excellent, his features regular, his eyes large, and above all he carried with him an air of assurance that was beauty in itself.

"Miss Emily Ellison," young Decker bowed very slightly, "may I present to you Lord George Ashworth."

Emily held out her hand and curtsied, eyes down to hide the colour of excitement she felt climbing up her cheeks. Really, she must behave as if she met lords every day, and cared not a whit.

He spoke to her; she hardly heard the words. She replied gracefully.

The conversation was formal, a little stilted, but it hardly mattered. Decker was an ass—she needed only half her attention to maintain a subject with him—but Ashworth was entirely different. She could feel his eyes on her, and it was both dangerous and exciting. He was a man who would reach boldly for what he wanted. There might be finesse, but there would be no fumbling, no diffidence. It brought her a tingle of fear to know that she was, at this moment, the object of his interest.

She danced with him twice within the next hour. He was not indiscreet. Twice was enough; more would have drawn attention, perhaps Papa's, which could spoil everything.

She saw Papa across the room, dancing with Sarah, and Mama trying to avoid the very open admiration of Colonel Decker, without at the same time offending him, or allowing the situation to arouse the jealousy of others. At a different time, Emily would have watched for the education it would have given her. Now she had business of her own that required all her wits.

She was standing talking to one of the Misses Madison, but she was conscious of Lord Ashworth's eyes on her from across the room. She must stand straight. A bent back was most unbecoming, made an ugly bustline, and did little for the chin. She must smile, but not seem to be vacuous, and move her hands prettily. She never forgot how ugly hands could spoil an otherwise graceful woman, having seen it all too disastrously demonstrated by the other of the Misses Madison, to the total loss of a promising admirer. That was something Sarah had never quite mastered and Charlotte had, which was odder still. Charlotte was so awkward with her tongue, but she had such beautiful hands. She was dancing now with Dominic, her face lifted, her eyes glowing. Really, sometimes Emily doubted she had the sense she was born with! There was nothing to be gained from Dominic. He had no friends of value, and certainly no relations. True, he was comfortably enough placed himself, but that was of no consequence to Charlotte. Only a fool travelled a road that led nowhere. Still, you could not tell some people!

By midnight Emily had danced with George Ashworth another two times, but nothing had been said about a further meeting, or about his calling on her. She was beginning to fear she had not been as successful as she had at first presumed. Papa would soon decide it was time to go home. She must do something within the next few minutes, or perhaps lose her chance, and that would be appalling. She could not lose so soon the first lord she had spoken to familiarly, quite the handsomest man; and, even more to her liking, a man of wit and boldness.

She excused herself from Lucy Sandelson on the pretext of being rather warm, and made her way towards the conservatory. It would doubtless be far too cold in there, but what was a little discomfort in the pursuit of such advance?

She had waited five minutes, which seemed like fifty, when at last she heard footsteps. She did not turn, pretending to be absorbed in the contemplation of an azalea.

"I hoped you would not have grown cold and returned to the ballroom before I had the chance to disengage myself."

She felt the blood surge through her. It was Ashworth.

"Indeed," she said as calmly as she could. "I had no idea you had observed my leaving. I did not intend to be obvious." What a lie. If she had not thought he observed her she would have had to return, and leave again. "I was finding the heat growing a trifle oppressive. So many people."

"Do you dislike crowds? I am most disappointed." He sounded it. "I was hoping I might invite you, and perhaps Miss Decker, to accompany me and one or two friends to the races in a week's time. There is a big meeting, and all fashionable London will be there. You would have graced the scene, especially if you were to have worn the same delightful shade as you are wearing now. It brings all springtime and youth to mind."

She was too choked with excitement to speak. The races! With Lord Ashworth! All fashionable London. Dreams flickered past her eyes in such profusion she could hardly distinguish one from another. Maybe the Prince of Wales would be there; he loved racing. And who knew who else? She would buy another dress in green, a dress for the races, fit to turn every head on the course!

"You are very silent, Miss Ellison," he said from behind her. "I should be dreadfully disappointed if you did not come. You are quite the most enchanting creature here. And I promise you, the crowds at the races will be nothing like as stifling as here in the ballroom. It will all be open air, and if we are lucky, sunshine as well. Please say that you will come?"

"Thank you, Lord Ashworth." She must keep her voice steady, as if she frequently were invited to the races by lords and it were no cause for ecstasy. "I should be most charmed to come. I have no doubt it will be a delightful occasion, and Miss Decker quite a proper companion. I understand she has accepted?"

"Naturally, or I should not have been so inconsiderate as to approach you." That was a lie, but she was not to know it.

When Papa came to inform her it was time to return home, she followed obediently, smiling, in a haze of delight.

Race day was fine, one of those cool, dazzlingly sunny days of late spring when the very air seems to sparkle. Emily had prevailed upon Papa to purchase yet another new dress, and in the very green she wished. She had hinted at the eloquent argument that if really successful she might attract a future husband—a thought which could not fail to impress Papa. Three daughters were a severe test of any man's connections and good fortune if he wished to see them satisfactorily married. Sarah had been matched, if not brilliantly, at least acceptably. Dominic had sufficient means, and was certainly more than personable. He was uncommonly handsome, and seemed of easy temper and good habits.

Charlotte, of course, was entirely another matter. Emily could not see Charlotte being nearly so easily settled. She was both far too unaccommodating in her nature—no man liked an argumentative woman—and far too impractical in her own desires. She wished for the most awkward and, in the long run, unrewarding attributes in a man. Emily had tried to speak to her regarding her ambitions, to point out that financial means and social standing, coupled with acceptable appearance and behaviour that was at any rate well-mannered, were all one could reasonably expect—indeed, were a very great deal more than most girls ever achieved. But Charlotte refused to be persuaded, or seriously to acknowledge that she even understood.

But today none of that mattered. Emily was at the race meeting with Lord George Ashworth and Miss Decker and some young man she barely noticed. He was of infinitely less promise than Ashworth, and therefore not to be considered at the moment.

The first race was already over, and George had won very nicely on it. He claimed to know the owner of the animal, which made the whole venture even more exciting. Emily paraded along the close grass, parasol in hand, luxuriating in an air of great superiority. She was on the arm of a member of the aristocracy, and an uncommonly handsome one. She looked both fashionable and lovely, and she knew it. And she had inside information on the winner of the previous race. What more could anyone ask? She was of the elite.

The second race was a smaller affair, but the third was the big event of the meeting. The crowd began to buzz in excitement, like a swarm of bees disturbed. The swirls of movement grew more violent as people elbowed their way towards bookmakers, calling odds, trying to induce higher and higher wagers. Men in elegant and rakish clothes laughed loudly, as fistfuls of money changed hands.

Once, while Ashworth was talking about horses' legs, good heart, jockeys' skill, and other things she did not understand, Emily observed an incident she could merely stare at, transfixed. A portly gentleman, somewhat red in the face, was chuckling to himself over his good fortune, clutching a note in his hand. He took one or two steps forward, moving towards a sallow man in dark clothes, lugubrious as an undertaker.

"Lose, old fellow?" the stout man asked cheerfully. "Never mind, better luck with this one! Can't lose 'em all. Keep at it, I say," and he gave a broad chuckle.

The thin man looked at him with polite dismay.

"I beg your pardon, sir, but were you addressing me?" His

voice was quite soft. Had Emily been less close she would not have caught the words.

"You look as if misfortune has visited you," the stout man went on heartily. "Happens to the best of us. Keep trying, I say."

"Indeed, sir. I assure you I have had no misfortune."

"Ah," the stout man grinned and winked. "Not wanting to admit it, eh?"

"I assure you, sir—"

The stout man laughed and clapped the other on the arm. At that moment a stranger missed his footing and staggered sideways, cannoning into the stout man. He in turn fell forward almost into the arms of the sallow man in the mourning clothes. The man put out both hands to steady the sudden weight, or to fend it off. There were profuse apologies all round, and an attempt at straightening clothes. The ill-footed stranger muttered something, then apparently saw an acquaintance in the distance, and still talking, took himself off. A smart young woman materialized next to the dark man and begged him to come immediately and witness some good fortune of hers, while two other fellows having a heated discussion on the merits or demerits of a certain horse, took over almost the same spot of ground.

The stout man brushed himself down, drawing a deep breath. Then his hand stopped convulsively, halfway down his body, dived into his vest pocket, and came out empty.

"My watch!" he howled in anguish. "My money! My seals! I had three gold seals on my watch chain! I've been robbed!"

Emily swivelled round and tugged on Ashworth's sleeve.

"George!" she said urgently. "George, I just saw a man robbed! He was robbed of his watch and seals!"

Ashworth turned round, a slightly indulgent smile on his mouth.

"My dear Emily, it happens all the time at the races."

"But I saw it! It was most cleverly done. This man bumped him from behind and forced him almost on top of another, who ran his hands over him, and like a conjuror must have removed his possessions! Aren't you going to do something?"

"What do you suggest?" His eyebrows rose. "The man who took them will be innocently engaged in something quite different by now, and the goods themselves will have been passed on to someone else neither you nor the victim has ever seen."

"But it only happened this moment!" she protested.

"And where is the thief?"

She stared round. There was no one she recognized, except the victim and the two arguers. She turned back to George helplessly.

"I can't see him."

He grinned.

"Of course not, and even if you tried to pursue him, there would be people specially detailed to block your way. That's how they work. It's quite an art, indeed nearly as great as the art of avoiding them. Don't think about it. There's really nothing you can do. Just don't carry money in your skirt pockets. They are excellently clever at robbing women, too."

She stared at him.

"Now," he said firmly. "Would you care to place a small wager on Charles's horse? I can promise a place at least."

She accepted. To wager money was exciting, part of the thrill, and since it was not her own money, she could lose nothing, and might even gain. But far more important than any small financial advantage was the knowledge she was actually part of this new, brilliant world that since adolescence she had dreamed about. Ladies of high fashion laughed and swirled their skirts as they flounced along on the arms of elegant gentlemen, gentlemen with money and titles, who gambled on horses, on the turn of a card or the fall of dice, gentlemen who took life by the throat and won or lost fortunes in a day. She overheard their talk and it conjured visions for her; a little blurred, of course, because she had never been to a gambling den or a dogfight or cockfighting

37

pit; she had never seen a gentlemen's gambling club, or, come to that, anyone more than very slightly the worse for drink.

But there was danger in it, and danger, risk, was the essence of fortune. Emily had youth and looks, and some ready wit, and above all she believed she had style, that indefinable quality that marked the winners from the losers. If she were to win something permanent, the chance must be taken now.

She succeeded as well as she could have hoped. Ten days later she was invited, again with Miss Decker, to a lawn tennis party, which she enjoyed enormously. Of course she did not play, but the purpose was purely social, and in this she accomplished much, including an invitation to ride in the park in a few days' time. She would, of course, have to be lent both horse and habit, but this presented no problem. Ashworth had arranged for the horse, and she could perfectly easily borrow Aunt Susannah's habit. They were much the same size, and the fact that Susannah was approximately two inches taller could be dealt with by tucking the skirt over at the waist. No one but herself would know.

The day was the first of June, cool and brisk with dazzling sky and rain-clean streets. Emily joined Miss Decker, whom she had grown to dislike, although she hid it excellently, Lord Ashworth, and a Mr. Lambling, who was a friend of Ashworth's, and who had taken a distinct fancy to Miss Decker. Heaven only knew why!

They rode together under the trees on the firm gravel of Rotten Row. Emily sat a trifle precariously on the side saddle. She was not used to horses, but determined to keep her balance and even manage a certain panache as she guided her horse cautiously between a group of solemn children on fat ponies. She looked good, and she heard it reflected in the approving murmurs of a bunch of gentlemen eight or ten yards away. The habit was half an inch tight, flatteringly so. Her high-crowned riding hat, very like a gentleman's top hat, sat rakishly to one side on her shining hair. Her fair skin was complemented perfectly by the hat's dark colour and her shirt's white lace ruffles.

The others caught up with her and rode more or less abreast. Conversation was sporadic until they passed quite the most elegant woman Emily had ever seen. She had the palest silver fair hair and broad, handsome face. Her habit was forest green and most exquisitely cut, with velvet on the collar. Her horse was an animal of obvious mettle. Emily was lost in admiration. One day she would dearly like to ride down Ladies' Mile with that air of assurance, of superiority so deep as to be casually assumed.

The woman smiled broadly as they drew level, and adjusted her hat fractionally with one finger, setting it at a still more dashing angle. She was looking at Ashworth.

"Good morning, my lord," she said with a faintly mocking air.

Ashworth looked through her for a long, chill moment, then turned slightly in the saddle to face Emily.

"You were telling me, Miss Ellison, about your aunt's visit to Yorkshire. It must be most pleasant country, from your account. Do you go frequently yourself?"

It was an astounding piece of rudeness. It had been at least a quarter of an hour since Emily had mentioned Yorkshire, and the woman quite plainly knew him. Emily was too astonished to speak.

"...although I'm surprised she found early spring a comfortable time of the year to visit so far north," he went on, still keeping his back to the Row.

Emily stared at him. The woman's face twisted in a small grimace, a touch of bitter amusement in it. Then she touched her horse with her crop and moved on.

"She was speaking to you!" Emily said boldly.

"My dear Emily," Ashworth's mouth curved downward slightly, "a gentleman does not reply to every harlot who importunes him," he said with a hint of condescension. "Most especially in such a public place as this. And certainly not if he happens to be in the company of ladies at the time."

"Harlot?" Emily stammered. "But she was—she was dressed—I mean—"

"There is every degree of harlot, just as there is every degree of just about everything else! The more expensive they are, the more elite their custom, the less they look like it, that's all. You must learn to be a little less simple!"

The thought flashed through her mind, but she forbore from asking him how he knew the woman's occupation. Obviously there was an entire world about which she had much yet to learn, if she were to thread her way through it successfully, and reach the prize she intended.

"Perhaps you will be good enough to teach me?" she said, with a smile that she hoped hid more than it revealed. Let him read into it what he wished. "It is an area in which I am totally unacquainted."

He gave her a hard look for a moment or two, then broke into a broad smile. He had extraordinarily fine teeth. Emily made up her mind right then that she would exert her utmost effort to end up as Lady Ashworth—regardless of—certain disadvantages. They would have to be dealt with in due course, but she had no doubt she would be equal to them.

"I'm not sure, Emily, if you are quite as mellow as you seem." He was still looking at her.

She affected total innocence and met his eyes with a charming smile. She considered inviting him to know her better and decided against it. It was too forward, and anyway, she was quite sure he intended to anyway.

It was the second week in June when George Ashworth actually came to the Ellison house to call. Naturally it had been planned, planned most meticulously. Even Caroline tried unsuccessfully to hide a certain bubble of excitement.

At quarter to four they were all sitting in the withdrawing room, the sun shining in across the floor, the first roses blooming outside. Lord Ashworth and Mr. and Miss Decker were expected at any moment. Sarah sat rather primly on the piano stool, playing something nondescript; Emily was sufficiently practiced herself to know she was playing it badly.

Emily was singing inside with anticipation. Caroline sat in the best hardbacked chair, as if already preparing to pour the tea which was not yet served. Charlotte alone seemed unaffected. But then, of course, Charlotte never had had the sense to know what was important.

Emily herself was very composed. She had already done everything she could to prepare; all that remained now was to play each phrase, each glance, as it came.

They arrived precisely on time, and were shown in with a flurry of introductions. They all sat down and began the usual ritual of small talk. Only George Ashworth looked totally comfortable.

A giggling and rather flushed Dora brought in their tea: all Mrs. Dunphy's most elegant sandwiches, little butterfly cakes, and others that defied category. Everything was served with even more than usual ceremony.

"Emily told us about the race meeting," Caroline said conversationally, proffering the sandwiches to Ashworth. "It sounds quite fascinating. I have been on only two occasions myself, and they were both some time ago, and in Yorkshire. London races are most fashionable, I hear. Do tell us more about them? Do you go often?"

Emily hoped he would be discreet, partly because she had told her mother very little about the races, and even that little had been definitely slanted, a strong accent on fashion, and nothing whatsoever about the gambling touts, the pickpockets, those who had taken more refreshment than was good for them, and those who she now realized were of the same basic occupation as the lady of the elegant riding habit in Rotten Row. Please heaven, George would have the sense to pick and choose his recollections also.

George smiled.

"I'm afraid there are not so very many race meetings that it would be possible to go more than two or three times a month, Mrs. Ellison. And not all of them are worth bothering with—not the sort of thing I enjoy, and certainly not for ladies."

"Do ladies not attend all of them?" Sarah asked curiously. "You mean they are for men only?"

"Not at all, Mrs. Corde. I used the term 'ladies' to distinguish from the various other females who do attend, for their own reasons."

Sarah opened her mouth, interest lighting her face, then remembered her propriety and closed it again. Emily caught Charlotte's eye with amusement. They all knew Sarah's love of the socially correct. Charlotte said it for her.

"You mean women of no virtue?" she said frankly. "The demimonde, I think they call it?"

George's smile broadened.

"They do indeed, among other things," he agreed. "There are the race-goers, and those who follow the race-goers, and those who follow the followers. Horse traders, gamblers, and I'm afraid thieves."

Caroline frowned.

"Oh dear. It does not sound as pleasant a place as I had imagined."

"Race meetings vary as much as people, Mrs. Ellison," George said easily, reaching for another sandwich. "I was explaining why I do not attend certain of them."

Caroline relaxed.

"Of course. I was concerned about Emily; unnecessarily, it seems. I hope you understand?"

"It would hardly become you to do less. But I assure you, I would not dream of taking Emily anywhere I would not be happy to see my own sister."

"I didn't know you had a sister?" Caroline was suddenly interested again; and so, from the looks on their faces, were the Deckers.

"Lady Carson," George said easily.

"We should be most delighted to meet her. You must bring her to visit us," Mr. Decker said quickly.

"I'm afraid she lives in Cumberland." George dismissed his sister with equal ease. "She very seldom comes to London."

"Carson?" Decker would not let it go. "I don't think I know him?"

"Do you know Cumberland, Mr. Decker?" Emily asked. She did not like Decker, and resented his curiosity.

Decker looked a little taken aback.

"No, Miss Ellison. Is it—pleasant?"

Emily turned to George, raising her eyebrows.

"Very beautiful, if a little rustic," he replied. "It lacks a good many of the amenities of civilized living."

"No gaslights?" Charlotte asked. "Surely they must have hot water, and fires?"

"Certainly, Miss Ellison. I was thinking of gentlemen's clubs, imported wines, tailors fit to patronize, theatres of anything but the most bucolic—in short, society."

"It must be most distressing for your sister," Miss Decker said drily. "I must be sure not to marry a man with the misfortune or the perversity to live in Cumberland."

"Then if such a gentleman should ask you, you will have to refuse him," Charlotte said tartly. Emily hid a smile. Apparently Charlotte did not like Miss Decker any more than she did. But, please heaven, she was not going to be rude! "Let us hope you have an offer more to your liking," Charlotte finished.

Miss Decker flushed in annoyance.

"I don't doubt I shall, Miss Ellison," she snapped.

George sat forward, his handsome face darkened, his lip tight.

"I doubt you will get an offer more favourable than Lord Carson's, Miss Decker. Not for marriage, at least!"

There was a moment's hot silence. It was inexcusable for him to have embarrassed a woman in such a fashion, whatever the provocation. Caroline was at a loss for words.

Emily had to do something.

"It is as well we do not all have the same tastes," she said quickly. "But I dare say Lord Carson's estates are very comfortable. Living in a place is quite different from visiting it.

One always finds plenty to do when one is at home. There are responsibilities."

"How perceptive you are," George agreed. "Lord Carson's estates are extremely wide. He breeds bloodstock, and runs a prize herd of cattle; and, of course there is extensive shooting and fishing. There are mills of some sort also——"

He stopped suddenly, realizing he was speaking of possessions, of money, in a manner that was vulgar. "Eugenie has more than enough to do, especially with three children."

"She must indeed be busy," Caroline said noncommittally.

And so the afternoon continued. The conversation recovered. Emily worked hard to see that it did so, and Sarah was sufficiently impressed to exercise her very best manners, which were excellent.

Afterwards Emily and Charlotte were alone in the withdrawing room. Charlotte opened the doors to let in the late afternoon sun.

"You were not a great deal of help," Emily said a little crossly. "You might have perceived what manner of creature Miss Decker is!"

"I also perceived what manner of creature he is," Charlotte replied, staring at the roses.

"Mr. Decker?" Emily said in surprise. "He is nothing."

"Not Decker. Your Lord Ashworth. That yellow rose is going to be out tomorrow."

"What on earth does that matter? Charlotte, I mean to have George Ashworth offer for me, so just control your tongue while he calls upon us!"

"You what?" Charlotte turned round in amazement.

"You heard me! I mean to marry him, so just play at being courteous at least for the present."

"Emily! You hardly know him!"

"I will, by the time it matters."

"You can't marry him! You're talking nonsense!"

"I'm speaking perfectly good sense. You may be happy to spend your life dreaming, but I am not. I have no illusions that George is perfect——"

"Perfect!" Charlotte said incredulously. "He's appalling! He's shallow, a gambler, and probably a rake! He's not—not a part of our world, Emily. Even if he married you, he would make you wretched."

"You're a dreamer, Charlotte. There is no man who won't make you wretched some time or other. I think George will have more to compensate for it than most, and I mean to marry him. I won't allow you to prevent me." She meant it. Standing in the withdrawing room in the gold evening sunlight, looking at Charlotte's face, the light on her heavy hair, she realized just how profoundly she did mean it. That which at the beginning of the afternoon had been an idea, had now become a quite irrevocable intention.

Chapter
Three

It was the end of July, and Caroline was arranging flowers in the withdrawing room, thinking about the household accounts she ought to be doing instead, when Dora came in without knocking.

Caroline stopped, a long, white daisy in her hand. Really, she could not allow this extraordinary behaviour. She turned to speak, then saw Dora's face.

"Dora? What is it?" She let the daisy drop.

"Oh, ma'am!" Dora let out a long wail. "Oh, ma'am!"

"Pull yourself together, Dora. Now tell me what has happened. Is it that butcher's boy again? I've told you to report him to Maddock if he continues to be impertinent. He'll soon sort out a tongue that runs away with a young man. Otherwise he'll lose his employment. Maddock will tell him that. Now stop sniffling and go back to your work. And Dora, don't come into the withdrawing room again without knocking. You know better than that." She picked up the daisy from the sideboard and considered the vase again. There was too much blue on the left side.

"Oh no, ma'am," Dora was still there. "It's nothing to do with the boy. I dealt with that all right—threatened to set the dog on him, I did, after all the meat, you see!"

"We don't have a dog, Dora!"

"I know that, ma'am, but he don't."

"You shouldn't tell lies, Dora," but there was no criticism in her voice. She considered it a fair retaliation. Her words were habit, those she thought she ought to say, certainly what Edward would expect of her. "Well, what is it then, Dora?"

Dora's face bunched into a howl again as she remembered.

"Oh, ma'am! The murderer's at it again! We'll all be strangled if we set foot outside the door!"

Caroline's immediate reaction was to deny it, to keep Dora from hysterics.

"Nonsense! You're perfectly safe as long as you don't go hanging around by yourself after dark, and no decent girl does that anyway! There's nothing for you to be afraid of."

"But ma'am, he tried it again!" Dora wailed. "He attacked Mrs. Waterman's Daisy! Right out in the daylight, he did!"

Caroline felt a shiver of fear.

"What are you talking about, Dora? Are you just repeating a lot of silly gossip? Where did you hear that, from some errand boy?"

"No, ma'am. Mrs. Waterman's Jenks told Maddock."

"Really? Perhaps you had better send Maddock to me."

"Now, ma'am?" Dora stood transfixed.

"Yes, Dora, right now."

Dora scuttled out and Caroline tried to compose herself to arrange the rest of the flowers. The result was unsatisfying. Maddock knocked at the door.

"Yes, Maddock," she said coldly. "Maddock, Dora tells me she was present when you and—Jenks, is it?—were talking about the two girls who were killed recently, and a new attack?"

Maddock stood stiffly, surprise showing on his usual poker face.

"No, ma'am! Mr. Jenks came round to bring a bottle of port from Mr. Waterman for Mr. Ellison. While he was in my pantry he told me I should keep our girls in, even in daylight, not send them on errands alone because their Daisy, or whatever her name is, had been attacked in the street the other day. Apparently she is a well-built girl, and not the fainting kind. She had a jar of pickles of some kind in her hand, and hit him over the head with it. She wasn't hurt, and seemed quite in control of herself until she got home. Then, of course, she realized what could have happened to her, and burst into tears."

"I see." She was glad she had not criticized him too obviously, allowing herself room to retreat. "And where was Dora?"

"I can only presume, ma'am, that she was in the passage outside the pantry door."

"Thank you Maddock," she said thoughtfully. "Perhaps you had better not send the girls on any errands, as Jenks suggests—at least for the time being. I wish you had told me this earlier."

"I told the master, ma'am. He said not to worry you with it."

"Oh." Her mind raced over reasons why Edward should have done such a thing. What if she, or one of the girls, had gone out alone? Did he think only servants were attacked? What about Chloe Abernathy?

"Thank you, Maddock. You had better see if you can calm Dora a little; and suggest she stop listening at doors, while you are about it!"

"Yes, ma'am, certainly." And he turned on his heel and went out, closing the door silently behind him.

She had intended this afternoon to go and see Martha Prebble. Without really understanding why, she always felt rather sorry for the woman, although she did not like her greatly. Perhaps it was because she disliked the vicar—which

49

was quite stupid! He was doubtless a very good man, and probably suited Martha as well as most husbands suit their wives. One could not sensibly expect a vicar to be romantic; if he was honest, sober, well-mannered, and respected in the community, that was a great deal. To demand more was unreasonable, and Martha was eminently reasonable; even if she had not been as a girl, she would be by now!

Which brought Emily to her mind. It was all very well for her to accept occasional social invitations from Lord Ashworth, but one or two things Emily had said lately led Caroline to believe that she entertained ideas of a more permanent relationship. For Emily's own sake she must be disabused of such romantic follies. Otherwise she would be quite seriously hurt later on, not only by the dissolution of her ambitions in that direction, but by the casting of very definite disadvantage on any future designs. People would be bound to think the worst. Other young men, less aristocratic, but far more practically within Emily's reach, might well be put off—or their mothers would be, which was more to the point.

In view of Maddock's warning it would be better not to go even as far as the vicar's alone. She would take Emily with her, giving them an opportunity to talk privately. It was a delightful afternoon for a walk. Far better than taking Charlotte, which had also crossed her mind. Charlotte disliked the vicar and seemed unable or unwilling to conceal it. That was another thing; somehow to school Charlotte in the art of dissembling, masking her feelings. Apart from anything else, those feelings were far too violent to be becoming in a lady. She loved Charlotte dearly; she was the warmest, the quickest to sympathize, and had by far the sharpest sense of humour among her daughters, but she was impossibly forthright. There were times when Caroline despaired of her! If only she could learn a little tact before she ruined herself socially with some totally unforgivable gaffe. If only she would think before she spoke!

What kind of man would take her as she was? She was practically a social liability at times!

She surveyed the vase of flowers with exasperation, and decided she was in that frame of mind when further effort would only make the arrangement worse. Better find Emily and advise her that they were going to the vicar's. Charlotte at least would be pleased!

The walk to Cater Street was a pleasure, full of sunlight and wind and the noise of leaves. They set out shortly after three, Emily a little reluctantly, but accepting it with good enough grace.

Caroline thought she had better approach the subject obliquely.

"Maddock tells me there has been another girl attacked in the street," she began in a businesslike manner. Better get this over with also.

"Oh," Emily seemed interested, but not as frightened as Caroline would have expected. "I hope she wasn't seriously hurt?"

"Apparently not, but that may be a matter of good fortune rather than lack of intent on her attacker's part," Caroline replied sharply. She must frighten Emily enough to make sure she took no risks. A risk was so easy; an injury could be so permanent.

"Who was it? Anyone we know?"

"A servant of Mrs. Waterman's. But that is hardly the point! You must not go out alone, any of you, until this lunatic is apprehended by the police."

"But that might be forever!" Emily protested. "I'd planned to call on Miss Decker on Friday afternoon—"

"You don't even like Miss Decker!"

"Liking her has nothing to do with it, Mama; she knows people whom I wish to know, or at least to be acquainted with."

"Then you'll have to take Charlotte or Sarah. You are not to go alone, Emily."

Emily's face hardened.

"Sarah won't come. She's going to Madame Tussaud's with Dominic. It's taken her a month to persuade him."

"Then take Charlotte."

"Mama!" Emily said with withering disgust. "You know as well as I do, Charlotte will ruin it. Even if she doesn't actually say anything, her face will give her away."

"I take it she doesn't care for Miss Decker either?" Caroline said a trifle drily.

"Charlotte has no sense of what is practical."

It was the perfect opening. Caroline took it immediately. "It seems to me that you have very little idea yourself, my darling. Your pursuit of Lord Ashworth is hardly destined for any permanent success, and you are seeing far too much of him for a temporary admiration. You will draw an unwelcome attention to yourself, you will find that you are remembered as Ashworth's..." she hesitated, trying to find the right word.

"I intend to be Ashworth's wife," Emily said with an aplomb that staggered Caroline. "Which seems to me to be excellently practical."

"Don't be ridiculous!" Caroline said sharply. "Ashworth won't marry a girl with neither family connections nor money. Even if he were minded to, his parents certainly wouldn't permit it."

Emily stared straight ahead of her and continued marching down the street.

"His father is dead, and he is quite equal to his mother. There is no point in trying to dissuade me. I have made up my mind."

"And you have the temerity to say that Charlotte is impractical," Caroline said in dismay as they turned into Cater Street. "At least keep your own counsel and don't say anything—committing—in front of the vicar."

"I shouldn't dream of saying anything of any sort at all in front of the vicar," Emily replied sharply. "He doesn't understand such things."

"I'm sure he understands them, but as a man of the cloth he would not be interested. All men are equal before God."

Emily gave her a look that stripped bare her own dislike of the vicar and made her feel a hypocrite. It was an uncomfortable feeling, especially when it was generated by one's own youngest child.

"Well, if you imagine you're going to be a lady, you'll have to learn to exercise good manners, even to those you dislike," Caroline said sharply, aware that the reminder was possibly as timely to herself as to Emily.

"Like Miss Decker," Emily looked sideways at her with a tiny smile.

Caroline could think of no reply, and fortunately they were at the Prebbles' door.

Ten minutes later they were in the back parlour. Martha Prebble had ordered tea and was sitting on the overstuffed sofa facing them. Incredibly, Sarah was also there, deep in conversation. She did not seem the least surprised to see them. Martha apologized for the vicar's absence in a tone that left Caroline feeling that in some way Martha Prebble was perhaps as relieved as they were.

"So good of you to help, Mrs. Ellison," Martha said, leaning forward a little. "I sometimes wonder how this parish would survive if it were not for you and your good daughters. Only last week Sarah was here," she smiled sideways at Sarah, "helping with our charity for orphans. Such a delightful girl."

Caroline smiled. Sarah had never been any concern, except perhaps briefly when both she and Edward had wondered if Dominic had been a wise choice. But it had proved excellent, and everyone was happy with it—except perhaps Charlotte. Once or twice she had thought . . . but Martha Prebble was talking again.

". . . course we must help these unfortunate women. In spite of what the vicar says, I feel some of them are the victims of circumstance."

"The poorer classes do not have the advantages of proper upbringing, such as we have," Sarah nodded in agreement.

Really, Sarah was pompous at times: just like Edward. Caroline had missed the beginning of the conversation, but she could guess. They were planning an evening lecture, with a collection plate and tea and refreshments afterwards, in aid of unmarried mothers. It was something Caroline had been drafted into in a moment of absentmindedness.

Martha Prebble's face showed a sense of loss for a moment, as if she had meant something quite different. Then she recollected herself.

"Naturally. But the vicar says it is our duty to help such people, whatever their station, however they came to—fall."

"Of course."

Caroline was delighted when the maid came in with the tea. "Perhaps we had better discuss the programme. Who did you say was going to address us? I'm afraid if you mentioned it I must have forgotten."

"The vicar," Martha replied, and this time her face was unreadable. "After all, he is best qualified to speak to us on the subjects of sin and repentance, the weaknesses of the flesh, and the wages of sin."

Caroline winced at the thought, and privately thanked providence she had brought Emily and not Charlotte. Heaven only knew what Charlotte would have made of that!

"Very suitable," she said automatically. It ran though her mind that it was also totally useless, except to those who felt better for expressing such sentiments. Poor Martha. It must at times be very trying to live with so much rectitude. She looked across at Sarah. Wonder if it had ever occurred to her to consider such things? She looked so bland, so satisfied to agree. What thoughts were there behind her pretty face? She turned to Martha again, who was staring at Sarah. Was that grief in her face, hunger for a daughter she had never had?

"Oh I do so agree with you, Mrs. Prebble," Sarah was saying eagerly. "And I'm sure the whole community looks to you for a lead. I promise you we shall all be there."

"My dear, you may promise for yourself," Caroline added in haste, "but you cannot for others. I shall certainly attend, but we cannot speak for Emily or Charlotte. I have an idea Charlotte has a previous engagement." And if she had not, Caroline would soon contrive one for her. The evening would be bad enough without the kind of disaster Charlotte could cause with a few ill-considered remarks.

They all turned to Emily, who opened her eyes with apparent innocence.

"When did you say the occasion was, Mrs. Prebble?"

"Next Friday week, in the evening, at the church hall."

Emily's face fell.

"Oh, how most unfortunate. I have promised to do a favour for a friend, to visit an elderly relation with her; you understand of course that she would not make the journey alone. And visits mean so much to the elderly, especially when they are not in the best of health."

Emily, you liar, Caroline thought, afraid lest it show in her face. But she had to concede, lie though it was, Emily did it uncommonly well!

And so the visit progressed: polite, largely meaningless conversation; excellent tea, hot and fragrant; rather gluey cakes; and everyone hoping the vicar would not return.

They all walked home together, Sarah and Emily talking, Sarah the more. Emily seemed a little short of temper. Caroline came a step or two behind them, her mind still on Martha Prebble, and what manner of woman she must be to enjoy living with the vicar. Had he perhaps been very different when he was young? Heaven knew, Edward was pompous enough at times; perhaps all men were. But the vicar was infinitely worse. Caroline had often ached to laugh at Edward, even at Dominic; only a lack of courage had prevented her. Did Martha also long to laugh? It was not a face of laughter. In fact the more she thought about it, the more it seemed a face of suffering: strong-boned, reflecting deep feelings; not a face of peace.

A month later the whole event was only an embarrassing memory. Charlotte was delighted to have been prohibited from attending and had agreed, as fervently as was politic, that she might well say something to cause ill-feeling—inadvertently, of course.

Tonight it was gusty and cold for August. Mama, Sarah, and Emily had all gone to a further affair at the church hall, and since Martha Prebble had a summer cold, it was all the more necessary that it should be well supported by people like Mama, capable of organizing, seeing that those in charge of the catering attended to details, that things were done on time, and all was adequately tidied up afterwards. Again, Charlotte was happy to remain at home, with a quite genuine headache.

She thought it might be caused by the heavy, stormy weather, and she opened the garden doors to let in the air. It worked surprisingly well, and by nine o'clock she felt much better.

At ten o'clock she closed the doors as it was now dark. Sitting with the darkness intruding she felt a little vulnerable, remembering that there was nothing between the garden and the street except the rose wall. She had been reading a book her father would not have approved of, but a perfect opportunity since both he and Dominic were also out.

It was half past ten, and quite dark outside, when Mrs. Dunphy knocked on the withdrawing room door.

Charlotte looked up.

"Yes?"

Mrs. Dunphy came in, her hair a little untidy, her apron screwed up in her fingers.

Charlotte stared at her in surprise.

"What is it, Mrs. Dunphy?"

"Perhaps I shouldn't ought to bother you, Miss Charlotte, but I don't rightly know what to do about it!"

"About what, Mrs. Dunphy? Can't it wait till tomorrow?"

"Oh no, Miss Charlotte. It's Lily." Mrs. Dunphy looked wretched. "She's gone out with that Jack Brody again, and she isn't back. It's gone half past ten, Miss Charlotte, and she'll have to be up at six in the morning."

"Well don't you worry about it," Charlotte said a little sharply. She loathed trying to sort out domestic wrangles. "If she feels terrible tomorrow, perhaps she'll learn not to stay out too late in future."

Mrs. Dunphy caught her breath in exasperation.

"You don't understand, Miss Charlotte! It's half past ten and she hasn't come home yet! I never did like that Jack Brody. Mr. Maddock has said a number of times he was no good, and Lily ought to tell him to be on his way."

Charlotte had noticed that Maddock had a very ready regard for Lily, which would predispose him to disapprove of Jack Brody, or anyone else with whom she stepped out.

"I wouldn't take Maddock's view very seriously, Mrs. Dunphy. He's probably harmless enough."

"Miss Charlotte, it's nearer eleven than ten, and it's dark outside and Lily's out there somewhere with a man that's no good! Mr. Maddock's been out to look for her. He's out there now, but I think you should do something."

Charlotte realized for the first time exactly what Mrs. Dunphy was afraid of.

"Oh, don't be foolish, Mrs. Dunphy!" she burst out, not because it was foolish, but because she was afraid now too. "She'll be back presently, and you can send her in here to me. I'll make it plain to her that if she does this again we shall dismiss her. You'd better tell Maddock when he comes back, and then go to bed yourself. Maddock will wait up."

"Yes, Miss Charlotte. Do you—do you think she'll be all right?"

"Not if she ever does this again. Now go back to the kitchen and don't worry about it."

"Yes, thank you, Miss," and Mrs. Dunphy went out, still twisting her apron in one hand.

It was half an hour later, after eleven, when Maddock came in.

Charlotte put down her book. She was just about to go to bed herself. There was no point in waiting up for the others. Although they were later than she had expected. Church hall affairs usually finished by ten. Perhaps there was a lot of clearing up to do, and then they would have to find a carriage home. Papa was at his club, and she could not remember where Dominic had said he was going.

"What is it, Maddock?"

"It's after eleven, Miss Charlotte, and Lily still isn't home. With your permission, I think we should contact the police."

"The police! Whatever for? We can't get the police out because our servant girl is out with an undesirable man! We'll be the laughingstock of the neighbourhood. Papa would never forgive us. Even if she is ..." she looked for the word "...loose enough to stay out all night."

Maddock's face tightened.

"Neither of our girls is immoral, Miss Charlotte. There is something wrong."

"All right then, if not immoral, foolish, thoughtless." Charlotte was beginning to be really frightened herself now. She wished Papa were here, or Dominic. They would know what to do. Was Lily really in danger, should she call the police? The very thought of speaking to the police was frightening, demeaning. Respectable people did not have to call the police. If she did, would Papa be furious? Her mind raced with possibilities, of rumours of disgrace, of Papa's face red with anger, of Lily lying in the road somewhere.

"All right, perhaps you'd better call them," she said very quietly.

"Yes, ma'am. I'll go myself, and lock the door behind me. And don't worry, Miss Charlotte. You'll be perfectly safe here with Mrs. Dunphy and Dora. Just don't let anyone in."

"Yes, Maddock. Thank you."

She sat down to wait. Suddenly the room seemed chill and she huddled further into the cushions on the sofa. Had she done the right thing? Wasn't it a little hysterical to send Maddock out for the police just because Lily was no better than she should be? Papa would be furious. It would be talked about. Mama would be thoroughly embarrassed. It reflected on the morality of the whole household.

She stood up to call Maddock back, then realized it was too late. She had only just sat back on the sofa, shivering, when the front door opened and closed. She froze.

Then Sarah's voice came clearly. "I've never been so tired in all my life! Does Mrs. Prebble normally do all that herself?"

"No, of course not," Caroline said wearily. "It's just that with her being ill she didn't contact the people who normally help."

The door to the withdrawing room opened.

"Why, Charlotte, what on earth are you doing sitting there like a child huddled in the half-dark? Are you ill?" Caroline came forward quickly.

Charlotte was so glad to see her she felt the tears prickle in her eyes. It was ridiculous. She swallowed hard.

"Mama, Lily hasn't come back. Maddock's gone to tell the police!"

Caroline stared.

"Police!" Emily said incredulously, and then her disbelief changed to anger. "What on earth are you thinking of, Charlotte? You must be mad!"

Sarah came up behind her.

"What will the neighbours say? We can't have the police here just because a servant girl has run off with someone!" She looked around as if she expected to see him materialize. "Where's Dominic?"

"He's out, of course!" Charlotte snapped. "Do you think if he were here he'd have gone to bed?"

"You should never have left Charlotte alone," Emily said, anger sharpening her tone.

"Well, possibly Mama didn't know Lily was going to pick tonight to get lost!" Charlotte could hear her voice cracking. In her mind she saw Lily lying in the street. "She might be dead or something, and all you are thinking of is making silly remarks!"

Before anyone could take it any further the door opened and closed again and Edward came in through the open doorway of the withdrawing room.

"What's the matter?" he said immediately. "Caroline?"

"Charlotte sent for the police because Lily has run away," Sarah said furiously. "I expect we'll be the talk of the street tomorrow!"

Edward stood aghast, staring at Charlotte.

"Charlotte?" he demanded.

"Yes, Papa." She could not look at him.

"What on earth possessed you to do such a foolish thing, child?"

"She was afraid something..." Caroline began.

"Be silent, Caroline," he said sharply. "Charlotte? I'm waiting!"

Charlotte felt her tears disappear in rebellion. She looked at him, as angry as he was now.

"If the whole street is going to talk about us," she replied distinctly, "I would prefer it were because we were worried unnecessarily than because we didn't care enough to see if she was all right when she was lying somewhere hurt!"

"Charlotte, go to your room!"

Wordlessly, head high, she went out and up the stairs. Her bedroom was cold and dark, but she could only think of the colder and darker streets outside.

She woke in the morning tired and heavy-headed. She remembered last night. Papa was almost certainly still angry, and poor Lily would reap the worst of it, possibly even a dismissal. Maddock was probably in for an unpleasant patch, too. She must remember not to make it worse for him by letting Papa know it was he who had suggested the police.

And of course if Lily were dismissed it would upset the whole household until a replacement was found. Mrs. Dunphy would be thoroughly aggrieved. Dora would be run silly. And Mama would discover all over again how hard it was to come by a respectable girl, never mind to train her.

It was still early but there was no point in lying in bed. Anyway, better to get it over with than to lie fearing and building it into ever larger proportions.

She had ventured as far as the downstairs hall when she saw Dora.

"Oh, Miss Charlotte!"

"What's the matter, Dora? You look terrible. Are you ill?"

"Not properly speaking, I'm not. But isn't it terrible, Miss?"

Charlotte's heart sank. Surely Papa had not turned Lily out into the street in the middle of the night?

"What is, Dora? I went to bed before Lily came back."

"Oh, Miss Charlotte," Dora swallowed, her eyes round. "She never did come back. She must be lying murdered in the street somewhere, and we all in our beds like we didn't care!"

"She doesn't have to be anything of the sort!" Charlotte snapped, trying to convince herself. "She's probably lying in bed, too, in some miserable room with Jack what's-his-name."

"Oh no, Miss, it's wicked of you to say—" She blushed violently. "I'm sorry, Miss Charlotte, but you didn't ought to say that. Lily was a good girl. She'd have never done that, and without giving notice even!"

Charlotte changed the subject.

"Did the police come, do you know? I mean, Maddock went for them."

"Yes, Miss, a constable came, but he seemed to be of a mind that Lily was no better than she should be, and had simply run off. But then I always reckon police is no better than they should be either. All the low sorts of people they mix with, I dare say. Stands to reason, don't it?"

"I don't know, Dora. I've never known any police."

Breakfast was a formal and very grim affair. Even Dominic looked unusually glum. He and Papa departed for the day, and Emily and Mama went to the dressmaker's for fittings. Sarah was in her room writing letters. Funny what an enormous correspondence she had. Charlotte could never find above two or three people to write to in a month.

It was half past eleven and Charlotte was painting surprisingly successfully, for the gray mood she was in, when Maddock knocked and opened the door.

"What is it, Maddock?" Charlotte did not look up from her palette. She was mixing a muted sepia for leaves in the distance, and wished to get it exactly right. She enjoyed painting, and this morning it was particularly soothing.

"A person, Miss Charlotte, to see Mrs. Ellison, but since she is not in, he insisted on seeing someone."

She abandoned the sepia.

"What do you mean, 'a person,' Maddock? What kind of a person?"

"A person from the police, Miss Charlotte."

Fear rippled through Charlotte. It was real at last! Or were they come to complain about having been bothered over a domestic matter?

"Then you'd better show him in."

"Do you wish me to remain, Miss, in case he becomes a nuisance? You can never tell with police persons. They are used to a different class of neighbourhood altogether."

Charlotte would very much have liked his moral support.

"No, thank you, Maddock. But stay in the hall so I can call for you, please."

"Yes, Miss."

A moment later the door opened again.

"Inspector Pitt, ma'am."

The man who came in was tall and looked large because he was untidy; his hair was unruly, and his jacket flapped. His face was plain, a little Semitic, although his eyes were light and his hair no darker than brown. He appeared intelligent. His voice when he spoke was unusually beautiful, quite incongruous against his somewhat scruffy appearance. He looked Charlotte up and down keenly, irritating her already.

"I'm sorry to have to tell you when you are alone, Miss Ellison, but we cannot afford to waste time. Perhaps you would like to sit down?"

Instinctively she refused.

"No, thank you," she said stiffly. "What is it you want?"

"I'm sorry, I have bad news. We have found your maid, Lily Mitchell."

Charlotte tried to stand quite still, upright, although her knees were weak. She could feel the blood drain from her face.

"Where?" her voice was a squeak. This wretched man was staring at her. She did not normally dislike people on sight— no, perhaps that was not quite true—but this man certainly inspired it. "Well?" she said, keeping her voice level.

"In Cater Street. Perhaps you had better sit down?"

"I'm perfectly all right, thank you." She tried to freeze him with a glance, but he seemed oblivious to it. Quite firmly he took her arm and guided her backwards into one of the hardbacked chairs.

"Would you like me to call one of your maids?" he offered.

That incensed her. She was not so feeble she could not conduct herself decently, even in the face of shocking news.

"What is it you wish to do that cannot wait?" she said with great control.

He wandered slowly round the room. Really, the man had no manners at all. Still, what could you expect of the police? He probably could not help it.

"Your butler reported last night that she had gone out walking with a man called Jack Brody, a clerk of some sort. What time did you require her to come home?"

"Half past ten, I think. I'm not sure. No, maybe ten o'clock. Maddock could tell you."

"With your permission, I shall ask him." It sounded more like a statement than a request. "How long was she in your employ?"

It all sounded so final, so much in the past.

"Four years, about. She was only nineteen." She heard her voice drop suddenly, and a sharp memory of Emily came back to her, Emily as a baby, Emily learning to walk. It was ridiculous. Emily had nothing in common with Lily, except that they were both nineteen.

The wretched policeman was staring at her.

"You must have known her fairly well?"

"I suppose so." She realized just how little she did know. Lily was a face around the house, something she was used to. She did not know anything about the girl behind the face at all, what she cared about, or was afraid of.

"Had she ever stayed out before?"

"What?" She had temporarily forgotten him.

He repeated the question.

"No. Never. Mister—?" She had forgotten his name, too.

"Pitt, Inspector Pitt," he filled in for her.

"Inspector Pitt, was she—was she strangled, like the others?"

"Garroted, Miss Ellison, with a strong wire. Yes, exactly like the others."

"And—and was she also—mutilated?"

"Yes. I'm sorry."

"Oh." She felt weakness overwhelm her, and horror, and pity.

He was watching her. Apparently he saw nothing but her silence.

"With your permission, I'll go and speak to the other servants. They probably knew her better than you did." There was something in his tone of voice that implied she did not care. It made her angry—and guilty.

"We don't pry into our servants' lives, Mr. Pitt! But in case you think we are not concerned, it was I who sent Maddock for the police last night." She coloured with anger as soon as she had said it. Why on earth was she trying to justify herself to this man? "Unfortunately you were not able to find her then!" she added sharply.

He accepted the rebuke silently, and a moment later he was gone.

Charlotte stood staring at the easel. The painting which had seemed delicate and evocative a quarter of an hour ago was now only so many gray-brown smudges on paper. Her mind was full of blurred images, dark streets, footsteps, fighting for breath, and above all fear, and the dreadful, intimate attack.

She was still staring at the easel when her mother came in. Emily's voice floated from the hall.

"I'm sure it will look perfectly dreadful if she leaves it as loose as that. I shall appear to be quite fat! It's so unfashionable."

Caroline had stopped, staring at Charlotte.

"Charlotte, my dear, what is it?"

Charlotte found her eyes filling with tears. In an agony of relief she ran into her mother's arms and almost crushed her, holding her so tightly.

"Lily. Mama, she's been strangled, like the others. They found her in Cater Street. There's a terrible policeman here now, this moment! He's talking to Maddock and the servants."

Caroline touched her hair gently. It was an infinitely soothing gesture.

"Oh dear," she said softly. "I was so afraid of that. I never really imagined Lily had run off; I suppose I just wanted to think so because it was so much preferable to this. Your Papa will be so angry at having the police here. Does Sarah know?"

"No. She's upstairs."

Caroline pushed her away gently.

"Then we had better collect ourselves and prepare to face a good deal of unpleasantness. I shall have to write to Lily's parents. It is only right that they should hear from a member of the family, someone that knew Lily. And we were responsible for her. Now go upstairs and wash your face. And you had better tell Sarah. Where did you say this policeman was?"

Inspector Pitt returned in the evening, when Edward and Dominic were home, and insisted on speaking to them all again. He was very persistent and authoritative.

"I've never heard of such nonsense!" Edward said furiously when Maddock came to announce him. "The fellow's impertinence is beyond words. I shall have to speak to his superior.

I will not have women involved in this sordid affair. I shall speak to him alone. Caroline, girls, please withdraw until I send Maddock for you."

They all stood up obediently, but before they could reach the door, it opened and the untidy figure of Pitt came striding in.

"Good evening, ma'am," he bowed to Caroline. "Evening," he said and took in everyone else, his eyes lingering a moment longer on Charlotte, to her annoyance. Sarah turned to look at her with disgust, as if she were somehow responsible for this creature coming into the drawing room.

"The ladies are just leaving," Edward said stiffly. "Will you be so good as to stand aside and let them pass."

"How unfortunate," Pitt smiled cheerfully. "I had hoped to speak to them in your presence, for moral support, as it were. But if you prefer I speak to them alone, then of course—"

"I prefer that you do not speak to them at all! They can know nothing of this affair whatsoever, and I will not have them distressed."

"Well, of course we shall be very grateful for anything that you know, sir—"

"I know nothing either! I don't interest myself in the romantic affairs of servant girls!" Edward snapped. "But I can tell you all that the family knows of Lily. I can tell you about her service record, her references, where her family lives, and so on. I imagine you will want to know that?"

"Yes, although I don't suppose it's in the least relevant. However, I do require to speak to your wife and daughters. Women are very observant, you know; and women observe other women. You would be surprised how much might miss your eye, or mine, but not theirs."

"My wife and daughters have more to interest them than the romances of Lily Mitchell." Edward's face was growing redder and his hands were clenched.

Sarah moved a little closer to him.

"Really, Mr...." She dismissed his name. "I assure you, I know nothing whatsoever. You would be better employed questioning Mrs. Dunphy, or Dora. If Lily confided in anyone, it would be one of them. Find this wretched man she was walking out with."

"Oh, Mrs. Corde, we already have done. He says he left Lily at the end of the street, within sight of this house, at ten minutes before ten. He had to be back at his lodgings himself at ten o'clock, or be locked out."

"You've only got his word for that," Dominic spoke for the first time. He was leaning back in one of the chairs, looking a little flushed, but the most composed of them all. Charlotte's heart lurched as she turned to him. He looked so calm; Papa was ridiculous beside him.

"He was in his lodging-house by ten o'clock," Pitt replied, looking down at Dominic with a faint pucker between his eyes.

"Well, he could have killed her before ten o'clock, couldn't he?" Dominic persisted.

"Certainly. But why should he?"

"I don't know," Dominic crossed his legs. "That's up to you to find out. Why should anyone?"

"That's right," Sarah moved closer to Dominic, visibly allying herself with his theory. "You should be there, not here."

"At least he had the discretion not to come in daylight," Emily whispered to Charlotte. "Poor Sarah's frying!"

"Don't be spiteful," Charlotte whispered back, although silently she agreed, and she knew Emily knew it.

"You believe it was him, do you, Mrs. Corde?" Pitt raised his eyebrows.

"Of course! Who else would it be?"

"Who indeed?"

"I think it's perfectly obvious," Edward found his tongue again. "They had some sort of lovers' quarrel, and he lost his temper and strangled her. We'll make all the arrangements for the funeral, of course. But I don't think you need to bother us again. Maddock can tell you anything else you need to know of a practical nature."

"Not strangled, sir, garotted." Pitt held his hands up, pulling tight an invisible wire. "With a wire he just happened to be carrying, no doubt in case of such a contingency."

Edward's face was white.

"I shall report you to your superiors for impertinence!"

Charlotte felt an idiotic desire to giggle. No doubt it was hysteria.

"Did he also kill Chloe Abernathy?" Pitt enquired, "and the Hiltons' maid as well? Or have we two hangmen loose in Cater Street?"

They stared at him in silence. He was a ludicrous figure in their quiet withdrawing room—with ludicrous, ugly, and frightening suggestions.

Charlotte felt Emily's hand creep into hers, and she was glad to hang on to it.

No one answered Pitt.

Chapter
Four

The following day was one of the worst that Charlotte could ever recall. Everyone was feeling wretched, although it showed variously in different people. Papa was shorter-tempered than usual, and very full of authority. Mama was endlessly seeing to practical details, as if sorting out the kitchen and the housework would somehow alter other events. Sarah kept repeating the comments of social acquaintances until Charlotte finally lost her temper and told her in no uncertain terms to be quiet. Dominic already was quiet, to the point of silence. Emily seemed least affected, her mind obviously on other things. The only good thing to be said was that Grandmama was still staying with Susannah, and as yet was not in a position to offer comment.

Since it was a Saturday there was no work, and no one felt like going out for any other purpose.

The vicar sent a small note, by messenger, to express his regrets.

"Very courteous of him," Sarah said, glancing at it when her father had read it.

"It's the least he could do," Charlotte said irritably. The very thought of the vicar was enough to make her spit.

"You don't expect him to come in person over a servant," Sarah was also annoyed now. "Besides, there really isn't anything he can do."

Charlotte searched for an argument to that, and could not find one. She saw Dominic's amused dark eyes on her, and felt the blood rush to her face. If only she could stop that happening! It made her feel so foolish.

Caroline came in at that moment, her face coloured from rushing, her hair a little astray. Edward looked up.

"What on earth have you been doing, my dear? You look like—there's something on your nose."

She brushed at it automatically, and made it worse.

Charlotte took a handkerchief and removed the mark from her. It was flour.

"Have you been cooking?" Edward asked with pained surprise. "What's the matter with Mrs. Dunphy?"

"She's got a headache. I'm afraid all this business has hit her very hard. She was fond of Lily, you know. Anyway, I rather like cooking. I came because I just remembered I promised to take a receipt for vegetable soup to Mrs. Harding, and I wondered if two of you would take it for me this afternoon?"

Charlotte liked Mrs. Harding. She was a sharp-tongued but very long-memoried old lady with endless recollections about all sorts of people she had known in her somewhat colourful youth, before she had married above herself, and settled to wealth and respectability. Charlotte doubted all the stories were true, but they were hugely entertaining.

"I'll be happy to go, Mama," she offered quickly.

"You must take Sarah or Emily with you." Caroline looked at them both.

"I'm busy," Emily replied. "I have sewing to do, since we are a maid short. There is linen to be mended."

"And if Mrs. Dunphy is sick," Sarah added, "then I shall

stay at home and see if there is anything I can do for her. Perhaps I can talk with her, take her mind off it."

Charlotte gave her a withering stare. She knew perfectly well her reasons were not to do with Mrs. Dunphy. Sarah thought Mrs. Harding was a disreputable old gossip, and she did not wish to know her socially. As far as the gossip went, she was perfectly correct. But had her stories been a little more up to date they might well have found her a readier audience.

"Charlotte doesn't need company," Edward said tartly. "It's less than two miles away. Go straight there, Charlotte, and return as soon as it is civil for you to do so. I doubt there will be any need to explain. I expect the news is all over the neighbourhood. And don't gossip! Old Mrs. Harding is an inveterate busybody. Give her the receipt, and wish her well, and then come home again."

"I won't have the girls walking in the street alone," Caroline said firmly. "Either someone goes with her, or Mrs. Harding will have to wait. The streets are too dangerous."

"Nonsense, Caroline! She'll be perfectly safe," Edward sat up straighter. "It's broad daylight."

"It was broad daylight when Mrs. Waterman's maid was attacked!" Caroline rejoined. "I wonder you didn't tell us about that, so we as well as the servants might have been warned."

"My dear Caroline, where is your sense of proportion? This lunatic, whoever he is, attacks servant girls, girls of loose morals. No one could take Charlotte to be such a creature."

"What about Chloe Abernathy? She wasn't a servant!"

"Yes, I was surprised about her myself. I had always considered her to be proper enough, if somewhat light-headed. It shows how one can be deceived."

"Because she was killed?" Caroline said with a lift of amazement in her voice.

"Precisely."

That is a completely circular argument, Charlotte thought, almost forgetting herself so far as to say so. "You are saying she was killed because she was immoral, and she was immoral because she was killed!" she finished aloud.

"I am saying she was killed because she kept immoral company," Edward looked at her with a frown, "and the fact that she was killed proves it. Are you frightened to go out alone?" This time there was concern in his voice. He was not unkind.

"Yes," she said honestly. "I would prefer not to."

Dominic stretched out his legs, and then stood up swiftly.

"If you like, I'll come with you. I doubt I should be of any assistance whatsoever here, either with the linen or with Mrs. Dunphy, and certainly not in the kitchen."

The journey with Dominic was marvellous, in spite of the heat which beat down from the August sun, and up in waves from the pavement. Mrs. Harding was delighted to see them, although for once her flow of gossip seemed to have been cut off at the source. Perhaps it was the very masculine presence of Dominic. She offered them refreshments, and they were glad to accept a lemonade before parting. She understood but regretted their need for haste; at least she said so, but Charlotte had the distinct feeling Dominic's presence hampered her, although she obviously admired him—as indeed what woman would not?

On the way home Dominic himself had seemed a little put out at her reticence. He said he had heard she was the best gossip in the district, and was greatly disappointed in her. Charlotte tried to explain what she felt to be the reason and ended up by regaling him with the best stories she could remember, to his vast entertainment. He laughed with pure delight, and Charlotte was blissfully, painfully as happy as she had ever been.

They arrived home to find Sarah in a rage, Papa white-faced, Emily silent, and Mama absent in the kitchen.

The happiness vanished as if a door had been closed on it, though Dominic was still smiling, as if he had not felt the change.

"What's the matter with everyone?" he asked, going over to open the French windows. "You need some air. It's a perfect day." Then he swung round, his face clouded. "You're not still thinking about Lily, are you? I'm sure she wouldn't want or expect us to stay glum for the rest of the summer."

"This is hardly the rest of the summer, Dominic," Sarah said tartly. "But it has nothing to do with Lily, at least not in the way you mean. The wretched police have been here again."

Charlotte felt only anger, until she saw her father's face. He seemed less angry than genuinely distressed.

"What for, Papa? Haven't we told them all we know?"

He frowned, looking away from her.

"It appears they are not satisfied that it was this fellow she was walking out with or, if it was not him, then some lunatic."

"Well, they can't imagine it has anything to do with us," Dominic said incredulously.

"I don't know what they imagine," Edward replied sharply. "I personally think they are using it as an excuse to be inquisitive, to exercise their curiosity."

"What have they been asking?" Charlotte looked from one to the other of them. "Surely if they are impertinent we don't have to answer them? Send them out of the house."

"It's all very well for you to speak!" Sarah snapped. "You were not here."

"You could have been out, if you'd been prepared to come with me." Charlotte was quite mild. She was delighted that Dominic had come instead, but a hint of resentment over the spoilt afternoon lingered at the back of her mind.

"Don't worry, you haven't escaped anything," Sarah tossed her head a little. "They are coming back to see you."

"I don't know anything!"

"And Dominic."

Charlotte turned to Edward. "Papa, what can I tell them? I never even saw Lily that day, that I can recall." She felt

73

a quick stab of shame. "And I didn't know her very well at any time."

"I don't know what they want." Once again Edward's anxiety was more apparent than his irritation. "They asked all sorts of odd questions, about myself, and Maddock, and they were very keen to speak to Dominic."

Dominic frowned, and a flicker of concern crossed his face. "What about the other victims—apart from Lily?"

"Don't be foolish!" Sarah said sharply. "They can hardly consider you had anything to do with it, except perhaps that you may have noticed something, some odd person hanging around the street perhaps. After all, you do travel up and down the street almost every day."

A new and appalling thought occurred to Charlotte. Could the police possibly be idiotic, blind enough to think one of them—? Dominic and Papa were out frequently, passed Cater Street—.

Sarah saw it in her face.

"I shall soon disabuse them of that lunacy," she said furiously. "I know Dominic far too well. He is not the sort of man even to look at servant girls, much less accost them. He is not some creature of uncontrollable passions. He is a civilized man. Such a thing would not enter into his head."

Charlotte turned to Dominic and saw for an instant in his face a look of hurt, of deep frustration, as if he had glimpsed and then lost something of inestimable value. She did not know then what momentary dream of sensuality or danger he had seen, and missed.

It was just over an hour later when Pitt returned, this time bringing with him a man Charlotte had not seen before, a man who was very briefly introduced to her as Sergeant Flack. He was a slight man of hardly average height, but looked even smaller beside Pitt. He remained absolutely silent, but his eyes wandered all over the room with consuming interest.

"Good afternoon, Mr. Pitt," Charlotte said calmly. She was

determined not to be ruffled by him, and to dismiss him as soon as possible. "I'm sorry you have taken the trouble to return, since I'm quite sure I can tell you nothing more. However, of course I will answer any questions you wish to ask." Perhaps that was a little rash. She must not let him be impertinent.

"You would be surprised what is sometimes useful," Pitt replied. He turned to his sergeant and briefly directed him to the kitchen to question Maddock, Mrs. Dunphy, and Dora.

He looked back to Charlotte. He seemed to be totally at ease, which in itself was irritating. He ought to have been a little...a little impressed. After all, he was a mere policeman and in the house of those considerably superior to him socially.

"What is it you wish to know?" she said coldly.

He smiled charmingly.

"The name and whereabouts of the lunatic who is garotting young women in the streets of this neighbourhood," he replied. "Of course that is presuming it is one person, and not a crime, and then another crime in imitation."

She was surprised into facing him, meeting his eyes.

"Whatever do you mean?"

"That sometimes people hear of a crime, especially if it is a gruesome one, and it gives them the idea to solve their own problems in the same manner: to dispose of someone that is in the way, from whose death they could benefit, financially or otherwise, and," he snapped his fingers, "you have a second murder, or a third, or whatever. The second murderer hopes the first will be blamed."

"You make it sound so matter-of-fact," she said with distaste.

"It is a matter of fact, Miss Ellison. Whether it is this fact or not, I have to enquire—but not until I have exhausted some of the more obvious possibilities."

"What possibilities do you mean?" she asked and then wished she had not. She did not desire to encourage him. And to be honest, she was a little afraid of the answer.

"Three young women have been garotted in this area over the last few months. The first thing that comes to mind is that there is a maniac loose."

"I would have thought that was the answer," she said with some relief. "Why should you imagine any other? Why don't you take your enquiries to the sort of place where you will find such people—I mean the sort of people who are likely to—" she fumbled for the exact phrase she wanted "—the criminal classes!"

"The underworld?" he smiled a little derisively. There was bitter amusement and a little patronage in his tone. "What sort of a place do you imagine the underworld is, Miss Ellison? Something I find by opening a sewer manhole?"

"No, of course not!" she snapped. "I have no knowledge of it myself, of course. It hardly comes within my social sphere! But I know perfectly well that there is a world of criminal classes whose standards are totally different—" she raked him up and down with a withering stare, "—at least from mine!"

"Oh, very different, Miss Ellison," he agreed, still smiling, but there was a hardness in his eyes. "Although whether you are referring to moral standards, or standards of living you didn't say. But perhaps it doesn't matter—they are not as far apart as the words imply. In fact I have come to think they are usually symbiotic."

"Symbiotic?" she said in disbelief.

He misunderstood her, supposing she did not know the meaning of the word.

"Each dependent upon the other, Miss Ellison. A relationship of coexistence, of mutual feeding, interdependence."

"I know what the word means!" she said furiously. "I question your choice of it under the circumstances. Poverty does not necessarily produce crime. There are plenty of poor people who are as honest as I."

At that he broke into a genuine grin.

"You find that amusing, Mr. Pitt?" she said icily. "I spoke forgetting that you do not know me well enough for that to be any standard. But at least you know that I do not garotte young women in the street!"

He looked at her, at her waist, at her slender hands and wrists.

"No," he agreed. "I doubt you would have the strength."

"Your sense of wit is impertinent, Mr. Pitt." She tried to stare him down, but since he was well over six feet and she was half a foot shorter, she failed. "And not in the least amusing," she finished.

"It was not intended to amuse, Miss Ellison, nor to be wit. I meant it quite literally." Now he was serious again. "And I doubt you have ever seen real poverty in your life."

"Yes, I have!"

"Have you?" His disbelief was quite apparent. "Have you seen children abandoned when they are six or seven years old to beg or steal to keep alive, sleeping in gutters and doorways, soaked to the skin by rain, owning nothing but the rags they stand in? What do you suppose happens to them? How long do you think it takes for an undernourished six-year-old, alone in the streets, to die of starvation or cold? When he has been taught nothing but to survive, when he cannot read or write, when he has been passed from one person to another until nobody wants him, what do you think happens to him? Either he dies—and believe me, I've seen a lot of their little bodies lying in the back streets, dead of cold and hunger!—or else he's lucky, and some kidsman or sweep takes him in."

In spite of herself she let her pity overcome her anger.

"A kidsman?"

"A kidsman is a man who picks up children like these," he went on, "and at first takes them in and feeds them, gives them shelter and some sort of security, a place to belong. Then gradually he prevails on their gratitude by teaching them to thieve, at least to thieve with skill. To begin with they go out with some of the older boys, watching them work, something simple to start with. It used to be silk handkerchiefs when they were more fashionable. Later they graduate to something more subtle; the clever ones even progress to inside pockets, watch chains or seals. A really first-class kidsman will run classes. He'll hang a row of old coats on a line across the room, a silk handkerchief trailing from each pocket, and the boys will take them one by one to try their skill. Or he might use a tailor's dummy, with bells sewn all over the coat, to tinkle at the slightest disturbance, or even stand with his back to them himself. Those who succeed are well rewarded, while those who fail are punished. A child with courage, or hunger, and nimble fingers can make himself and his master a good living, until he grows too large or loses the agility of his hands."

She was horrified, and through her distress for the child she was angry with him for making her look at such things.

"What happens then? Does he starve?" she asked. She did not want to know, and yet she could not bear not to.

"Probably he graduates to being a footpad, or if he's smart, joins a band of pickpockets, the swell mob—"

"The what?"

"The swell mob—the best end of the pickpocketing business, well-dressed, usually having rooms in a moderate neighbourhood, a mistress, which they pick up when they are about thirteen or fourteen, almost always an older girl. Oddly enough they are very faithful and regard it as a sort of marriage. They work in gangs of three to six, each taking his part in the maneuvering and execution of a robbery. They very often rob women."

"How do you know all this? And if you know about it, why don't you arrest them, prevent it?"

He snorted slightly.

"We do arrest them. Nearly all of them spend some of their time in prison."

She shivered.

"What a terrible life. Surely it would be better to be a sweep. Didn't you say something about sweeps? That at least would be honest."

"My dear Miss Ellison, it would take a wiser and considerably more experienced woman than you are to find an honest sweep. Have you ever been up a chimney?"

She raised her eyebrows in disdain as frigid as she could make it.

"You have a curious idea of the occupations of a gentlewoman, Mr. Pitt. But if you need an answer, then no, I have never climbed up inside a chimney."

"No." He did not seem in the least perturbed by her tone. He looked her up and down again and she found herself colouring under his gaze. "You would not fit," he said frankly. "You are far too tall, and far too big."

She blushed furiously.

"Oh, you have an excellent waist, but," his eyes went to her shoulders and bust, then on down, "the rest of you would most certainly get stuck in the vertical tunnels, the dogleg bends, and soot would get in your nose and mouth, your eyes, your lungs—"

"It sounds horrible, but not dishonest, except for the sweep, because he gets someone else to do the labour. But as you pointed out, they could hardly do it themselves."

"Miss Ellison, no professional cracksman robs a house without first obtaining information as to the layout, and where the valuables are kept. Can you think of a better way of doing that than by going through the chimney system?"

"You mean—but that's terrible!"

"Of course it's terrible, Miss Ellison. It's all terrible!" he said furiously, "poverty and crime, loneliness, dirt, chronic disease, drunkenness, prostitution, beggary! They steal, forge money and letters, practice fraud and prostitution, but seldom murder unless pushed to it. And they don't come out of their own world except for profit. There's no profit in garotting three helpless girls in Cater Street. They were not even robbed."

She could not look away from him; she was held by a mixture of fascination and horror. She disliked him acutely, and what he was saying frightened her.

"What do you mean? What are you suggesting? They are dead!"

"Oh, very. I'm saying that the kind of garotter you are thinking of, from the underworld, the criminal classes, kills for gain. He would not risk his neck for fun. He kills to escape capture, and only if it is necessary. Far better to merely immobilize or stun. He first marks his victim, choosing only those who have money."

"Then why—?" A new world had opened in front of her, ugly and confused, intruding into the safety of her beliefs, the things she had considered certain, fixed.

He looked at her with a very slight smile, as if there were understanding between them.

"If I knew that perhaps I should know who it is. But his reason is not a simple one—and not a clean one, like a robbery or revenge. It is something darker than that, twisted deeper into the soul."

She was frightened, and she disliked him, disliked his familiarity, his intrusion into her emotions, forcing her to know things she did not want to know.

"I think you had better go, Mr. Pitt. There is nothing whatsoever I can tell you. And I believe you wished to see Mr. Corde, although I'm sure he can tell you nothing either. Perhaps you had better consider the other girls—who were killed." She drew breath and tried to steady herself.

"I shall consider everything, Miss Ellison. But yes, I would like to see Mr. Corde. Perhaps you would be good enough to call Maddock, and send for him?"

The evening was not a pleasant one. Dominic would not tell anyone what Pitt had asked him, although Edward did press him as far as discretion would allow. Dominic remained almost silent which was worrying in itself because it was out of character. Charlotte was afraid even to entertain her thoughts. She kept just beyond framing the possibility that Pitt had discovered something that embarrassed Dominic, something to be ashamed of. Of course, it could have nothing to do with the death of Lily, or the others, but everyone knew that men, even the best of them, occasionally did other things that were not known. It was the nature of men, and to be expected but not acknowledged, for one's own peace of mind.

She talked determinedly of other things, aware that sometimes what she said was nonsense, but better nonsense than the long gaps in conversation when thoughts intruded.

In spite of being tired, she slept badly and woke late, causing her to have to rush to get ready for church. She had never particularly enjoyed church, the formality of it, the atmosphere of rigid propriety, the polite greetings that were a ritual rather than a matter of friendship, the form of service that was always the same till she found herself saying the words and singing the responses like a parrot. She could go through the whole thing automatically, providing she did not stop to think where she was. Once she stopped she had to look at the words to get herself started again until habit took over. And, of course, the vicar would preach a sermon. It was usually on sin, and the need for repentance. The woman taken in adultery was his favourite story, although he never drew from it the same meaning that Charlotte did. And why was it always the woman? Why were men never taken in adultery? In all the stories she had ever heard it was women who committed the adultery, and men who found them and commented on it! What about the men with whom they were found? Why didn't the women throw stones at them? She had asked Papa that, a long time ago, and been told with some surprise not to be ridiculous.

The vicar gave his usual sermon today; in fact, if anything, it was even worse. His text was "Blessed are the pure in heart" but his message was more "blessed are the clean of action." He went to great lengths to condemn unclean actions. And the more he spoke about harlots and prostitutes, the more Charlotte found her mind seeing the poor that that wretched Pitt had described; children left to starve at the age when she and her sisters were just learning to read and write, being taught by Miss Sims in the schoolroom. She thought of young women left alone with babies. How else could they live?

She very seldom swore, but this morning she would have consigned Mr. Pitt to hell for having forced her to know of such things. She sat on the hard pew and stared at the vicar. Everything he said made her feel worse. She had always disliked him, and by the end of this morning she hated him with a vehemence that depressed and frightened her. She was sure it was very unchristian, and unfeminine to hate anyone this way, and yet she felt it with a depth and rightness she could not deny.

She looked up at the organ loft and saw Martha Prebble's pale face as she played the closing hymn. She looked bored and unhappy, too.

Sunday lunch was a miserable affair and the afternoon must, of course, be spent suitably for the Sabbath. Tomorrow Grandmama was returning from Susannah's, which was not greatly to be looked forward to either.

It would have seemed impossible, but Monday was worse. Grandmama arrived at ten o'clock, muttering dark prognostications about the downfall of the neighbourhood, of the gentle classes, of the world at large. Morality was going downhill at a great rate, and they were all destined for disaster.

They had no sooner got her unloaded and upstairs in her own sitting room, when Inspector Pitt arrived again, bringing with him the silent Sergeant Flack. Sarah was out—something to do with some charitable cause or other. Emily was at the dressmaker's being fitted for another occasion with George Ashworth. Really, she ought to have more sense! It was time she realized he was a gambler, a philanderer, or worse, and that nothing would come of it for her but the ruin of her reputation. And all the time Mama was upstairs trying to soothe Grandmama into a state where she could be left without making everyone's life a plague.

There was no one Charlotte wished to see less than Inspector Pitt.

He came into the morning room, filling the doorway, coat flapping, hair untidy as always. His affability irritated Charlotte almost beyond bearing.

"What do you want, Mr. Pitt?"

He did not bother to correct her, to say that he was *Inspector* Pitt. This also annoyed her for she had intended it to slight him.

"Good morning, Miss Ellison. The most perfect summer day. Is your father at home?"

"Of course not! This is Monday morning. Like most other respectable people, he is in the city. Just because we are not working class does not mean we are idle!"

He grinned broadly, showing strong teeth.

"Charmed as I am by the pleasure of your company, Miss Ellison, I am here working also. But if your father is out, then I shall have to speak to you."

"If you must."

"I don't investigate murder for pleasure." His smile vanished, although his good humour remained. There was a hint of tragedy, even anger, in his voice. "There is little pleasure in it for anyone, but it must be done."

"I have already told you what little I know," she said exasperatedly. "Several times. If you cannot solve it, then perhaps you had better give up, and pass it over to someone who can."

He ignored her rudeness.

"Was she a pretty girl, Lily Mitchell?"

"Didn't you see her?" she said in surprise. It seemed a most elementary thing to have omitted.

His smile was sad, as if he were sorry for her, as well as patient.

"Yes, Miss Ellison, I saw her, but she was not pretty then. Her face was swollen and blue, her features distorted, her tongue—"

"Stop it! Stop it!" Charlotte heard her own voice shouting at him.

"Then will you be good enough to step off your dignity," he said quite calmly, "and help me to find out who did that to her, before he does it to someone else?"

She felt angry and hurt and ashamed.

"Yes, of course," she said quickly, turning away so he could not see her face, and even more, so she could not see him. "Yes, Lily was quite pretty. She had very nice skin." She shivered and felt a little sick as she tried to picture that skin bloated and marked by violent death. She forced it out of her mind. "She never had spots or looked sallow. And she had a very soft voice. I think she came from somewhere in the country."

"Derbyshire."

"Oh."

"Was she friendly with the other servants?"

"Yes, I think so. We never heard of any trouble."

"With Maddock?"

She swung round to face him, her thoughts coming too quickly to disguise.

"You mean . . . ?"

"Precisely. Did Maddock admire her, fancy her?"

She had never before considered the possibility of Maddock having such feelings. Possessiveness over his servants perhaps, but desire, jealousy? Maddock was the butler, in formal clothes, polite, in charge of the house. But he was a man, and now that she thought about it, probably not more than thirty-five or so, not much older than Dominic. What a preposterous thought! To think of him in the same breath as Dominic.

Pitt was waiting, watching her face.

"I see the thought is a new one to you, but not unlikely, when you weigh it."

There was no point in lying to him.

"No. I remember someone saying something. Mrs. Dun-phy—the night Lily—disappeared. She said Maddock—liked Lily, that he would be bound to disapprove of Jack Brody because he took Lily out, whatever he was like. But that could mean no more than that he was afraid of losing a good girl. It takes a long time to train a new one, you know." She did not want to get Maddock into trouble. She could not really imagine he had followed Lily out and done *that* to her. Could she?

"But Maddock went out that evening, into the streets?" Pitt went on.

"Yes, of course! You already knew that. He went to look for her, because she was late. Any good butler would do that!"

"What time?"

"I'm not sure. Why don't you ask him?" She was aware as soon as she said it that it was foolish. If Maddock were guilty of anything, not that he was of course, but if he were he would hardly be likely to tell Pitt the truth about it. "I'm sorry." Why should she apologize to this policeman? "Ask Mrs. Dunphy," she went on stiffly. "I believe it was a little after ten, but naturally I was not in the kitchen to know for myself."

"I have already asked Mrs. Dunphy," he replied, "but I like to get corroboration from as many sources as possible. And her memory, on her own admission, is not very reliable. She was very upset by the whole business."

"And you think I'm not? Just because I don't weep all over the place?" The intimation that she had *not* cared as much as she should have.

"I would hardly expect you to be as fond of a servant girl as the cook might be," Pitt said with his mouth twitching slightly, as if there were a smile inside him. "And I would think your nature excites to anger rather more readily than to tears."

"You think I am ill-tempered?" she said, then immediately wished she had not. It implied she cared what he thought of her, which was absurd.

"I think you are quick-tempered and take little trouble to hide your feelings," he smiled. "A not unattractive quality and uncommon in women, especially of gentle birth."

She found herself blushing hotly.

"You are impertinent!" she snapped.

His smile broadened; he was looking straight at her.

"If you didn't wish to know what I thought of you, why did you ask?"

She could think of no answer to that. Instead she summoned all the dignity she could and faced him squarely.

"I believe it is quite possible Maddock was fond of Lily, but you surely cannot imagine he held the same regard for the Hiltons' maid, and still less for Chloe Abernathy. Therefore, to suppose that he might have killed them all is faulty reasoning in the extreme, if you attribute his motive to fondness. If not, then you have no motive at all. I think perhaps you had better begin again, on a more promising line of enquiry." She intended it as a dismissal.

He did not move.

"You were the only one here at the time?" he asked.

"Apart from Mrs. Dunphy, and Dora, of course. Why?"

"Your mother and sisters were at some church function. Where were your father and Mr. Corde?"

"Ask them."

"You don't know?"

"No, I don't."

"But they came home passing close to Cater Street, if not actually through it?"

"If they had seen anything, I'm sure they would have told you."

"Possibly."

"Of course they would! Whyever not?" A terrible thought hit her like a blow. "You can't—you can't imagine that one of them would—"

"I imagine everything, Miss Ellison, and believe nothing until there is proof. But I admit, there is no cause to suppose——," he left it hanging a second. "But someone did. I would like to have another talk with Maddock—undisturbed."

That evening everyone was at home, even Emily. They sat with the French windows open onto the lawn and the late sun in the garden, but instead of the balmy air of evening, filled with the scents of the day, it seemed only heavy with oppression.

It was Sarah who said what they were all thinking, or something close to it.

"Well, I'm not worried," she lifted her chin a little. "Inspector Pitt seems a sensible man to me. He'll soon discover that Maddock is as innocent as the rest of us. I dare say he'll even decide so tomorrow."

Charlotte spoke her thoughts, as usual, before she considered.

"I have no faith at all in his good sense. He is not like us."

"We all know he is a different class of person," Sarah said quickly. "But he is used to dealing with criminals. He must know the difference between a perfectly respectable servant like Maddock, and the kind of ruffian who goes around strangling girls."

"Garotting," Charlotte corrected. "And there is a lot of difference between ruffians, as you put it, who attack and rob people, and the sort of person who garottes women, especially servant girls who have nothing worth stealing."

Dominic smiled widely.

"And how would you know, Charlotte? Have you become an expert on crimes of passion?"

"She doesn't know!" Edward said very sharply. "She is being contrary, as usual."

"Oh, I don't agree," Dominic was still smiling. "Charlotte's not contrary; she's just forthright. And she has been spending a lot of time lately with that police fellow. Perhaps she's learned something?"

"She could hardly learn anything of value, or suitable for

a lady to know, from such a person," Edward said with a frown. He turned to her. "Charlotte, is this true? Have you been seeing this person?"

Charlotte found herself colouring with confusion and anger.

"Only when he called here on police business, Papa. Unfortunately he has come on two occasions when no one else was in."

"And what have you been saying to him?"

"Answering his questions, of course. We hardly have social conversations."

"Don't be impertinent! I meant, what has he asked you?"

"Not a great deal." Now that she came to think of it, their conversations had been of no immediate relevance to his investigations. "He asked me a little about Lily, and about Maddock."

"He's a perfectly awful man," Sarah shivered. "It really is appalling that we should have to have him in the house. And I think we should be very careful about letting Charlotte talk to him. You never know what she may forget herself and say."

"Do you suggest we should stand in the street and answer his questions?" Charlotte lost her temper completely. "And if you don't let him speak to me, he will suspect I know something shameful that you are afraid I will let slip."

"Charlotte," Caroline's voice was quite soft, but there was an edge of firmness in it that had the desired effect.

"I don't think he's awful," Dominic said casually. "In fact, I rather like him."

"You what?" Sarah was incredulous.

"I rather like him," Dominic repeated. "He has a dry sense of humour, which must be difficult enough in his job. Or perhaps it's the only way to retain his sanity."

"You have a peculiar taste in friends, Dominic," Emily said tartly. "I should be obliged if you didn't entertain him at home."

"It would seem redundant at present," Dominic said pleasantly. "Charlotte appears to be doing very well. I doubt he has time to spare."

Charlotte was about to reply, when she realized he was teasing. She blushed with confusion. Her heart was beating so violently she worried in case someone else noticed it.

"Dominic, this is not a suitable occasion," Caroline said clearly. "It seems this person really does consider that Maddock might be involved."

"More than involved," Edward was totally serious now. "I gather he actually thinks he might have killed Lily."

"But that's ridiculous." Sarah was not yet more than superficially worried. Her concern was still only a matter of social inconvenience, a stigma to be circumvented with care, to be talked away. "He couldn't have."

Emily was thinking hard, frowning.

Edward folded his hands together, staring at them. "Why not?"

Sarah looked up, startled, but no one else spoke.

"After all," Edward went on, "it is inescapable that someone did. It would also appear that it might well be someone who lives around this area, which precludes the sort of criminal who ordinarily attacks people in the street, robbers and so forth. And no robber of any efficiency attacks a servant girl out late, such as Lily. She could have nothing worth taking, poor child. Perhaps Maddock became infatuated with her, and when she rejected him for this young Brody, he lost his head. We have to consider that that may be the truth, however disagreeable."

"Papa, how can you?" Sarah burst out. "Maddock is our butler! He has been for years! We know him!"

"He is still a human being, my dear," Edward said gently, "and subject to human passions and weaknesses. We must face the truth. Denying it will not alter it, nor can it help anyone, not even Maddock; and we have to consider the safety of others, especially Dora and Mrs. Dunphy."

Sarah's face dropped.

"You don't think—"

"I don't know, my dear. It is for the police to decide, not us."

"I don't think we should leap to conclusions." Caroline was obviously unhappy. "But we must be prepared to face the truth, when it becomes inevitable."

Charlotte could no longer keep silent.

"We don't know that it is the truth! She was garotted, not strangled: killed with a wire. If Maddock suddenly lost his temper, why did he have a wire with him? He doesn't walk around carrying a garotting wire!"

"My dear, it's quite possible he lost his temper before he left the house," Edward said quietly. She was not looking at them. "Refusing to face it will not help."

"Face what?" Charlotte demanded. "That Maddock could have killed Lily? Of course he could! He was out in the street at the right time. So were you, Papa. So was Dominic. I dare say there were a hundred other men who were, and we shall never know three-quarters of them. Any one of them could have killed her."

"Don't be foolish, Charlotte," Edward said sharply. "I don't doubt the other households can account for their men-servants at the relevant time. And there is no reason to suppose any of them were acquainted with poor Lily anyway!"

"And did Maddock now the Hiltons' maid?" Charlotte demanded.

Caroline winced.

"Charlotte, your behaviour is becoming offensive." Edward's face was stern; it was obvious he wished to end the matter. "We understand that you would prefer it to be someone we don't know, a wanderer from some slum region, but as you pointed out yourself, the motive of robbery doesn't stand. Now let us consider the matter closed."

"You can't just say that Maddock killed Lily, and leave it at that!" She knew she was risking his very real anger, but the indignation inside her would not let her be silent.

Edward opened his mouth, but before he could muster words, Emily broke in.

"You know, Papa, Charlotte has a certain truth. Maddock might have killed Lily, although it seems rather pointless if he was fond of her. In fact, self-defeating! But why on earth should he kill the Hiltons' maid, or Chloe Abernathy? And they were killed first, before Lily. It doesn't make sense."

Charlotte felt a rush of warmth towards Emily. She hoped Emily knew it.

"Murder itself is hardly sensible, Emily," Edward's colour heightened with anger. To be defied by Charlotte was becoming habit, but by Emily as well was intolerable. "It is a bestial crime, a crime of animal passion, and unreason."

"Are you saying he's mad?" she looked at her father. "That Maddock is bestial, or passionately, unreasonably insane?"

"No, of course not!" he snapped. "I am not an expert in criminal insanity, and neither are you! But I presume Inspector Pitt is; it is his job, and he believes Maddock is guilty. Now you will not discuss the subject any further. Is that understood?"

Charlotte looked at him. His eyes were hard, and could it possibly be that they were also frightened?

"Yes, Papa," she said obediently. She was used to obedience. It was habit. But her mind rebelled, whirling with new thoughts, with new fears finding shapes, with something very dreadful.

Chapter
Five

The wretched policeman returned the following day, questioning Maddock first, then Caroline, then finally asking if he could see Charlotte again.

"Why?" Charlotte was tired and this morning the deep unhappiness of fear and the reality of death had settled upon her. The blindness of the first shock had passed. She had gone to sleep on tragedy, and wakened to find it still with her.

"I don't know, dear," Caroline replied, still in the doorway. She held the door open for her daughter. "But he asked for you, so I suppose he must think you can help somehow."

Charlotte stood up and walked out slowly. Caroline touched her arm gently.

"Do be careful before you speak, my dear. We have had a great tragedy; don't let your distress, or your concern for

Maddock, provoke you into saying something you may afterwards regret because it has led to conclusions you did not foresee. Do not forget he is a policeman. He will remember everything you say, and try to see meanings beneath it."

"Charlotte never thought before she spoke in her life," Sarah said crossly. "She'll lose her temper, and I can't blame her. He is a most disgusting person. But the least one can do is behave like a lady, and say as little as possible."

Emily was sitting at the piano.

"I think he admires Charlotte," she said, touching the top note lightly with her finger.

"Emily, this is no time for levity!" Caroline said sharply.

"Can't you ever think of anything but romance?" Sarah glared at her.

Emily smiled with a small uplift of the corners of her mouth.

"Do you think policemen are romantic, Sarah? I think Inspector Pitt is excessively plain, and of course he must be common, or he wouldn't be a policeman. But he has the most beautiful voice, sort of surrounds you like warm treacle, and his diction and grammar are excellent. I suppose he is trying to better himself."

"Emily, Lily is dead!" Caroline gritted her teeth.

"I know that, Mama. But he must be used to that kind of thing, so it won't prevent him from admiring Charlotte." She turned to her sister and regarded her objectively. "And Charlotte is very handsome. I dare say he doesn't mind her tongue. He is probably used to indelicacy."

Charlotte felt her face flaming. The thought of Inspector Pitt's even entertaining such an idea about her was unbearable.

"Hold your tongue, Emily!" she fumed. "Inspector Pitt has no more chance of enjoying my attentions than—than you have of marrying George Ashworth. Which is just as well, because Ashworth is a gambler and a cad!" She pushed past Caroline and into the hall.

Pitt was in the smaller, rear sitting room.

"Good morning, Miss Ellison," he smiled widely; it would have been charming in anyone else.

"Good morning, Mr. Pitt," she said coldly. "I cannot think why you should have sent for me again, but since you have, what is it you want?"

She stared at him, trying to make him feel awkward, and instead thought for an appalling moment that she saw in his eyes the admiration Emily had spoken of. It was intolerable.

"Don't stand there staring like a fool!" she snapped. "What do you want?"

His smile vanished.

"You seem very disturbed, Miss Ellison. Has something further happened to distress you? An event, a suspicion, something you remembered?" His light, intelligent eyes were on her face, waiting.

"You appear to suspect our butler," she replied icily. "Which is naturally distressing to me, both because you are blaming someone in my home, and no doubt you will arrest him and put him in prison, and because, since I'm perfectly sure he didn't do it, whoever did is still out in the streets. I would have thought that such a situation would be enough to distress any person of the slightest sensibility."

"You leap to conclusions with the greatest of mental athleticism, Miss Ellison," he smiled. "To begin with, we frequently arrest people, but we take them to court; we do not put them in prison. You might feel sure he is not guilty, and I am inclined to agree with you, but neither you nor I has the right to dismiss anyone from consideration until something is proved or disproved regarding their involvement in the affair. And to conclude, you are wrong in assuming that because I am still looking at Maddock, I have ceased to look elsewhere."

"I do not wish for a lecture on police procedure, Mr. Pitt." She could see his point, even that he was right, and it did nothing to help her temper.

"I thought it might be reassuring."

"What is it you want, Mr. Pitt?"

"The night that Lily was killed, when was the last time you saw Maddock before he went to look for her?"

"I've no idea."

"What did you do that evening?"

"I read. What can that possibly have to do with it?"

"Oh?" His eyebrows rose with interest. He smiled. "What did you read?"

She could feel herself colour with annoyance because her father would have disapproved of her books as something that was not becoming for a lady to wish to know about.

"That is not your concern, Mr. Pitt."

Her answer seemed to amuse him. It suddenly occurred to her that he might have thought it was a romance, or old love letters.

"I was reading a book on warfare in the Crimea," she said angrily.

His eyes widened in surprise.

"An unusual interest for a lady."

"Possibly. What has it to do with Lily, which I'm told is your job here?"

"I take it you chose that opportunity because your father does not approve of your interest in such bloody and unfeminine subjects?"

"That is none of your concern either."

"So you read alone; you did not call in Maddock or Dora to fetch you any refreshment, or alter the gas, or lock the doors?"

"I didn't wish for any refreshment, and I'm quite capable of turning the gas up or down myself, or locking the doors."

"Then you didn't see Maddock at all?"

At last she realized what he was seeking. She was annoyed with herself for not having seen it before.

"No."

"So he could have been out any time during the evening, as far as you know?"

"Mrs. Dunphy said he spoke to her. He only went out when Lily was late home, and—and he became worried."

"So he says. But Mrs. Dunphy was alone in the kitchen. He could actually have gone out earlier."

"No, he couldn't. If I had called for anything I should have noticed his absence."

"But you were reading a book your father did not approve of." He was looking at her closely. His eyes were frank, as if there were no wall between them.

"He didn't know that!" But even as she said it the sickening thought came that Maddock probably had known it. She had taken the book from her father's study. Maddock knew the books well enough to spot which one was missing, and he knew her. She turned to face Pitt.

He merely smiled. "However," he went on, dismissing the book with a wave of his hand. Really, he was a most untidy creature, so different from Dominic. He looked like a wading bird flapping its wings. "I can think of no reason why he should harbour any feelings against Miss Abernathy." His voice lifted. "Was Miss Abernathy a friend of yours?"

"Not especially."

"No," he said thoughtfully. "From what I have been told, she would hardly have been your choice of company. A somewhat flighty girl, much given to laughter and rather frivolous pursuits, poor child."

Charlotte looked at him. He was quite grave. Was he not sufficiently used to death in his job that it no longer moved him?

"She was not an immoral girl," she said quietly, "just very young, and still a little foolish."

"Indeed." He gave a tight little grimace. "And not in the least likely to have had a liaison with someone else's butler. I imagine her sights were set a good deal higher. She could hardly have remained in the kind of society she sought were she in any way engaged with a servant, even a superior one!"

"Are you being sarcastic, Mr. Pitt?"

"Quite literal, Miss Ellison. I do not always observe the rules of society, but I am quite aware of what they are!"

"You surprise me!" she said cuttingly.

97

"Do you disapprove of sarcasm, Miss Ellison?"

She felt her face flush; it had been the perfect barb.

"I find you offensive, Mr. Pitt. If you have some question to ask in connection with your business, please do so. Otherwise permit me to call Maddock to have you shown out."

To her surprise he also blushed, and for once he did not look at her.

"I apologize, Miss Ellison. The last thing I wished was to offend you."

Now she was confused. He looked unhappy, as if she had actually hurt him. She was at fault, and she knew it. She had been intolerably rude and he had so far forgotten himself as to give her as good in return. She had used her social advantage to fire the last shot. It was not something to be proud of; in fact it was an abuse of privilege. It must be rectified.

She did not look at him either.

"I'm sorry, Mr. Pitt. I spoke hastily. I am not offended at you, but a little more disturbed by . . . by circumstances than I had allowed for. Please pardon my rudeness."

He spoke quietly. Emily was right; he had a beautiful voice.

"I admire you for that, Miss Ellison."

Again she felt acutely uncomfortable, knowing he was staring at her.

"And there is no need to fear for Maddock. I have no evidence on which to arrest him, and quite honestly, I think it is very unlikely he had anything to do with it."

Her eyes flew up to meet his, to search and see if he were being honest.

"I wish I did have some idea who it was," he went on seriously. "This kind of man does not stop at two, or three. Please, be most careful? Do not go out alone, even for the shortest distance."

She felt a confusion of horror and embarrassment run through her: horror at the thought of some nameless madman stalking the streets, just beyond the darkened windows, and embarrassment over the depth of feeling in Pitt's eyes. Surely it wasn't conceivable that he actually—? No, of course not! It was just Emily's stupid tongue! He was a policeman! Very ordinary. He probably had a wife somewhere, and children. What a big man he was, not fat, but tall. She wished he would not look at her like that, as if he could see into her mind.

"No," she said with a quick swallow. "I assure you I have no intention of going out unaccompanied. We none of us shall. Now if there is nothing more I can tell you, you must persist in your enquiries—elsewhere. Good day, Mr. Pitt."

He held the door open for her.

"Good day, Miss Ellison."

It was late afternoon and she was alone in the garden, picking off dead rose heads, when Dominic came over the grass towards her.

"How very tidy," he looked at the rose bushes she had done. "Funny, I never thought of you as so—regimented. That's more like Sarah, tidying up after nature. I would have expected you to leave them."

She did not look at him; she did not want the disturbing emotion of meeting his eyes. As always, she said what she meant.

"I don't do it to be tidy. Taking off the dead heads means the plant doesn't put any more goodness into them, seeds and so forth. It helps to make them bloom again."

"How practical. And that sounds like Emily." He picked a couple off and dropped them into her basket. "What did Pitt want? I would have thought he'd asked us everything possible by now."

"I'm not really sure. He was very impertinent." Then she wished she had not said it. Perhaps he had been, but she had also been rude, and it was less forgivable in herself. "It may be his way of...of surprising people into frankness."

"A little redundant with you, I would have thought?" he grinned.

Her heart turned over. Habit, familiarity all vanished and it was as if she had just met him again, enchanted. He was everything that was laughing, masculine, romantic. Why, oh why could she not have been Sarah?

She looked down at the roses in case he read it all in her eyes. She knew it must be naked there. For once she could think of nothing to say.

"Did he go on about Maddock?" he asked.

"Yes."

He snapped off another dead head and dropped it into the basket.

"Does he honestly think the poor devil was so besotted by Lily that when she chose Brody instead he followed after her and killed her in the street?"

"No, of course not! He wouldn't be so stupid," she said quickly.

"Is it so stupid, Charlotte? Passion can be very strong. If she laughed at him, mocked him—"

"Maddock! Dominic?" she faced him without thinking. "You don't think he did, do you?"

His dark eyes were puzzled.

"I find it hard to believe, but then I find it hard to believe anyone would strangle a woman with a wire like that. But someone did. We only know one side of Maddock. We always see him very stiff and correct: 'yes, sir,' 'no, ma'am.' We don't ever think what he feels or thinks underneath."

"You *do* think so!" she accused.

"I don't know. But we have to consider it."

"We don't! Pitt might have to, but we know better."

"No we don't, Charlotte. We don't know anything at all. And Pitt must be good at his job, or he wouldn't be an inspector."

"He's not infallible. And anyway, he said he didn't think that Maddock was involved; he just had to exhaust all the possibilities."

"Did he say that?"

"Yes."

"Then if he doesn't think it's Maddock, why does he keep coming here?"

"I suppose because Lily worked here."

"What about the others, Chloe and the Hiltons' maid?"

"Well, I suppose he goes there, too. I didn't ask him."

He stared at the grass, frowning.

She longed to say something wise, something he would remember, but nothing came to her but a storm of feelings.

He took off the last rose and picked up the basket.

"Well, I suppose he'll either arrest someone, or declare it an unsolved crime," he said drily. "Not a very comforting thought. I think I'd rather anything than that." And he walked back into the house.

She followed after him slowly. Papa and Sarah and Emily were all in the withdrawing room, and as she came in after Dominic, Mama also entered from the other door. She saw the basket of flower heads.

"Ah, good. Thank you, Dominic." She took them as he held them out.

Edward looked up from the newspaper he was reading.

"What did that policeman ask you this morning, Charlotte?" he asked.

"Very little," she replied. Actually all she could clearly remember was how rude she had been, and the relief that he did not seriously suspect Maddock.

"You were in there long enough," Emily observed. "If he was not asking you questions, what on earth were you doing?"

"Emily, don't be foolish!" Edward said tersely. "And your comments are in poor taste. Charlotte, please answer me a little more fully. We are concerned."

"Really, Papa, he seemed only to be going over the same things again, about Maddock, what time he went out, what Mrs. Dunphy said. But he did admit that he did not believe Maddock guilty himself, only that he had to pursue every possibility."

"Oh."

She had expected relief, even joy; she could not understand the silence that greeted her.

"Papa?"

"Yes, my dear?"

"Are you not relieved? The police do not suspect Maddock. Inspector Pitt said as much."

"Then whom do they suspect?" Sarah asked. "Or didn't they tell you that?"

"Of course they didn't!" Edward frowned. "I'm surprised they told her so much. Are you sure you understood correctly? It was not perhaps wishful thinking?"

It was almost as if they did not want to believe her.

"No, I didn't misunderstand. He was perfectly plain."

"What exactly did he say?" Caroline asked quietly.

"I can't remember, but I was not mistaken in his meaning, of that I am perfectly sure."

"Well, that's a relief," Sarah said, putting down her sewing. She sewed very beautifully; Charlotte had envied her that for as long as she could remember. "Now perhaps the police won't return."

Emily smiled. "Yes, they will."

"What for, if they don't suspect Maddock?"

"To see Charlotte, of course. Inspector Pitt admires Charlotte greatly."

Edward drew in a sharp breath. "Emily, this is not an occasion for frivolity. And the less fortunate imaginings of some policeman are not of interest to us. No doubt many men of ordinary background admire women who are above them, but have more sense than to let it be known."

"But the police have no reason to come back, no real reason," Sarah pressed.

"That is the most real of reasons," Emily was not easily suppressed. "Crimes come and go; loves last longer."

"Some do," Dominic said drily.

"Well, it's obviously someone from the criminal classes," Sarah said, ignoring them both. "I don't know why they even considered it could be otherwise. It seems incompetent to me."

"No," Charlotte said quickly. "It isn't!"

Edward turned to her in surprise.

"Isn't what, my dear?"

"Isn't someone from the criminal classes. They only kill if they can't help it, either to escape or something of that sort, or else for revenge. They only attack people they don't know in order to rob. And Lily was not robbed."

"How do you know all this?"

Charlotte was conscious that they were all looking at her. "Inspector Pitt told me. And it makes sense."

"I don't know why you should expect the criminal classes to make sense," Sarah was impatient. "It will be some lunatic, someone who is quite depraved and does not know what he is doing." She shivered.

"Poor devil," Dominic spoke with feeling, and Charlotte was surprised by it. Why should he have such pity for a creature who had horribly killed three times?

"Spare your concern for Lily and Chloe and the Hiltons' maid," Edward said with a little snort.

Dominic looked around.

"Why? They're dead. This poor animal is still alive, at least I presume he is."

"Stop it!" Edward said sharply. "You'll frighten the girls."

Dominic gazed round at them. "I'm sorry. Although I think this is a time when a little fear might save your life." He turned his head to Charlotte. "So Pitt doesn't think it's some madman from the underworld. What *does* he think?"

There was only one conclusion. She faced it as calmly as she could, but her voice still shook.

"He must think it is someone who lives here, somewhere near Cater Street."

"Nonsense!" Edward sat up sharply. "I've lived here all my life. I know just about everyone within a radius of—of miles. There is no—lunatic of such monstrous proportions

in this neighbourhood. Good heavens, if there were, does he
not think we should know it? Such a creature could hardly
pass unnoticed! He could not appear to be like the rest of
us."

Couldn't he? Charlotte looked at him, then surrepti-
tiously at Dominic. How much of people really showed in
their faces? Did any of them even guess the wildness of feeling in her? Please heaven, no! If such madness, such tor-
mented hatred as this creature felt was there to see, why
was this man not known already? He must be seen by someone—family, wife, friends? What did they think, if they
knew? Could you know something like that about someone,
and not speak? Or would you refuse to believe it, turn away
from the evidence, construe it as meaning something else?

What would she do—if she loved someone? If it were
Dominic, would she not protect him from everything, die to
do it, if necessary?

What a monstrous thought! As if anyone remotely like
Dominic could have been involved in violence, the obscene
anger that drove one to terrify and destroy, to linger in
shadows along the street walls, hungering after fear.

What kind of man was he? She could only see him as a
black shadow against mists. Had Lily seen his face? Had any
of them? If she saw it herself, would it be a face she knew—a
new nightmare, or a familiar one?

They were talking round her. She had missed it. Why did
they accept that it could be Maddock so easily? It was almost
as if they were grateful for a solution, as if any solution were
better than none.

No, that was dreadful. But in spite of herself she could
understand it. The suspicion was gone. Any knowledge, any
fact to face was better than wondering, knowing he was still
out there in the gaslit streets. Whatever the known was, it
was better than the unknown, better than the police here,
asking questions, suspecting.

She could understand, but at the same time she was
ashamed of them for it, of herself for not saying something,

exposing it. In a way she was allowing it, allowing them all to deceive themselves.

The conversation flowed round her and she had no heart to join in.

Emily had no such thoughts. And the following day the whole sordid business had receded to the dimension of a mere practical problem. Of course she was sorry about Lily, but Lily was beyond help now, and grieving would do her no good. Emily had never understood mourning. The most peculiar thing about it was that it was the most pious people who indulged in it, those who should have been the ones to rejoice! After all, they preached heaven and hell loudly enough. Surely to mourn was the gravest insult one could pay to the dead? It presupposed judgment was going to find them light in the balance.

Lily had been ordinary enough, but there was nothing in her to warrant damnation, so one could presume she was in a better place. Whatever sins she had committed, and they could only be small, were surely washed clean by the payment of her life.

So the whole matter was better forgotten, except for the rather squalid business of discovering who killed her. And that was the job of the police. All she and her family could do was take sufficient care to see they did not get in the way of this lunatic's garotting wire.

The practical matters of real importance were the positive ones, such as discovering what everyone might wear at the party to be given by a certain Major and Mrs. Winter, to which George Ashworth was to escort her. It would be a serious setback if she were to find her dress duplicated, or nearly so. She aimed ultimately to set fashion rather than follow it, but in the meantime she must judge it to a nicety, so as not to appear merely eccentric. She would have to consult the Misses Madison, and Miss Decker—without their being aware of it, of course.

The police did not return for several days. Apparently they

were conducting their investigations elsewhere, probably going back to the earlier deaths, talking to the Abernathys and the Hiltons. The whole affair was not discussed openly again, although they nearly all found themselves saying small things, letting thoughts slip out. They were mostly expressions of relief that the police were out of the house and had transferred their unwelcome presence, with its attendant speculation and scandal, to someone else. The other feeling that came through was the continuing anxiety about what might happen next, where this creature might be, if it were actually conceivable that he came from the immediate neighbourhood—someone's manservant, or a small trader?

Emily gathered all her information, and procured a magnificent gown in the palest lilac, with delicate silver trim. She was in particularly good health; her skin was clear, far better than the elder Miss Madison's, and her eyes bright. She had excellent colour, not too high, and her hair for once did everything she wished.

Ashworth called for her in his coach, naturally paying his respects to the family before departing. Mama was very civil, Papa even more so, but Charlotte was as uncompromising as usual.

"Your sister Charlotte has little liking for me, I think," Ashworth observed as soon as they were alone. "It's a pity. She's a handsome creature."

Emily knew she had nothing to fear from Charlotte, but it might be wise not to be too readily available to Ashworth. It was more than possible he hankered more for the chase than for the prize.

"Indeed she is," she agreed. "And you are not the only one to have noticed it."

"I should hardly think so." Then he looked at her with a smile. "Or were you being particular? Tell me, if you know a nice piece of gossip?"

"Only that our police inspector seems much taken with her, to Charlotte's fury!"

He laughed outright. "And knowing you, you have not let

it go unmarked. Poor Charlotte, how very irritating to be admired by a policeman, of all things!"

Their arrival was all Emily could have hoped for, indeed have planned. And thereafter for at least the first two hours all went well; but later she found Ashworth's attention wandering not only to his drinking and gambling companions, but especially to one Hetty Gosfield, a conspicuous girl of somewhat indelicate charms, but influential parentage and, worse than that, money. She had always known that Ashworth had an admiring eye for a pretty woman, and she had not expected to hold his entire attention, or even the larger part of it, without considerable work. But this Gosfield woman was beginning to be a threat.

Emily watched as Ashworth, at the far side of the room, smiled into the eyes of Hetty Gosfield, and Hetty laughed happily back. A quarter an hour later the situation was much the same.

Emily took a deep breath and considered. Above all things she must not make a scene. Ashworth abhorred any vulgarity that was not his own; even when he found it amusing, he still despised it. She would have to be far subtler than that; put the Gosfield woman in the wrong.

It took her some time to work it out, as her attention was divided between carrying on a conversation with Mr. Decker without talking too apparent nonsense, controlling her temper, and coming to a satisfactory plan of action.

When at least she moved it was with decisiveness. She knew one of Ashworth's young friends passably well, the Honorable William Foxworthy—empty-headed, possessing more money than good taste, and of an exhibitionistic temperament. It was not hard to attract his attention. He was at one of the tables playing cards. He saw her watching him. She waited until he won.

"Oh, excellent, Mr. Foxworthy!" she applauded. "What skill you have. Indeed, I swear I have never seen anyone cleverer—except Lord Ashworth, of course."

He looked up sharply.

"Ashworth? You think he is cleverer than I?"

She smiled sweetly.

"Only at cards. I have no doubt you excel him in many other things."

"I don't know about other things, Miss Ellison, and I assure you I have a greater skill at cards."

She gave him a gentle look, full of patience and total disbelief.

"I'll show you!" He stood up, the pack in his hand.

"Oh, pray, don't trouble yourself," she said quickly. It was going extremely well, exactly as she had intended. "I'm sure you are most able."

"Not able, Miss Ellison." He was stiff now, full of outraged pride. "That implies mere indifference. I am better than Ashworth. I'll prove it."

"Oh, please. I didn't mean to disturb your game," she protested, still loading her voice with disbelief.

"You doubt me?"

"Do you wish me to be honest?"

"Then you leave me no option but to beat Ashworth, and oblige you to believe me!" He strode across the room towards Ashworth, who was still totally engaged with Hetty Gosfield.

"George!" he said loudly.

"Oh, please!" Emily cried plaintively, but did not follow him beyond the first few paces. She must not be seen to have instigated this, or the whole purpose would be destroyed.

It worked marvellously. Foxworthy disrupted the tête-à-tête, demanding to prove his superiority. Ashworth could not resist, and Hetty Gosfield argued at first, but as Ashworth became annoyed with her because she was being tiresome and drawing a vulgar attention to them, she sulked and went away with someone else.

After it was all over Emily found herself with Ashworth again.

"Beat him," he said with satisfaction.

"Of course," Emily smiled. He apparently had no idea that

the exercise had nothing to do with skill at cards. "I had presumed you would."

"I can't bear vulgarity," he went on aggrievedly. "Bad taste for a woman to make an exhibition of herself."

Again Emily agreed, although privately she thought it was no worse for a woman than for a man; but that was not the way society saw it, and she knew the rules well enough to play by them, and *too* well to imagine one could break them and still win.

It was only when she was at home, lying in bed staring at the gaslight patterns on the ceiling, reflected from the lamps outside, that she reviewed the evening. There was no question in her mind that she still intended to marry George Ashworth, but there must be a weighing of his faults, a decision as to which might reasonably be changed, and which she would have to learn to live with, and herself change. Perhaps it was too much to require of any man of breeding and wealth that he should be faithful, but she would most certainly require that he be discreet in his liaisons. He must never make her an object of public sympathy. When the time was right, she must make that quite clear.

Again, he might gamble his own money as much as he chose, but never mortgage that which she might in good conscience regard as his provision for her—in other words their house, the wages of servants, a carriage and good horses, and a dress allowance sufficient to permit her to appear as becomes a lady.

She fell asleep, still thinking of the practicalities.

The following Thursday she went with Sarah to visit the vicar and Mrs. Prebble for tea, and to discuss the forthcoming church bazaar.

"But what if the weather is inclement?" Sarah asked, looking from one to another of them.

"We must trust in the Lord," the vicar replied. "And September is frequently the most delightful month of the year.

Even if it rains, it is unlikely to be cold. I don't doubt our faithful parishioners will suffer it with good grace."

Emily profoundly doubted it, and was glad that Charlotte was not there to express her opinion.

"Is it not possible to arrange some form of shelter, in case of misfortune?" she asked. "We can hardly rely upon the Lord to favour us above others."

"Us above others, Miss Ellison?" The vicar raised his eyebrows. "I fear I have not grasped your meaning."

"Well, perhaps others may require rain," she explained. "Farmers?"

The vicar looked at her coolly. "We are about the Lord's business, Miss Ellison."

There was no courteous answer to that.

"It may be quite easy to arrange to borrow some tents," Martha said thoughtfully. "I believe they have some at St. Peter's. No doubt they will be happy to lend them to us."

"It will be something of a social occasion," Sarah observed. "People will be wearing their best clothes."

"It is a church bazaar, Miss Ellison, to raise money for charity, not for women to disport themselves." The vicar was cold, his disapproval obvious.

Sarah blushed in embarrassment, and Emily charged to her defence in a manner worthy of Charlotte.

"Surely to appear on the business of the Lord one would wish to wear one's best, Vicar," she said blandly. "We can still behave with decorum. We do at church, where you would not expect us to come higgledy-piggledy."

A curious expression flickered across Martha's face, something like triumph and fear at the same time, and an obscure humour also, gone before it could be recognized.

"True, Miss Ellison," the vicar said piously. "Let us hope everyone else has the sense of duty and fitness that you do. We must set an example."

"We must also hope that people enjoy themselves," Martha offered. "After all, they will be little likely to part with their money if they feel miserable."

Emily glanced at the vicar.

"We are not a public amusement," he said icily.

Emily could think of nothing less likely to amuse the public than the vicar's frozen face. "Surely we can be happy," she said deliberately, "without being remotely like a public amusement?" As if Charlotte were at her elbow, she went on. "In fact, the very knowledge that we are in the service of the Lord will be a source of joy to us."

If it ever occurred to the vicar's mind that she was being sarcastic, there was no sign of it in his face. But she caught Martha's eye, and wondered if perhaps Martha would like to have said the same herself?

"I'm afraid you are not wise in the ways of the world," the vicar said, looking down at her, "as indeed it becomes a woman not to be. However, I must advise you that people are not as happy in the Lord's work as they should be, else the world would be a far better place, instead of the vale of sin and frailty it is. Alas, how weak is the flesh, even though the spirit would have it otherwise!"

There was no answer to that either. Emily turned her attention to the practical details; these at least she was extremely good at, although they interested her not at all. But it was only fair she did not leave them all to Sarah.

On the way home they were both quiet for a long time, till they were within half a mile of their own house. Sarah pulled her wrap a little closer round her.

"It is far cooler than I expected," she said with a little shiver. "It looked as if it would be warm."

"You're tired," Emily sought the obvious explanation. "You have been working very hard on this—affair." She decided to omit the adjective that came to her tongue.

"I can't leave poor Mrs. Prebble to do everything. You have no idea how hard that woman works." Sarah walked a little more quickly.

She was quite correct. Emily had very little idea of what Martha Prebble might do with her time. It had never interested her to think of it.

"Does she? At what?"

"At raising money for the church, at visiting the sick and the poor, at running the orphanage. Who do you suppose arranged the outing for them last month? Who do you think laid out old Mrs. Janner? She had no family and she was as poor as a mouse."

Emily was surprised.

"Martha Prebble did?"

"Yes. Sometimes others help, but only when they feel like it, when it suits them, or when they think someone else is watching who will praise them for it."

"I didn't know that."

Sarah pulled her shawl closer round her again.

"I think that's why Mama sometimes puts up with her rather funny ways, and with the vicar. I must admit myself, they are a little trying at times; but one must bear in mind the work they do."

Emily stared ahead of her. Such thoughts obliged her admiration, in spite of her profound dislike of the vicar and, by association, of Martha also. People were full of the most curious traits.

Caroline also was thinking of the vicar and Martha Prebble, but less kindly. She had been aware of Martha's work, especially with orphans, long enough for the surprise to have faded. She also understood some of the loneliness of a woman who has had no children and who is driven by both family and circumstances to labour for those who are not her own. It must frequently be an anonymous, thankless task.

But a little of their company, especially the vicar's, was sufficient for a long time.

"A very worthy woman," Grandmama observed. "A fine example to others of the parish. A pity there are so few who follow her. You must be pleased with Sarah. She's turning out very well."

Caroline thought it made her sound like a cake or a pudding, but she knew Grandmama did not appreciate levity at her expense.

"Yes," Caroline agreed, still looking at her sewing. There seemed to be far more linen to mend than she had remembered. But it was a long time since they had been short of a maid, in fact since before Sarah was married.

"Pity you can't do something about Charlotte," Grandmama went on. "I really don't know how you're ever going to get that girl married. She doesn't appear even to be trying!"

Caroline rethreaded her needle. She knew why Charlotte did not try, but it was none of Grandmama's business.

"She certainly is different in her tastes from Emily," she said noncommittally. "And in her tactics. But then there is no reason why they should be the same."

"You ought to speak to her," Grandmama insisted. "Point out the practicalities to her. What is going to happen to her if no one marries her? Have you considered that?"

"Yes, Grandmama, but frightening her will do no good, and even if she does not marry, she will survive. Better single than married to someone disreputable, or loose-living, or who could not provide for her satisfactorily."

"My dear Caroline," Grandmama said exasperatedly, "it is your duty as her mother to see that she does not! And it is also your duty to control this house in an organized fashion. When are you going to get another maid?"

"I have already made enquiries and Mrs. Dunphy has seen two, but they were not satisfactory."

"What was the matter with them?"

"One was too young, no experience; the other had a reputation that was undesirable."

"Perhaps if you'd checked Lily a little more closely she wouldn't now be murdered! This sort of thing doesn't happen in a well-ordered house."

"It didn't happen in the house!" Caroline was stung to sharpness at last. "It happened in Cater Street. And you are quite irresponsible to suggest, even by implication, that Lily brought it upon herself in any way, or that she was immoral. And I won't have it said in my house."

"Well, really!" Grandmama stood up, her hands tight, her face flushed. "No wonder Charlotte doesn't know how to keep a civil tongue in her head, and Emily's chasing after that ne'er-do-well just because he has a title. She'll do nothing but make a fool of herself, and you'll be to blame. I told Edward when he married you that he was making a mistake, but of course he was enamoured of you and didn't listen. Now Charlotte and Emily will have to pay for it. Well, don't say afterwards that I didn't warn you!"

"I wouldn't dream of it, Grandmama. Do you want dinner upstairs or will you be sufficiently recovered in time to come down for it?"

"I am not ill, Caroline. I am merely very disappointed, though not surprised."

"One can recover from disappointment as well as illness," Caroline said drily.

"You are immodest, Caroline, and unfeminine. No wonder Charlotte is a shrill. If you'd been my daughter, I would have seen to it that you grew up to be a lady." And without giving Caroline a chance to reply to that, she went out and closed the door behind her with a sharp clack.

Caroline sighed. There was more than enough to do, enough trouble, without Grandmama aping a prima donna. Still, she ought to be used to it by now, only she resented the criticism of Charlotte. The slander against Lily was painful in a different and deeper way.

What kind of person would kill a harmless, penniless girl like Lily Mitchell? Only a madman. A madman straying from the criminal world, or a madman who looked like any of the rest of them, except at night, when he saw a young woman alone in the streets? Could it even be someone she herself had seen?

Her thoughts were interrupted by Edward coming in.

"Good evening, my dear." He kissed her on the cheek. "Have you had a pleasant day?" He looked at the linen and frowned. "Still no replacement for Lily? I thought you were seeing one or two today."

"I did. Nothing suitable."

"Where are the girls? And Mama?" He sat down, stretching comfortably.

"Do you wish some refreshment before dinner?"

"No, thank you. I stopped at my club."

"I thought you were a little late," she said as she glanced at the clock.

"Where are they?" he repeated.

"Sarah and Dominic are dining with the Lessings—"

"The who?"

"The Lessings, the sexton and his family."

"Oh. And the others?"

"Emily is with George Ashworth again. I wish you would speak to her, Edward. I don't seem to make any impression."

"I'm afraid, my dear, she will have to learn by the bitterness of experience. I doubt she will listen to anyone. I could forbid her, of course, but they would be bound to see each other at social occasions, and it would only lend an air of romance to the affair, which would strengthen it in her eyes. It would defeat its purpose in the end."

She smiled. She had not credited him with such perception. She had made the suggestion only to safeguard herself.

"You are quite right," she agreed. "It will probably blow past of its own accord, in time."

"And Charlotte and Mama?"

"Charlotte is to dinner with young Uttley, and Grandmama is upstairs, in something of a temper with me, because I would not let her say that Lily was immoral."

He sighed.

"No, we must not say so, although I fear it may well be true."

"Why? Because she was killed? If you believe that, then what about Chloe Abernathy?"

"My dear, there are many ways of the world that you do not know, and it is better that it should be so. But it is more than possible that Chloe brought it upon herself also. Unfortunately," he hesitated, "even well-born girls form liaisons, alliances—," he left it hanging. "One doesn't know—there may be—jealousies, revenges. Things it is better we do not discuss."

And Caroline had to be content with that, although she found herself unable to believe it wholly or to dismiss it from her thoughts.

Chapter
Six

It was a week later that Caroline finally succeeded in engaging a new maid to take Lily's place. It had not been easy because although there were plenty of girls seeking a good position, many of them were unskilled, and many had reputations and references that were less than satisfactory. And, of course, since Lily's death and the manner of it were known, it was not the most pleasing prospect for a respectable girl seeking employment.

However, Millie Simpkins seemed the best applicant they were likely to get, and the situation was becoming most awkward without someone in the position. The next thing would be that Mrs. Dunphy would find she could not cope, and use the shortage of help as an excuse to give her notice as well.

Millie was a pleasant enough girl, sixteen years old. She appeared to have an accommodating and willing nature, and was clean and passably neat. She lacked any great experience, this being only her second position, but that could be all to the good. If she had few set ways, then she could be taught, moulded into the pattern of this household. And perhaps most important of all, Mrs. Dunphy took to her immediately.

It was Wednesday morning when Millie knocked on the door of the rear sitting room.

"Come in," Caroline replied.

Millie came in, a coat over her arm, and dropped a funny little curtsey.

"Yes Millie, what is it?" Caroline smiled at her. Poor child was nervous.

"Please, ma'am, this coat is—rather spoiled, ma'am. I don't rightly know how to mend it. I'm sorry, ma'am."

Caroline took it from her and held it up. It was one of Edward's—smart, a formal jacket with velvet collar. It was a moment or two before she found the tear. It was in the sleeve, in the lower section at the back of the arm. How on earth could anyone tear themselves in such a place? She explored it with her fingers, pulling the pieces apart. It was almost as if a sharp claw had ripped it, about two inches long.

"I'm not surprised," Caroline agreed. "Don't worry about it, Millie. I'll see what I can do with it, but we might well have to send it to a tailor, get a new piece set in."

"Yes, ma'am." Millie's relief was almost painful.

Caroline smiled at her. "You did the right thing to bring it to me. Now you'd better go back and get on with the plain linen, and I believe there's a petticoat of Miss Emily's that's torn."

"Yes, ma'am." She dropped another awkward little curtsey. "Thank you, ma'am."

After she had gone Caroline looked at the coat again. She could not remember Edward's having worn that coat for a long time, weeks in fact. Where could he have done that? Obviously he would not have worn it with such a tear. Why had he not asked her to do something about it at the time? He could not have failed to notice it. It was a coat he frequently wore to his club. In fact he had worn it—the night Lily was killed. She could remember quite clearly his coming in and being so angry with Charlotte for having sent for the police. The picture came to her mind: the gaslight on the wall hissing a little, throwing a yellowish light on the claret-coloured velvet. They had all been too busy with fear and anger to think of clothes. Perhaps that was why he had forgotten it?

It took her most of the afternoon to mend the tear. She had to pull threads from the seams to darn it invisibly, and even so she was not entirely satisfied with it. Edward was home fairly early and she mentioned it straight away, more or less in the way of an apology.

"I'm afraid it is still noticeable," she held it up. "But only if you catch it in the light, which of course you won't, since it is on the back of the arm. How in goodness' name did you come to tear it?"

He frowned, looking away from her. "I'm not sure that I can remember. It must have happened ages ago."

"Why didn't you mention it at the time? I could have mended it as easily then as now. In fact more easily: Lily would have done it. She was extremely clever at such things."

"Well, it probably happened since Lily's death, and I dare say I thought you had enough to do, being short a maid, without this. After all, I have plenty of other clothes."

"I haven't seen you in it since the night of Lily's death." She did not know why she said it.

"Well, maybe that's the last time I wore it. That explains very completely, I should think, why I didn't mention it. It was hardly of importance, compared with Lily, and the police in the house."

"Yes, of course." She folded it over her arm, meaning to tell Millie to take it upstairs. "How did you do it?"

"What?"

"The tear!"

"I really don't remember, my dear. Whatever does it matter?"

"I thought you were at your club all evening, and that that was why you were so late?"

"I was," his voice was becoming a little shorter. "I'm sorry if the new maid is unable to do these chores, but, my dear Caroline, there is no need to make such an issue of it. I don't intend to discuss it the whole evening."

She put it over her arm and opened the door.

"No, of course not. I just wondered how it happened. It is such a large tear." And she went out into the hall to call Millie. It would be a good idea for her to steam-press it to make it lie flat.

It was Dominic who quite unintentionally shattered her peace of mind and set her in a turmoil she could not control. He came to her a couple of days later holding out a waistcoat with his forefinger poked through a tear on the pocket.

"How did you do that?" she took it from him and examined it.

"Shoved my hand in it too far." He smiled. "Sheer stupidity. Can you mend it? I saw the marvellous job you did on Papa-in-law's coat."

She was pleased he should say so, because she was still not totally satisfied with it herself.

"Thank you. Yes, I think so. I'll try this evening."

"If you can do Papa's, I'm sure you can do that."

A thought occurred to her as he turned away.

"When did you see it?"

"What?" he looked back.

"When did you see the tear in Edward's coat?"

He frowned very slightly.

"The night Lily was killed."

"How observant of you. I wouldn't have thought in all the excitement you'd have seen it. Or did you see it at the club? That was where he did it."

He shook his head fractionally.

"I think you must have misunderstood. I was at the club, but Papa left very early, and his coat certainly wasn't torn then. I remember it clearly: Belton, the footman, gave him his hat and his cane. He would have noticed, couldn't have failed to."

"You must have the wrong night!"

"No, because I had dinner with Reggie Hafft. He dropped me off in Cater Street and I walked the last half mile or so. I saw Papa coming from the opposite end of Cater Street and called out to him, but he didn't hear me. He got home just a little while before I did."

"Oh." It was a stupid remark, but she was too stunned to think clearly. Edward had lied to her, over something completely trivial—but on the night Lily had been murdered. Why? Why had he not told her the truth? Was it something he was ashamed of, or afraid of?

What on earth was she thinking? This was preposterous! He must have been to call on some friend, and forgotten. That was it. It would be explained quite easily, and then she would be ashamed of the thoughts that crossed the back of her mind now.

The first time she saw him alone was when they retired to bed. Caroline was sitting on the stool in front of the mirror, letting down her hair and brushing it. Edward came in from the dressing room.

"Whom did you call on, the night Lily was killed?" she said lightly, trying to make it sound as if it did not matter.

She saw his face reflected in the mirror. He was frowning.

"Whom did I what?"

She repeated it, her heart beating strongly, her eyes avoiding his.

"No one," he said a little sharply. "I've already told you, Caroline, I was at my club! I came straight from the club home. I don't know why you are continuing to discuss the matter. Do you imagine I was lurking in Cater Street after my housemaid?" He was thoroughly angry now.

"No, of course not," she replied quietly. "Don't be foolish."

His face hardened into the white temper she knew very well. She had offended him profoundly by using the word *foolish.* Or had he chosen to pretend it was so, in order to avoid having to tell the truth, or think of another lie?

She must be overwrought; her mind was quite off the rails, becoming ridiculous. Better try to dismiss it and go to bed. Edward was still observing an icy silence. She thought for a moment of apologizing, then something within her acknowledged that she would think of it again, pursue it again, which would make any apology a lie.

They both got into bed without speaking. He lay perfectly still, breathing regularly. She had no idea whether he was asleep, trying to sleep, or merely pretending to be to avoid further involvement.

Why was she even entertaining such thoughts? She knew Edward, knew that for whatever reason he lied, it could have nothing to do with what had happened in Cater Street. She knew that. Yet he must have been doing something that he did not want her to know? Such as what? Nothing good, or he would have told her the truth, or at least whom he was with, if not the reason. Where could Edward have been to return via the opposite end of Cater Street? Where could he have been that needed lying about?

She tried to think of his pattern of life, the things he did daily, whom he knew, the other places he visited. The more she thought about it, the more she realized how little she knew. At home she knew him so well she could often tell beforehand what he would say, how he would feel about any event, whom he would like, or dislike. But when he left for the city he walked into a different part of his life, and she actually knew nothing about it except what he told her.

She went to sleep deeply unhappy.

The next day was appalling. Caroline woke with a dull headache and felt so fearful and depressed she spoke only when necessity forced her. She was busy in the linen cupboard checking Millie's work when Dora came to say that Inspector Pitt from the police was back again, and would she see him?

Caroline stared at the pile of pillowcases in front of her, her heart pounding, her mouth dry. Had Pitt been to the club and found out that Edward was lying? It was impossible that he had killed Lily, for any reason. But he must be hiding something. She would have to try to protect him. If only she knew the truth!

"Ma'am?" Dora was still waiting.

"Oh yes, Dora. Tell him I shall be there in five minutes. Put him in the withdrawing room."

"Yes, ma'am."

Pitt was standing staring out of the window when she opened the door. He swung round to face her.

"Good morning, Mrs. Ellison. I'm sorry to disturb you again, but I'm afraid I have to pursue everything."

"You seem to be pursuing us rather extensively, Mr. Pitt. Do I presume from your remark that you pursue everyone else as diligently?"

"Certainly, ma'am."

What an odd-looking man he was, so inelegant. His presence dominated the room. Or did she just feel that way because she was frightened of him?

"What is it you wish this time, Mr. Pitt?" Better to get it over with.

"Your husband came home unusually late on the evening Lily Mitchell was murdered." It was more of a statement than a question, as if he were reaffirming something he already knew.

"Yes." Did her voice sound as strained as she felt?

"Where had he been?"

What should she say? Should she repeat what Edward had told her? Or the truth that Dominic had subsequently let slip? She realized as she put the problem to herself that she had not even questioned Dominic's version! If she told him Edward was at the club the whole evening she would be saying at the same time that Edward had lied to her. It would make it that much harder for him to—to negotiate himself out of the lie. But if she said he had been elsewhere, then she obliged him to explain something he would not, or could not.

Pitt was staring at her with those light, intelligent eyes. She felt transparent, like a child caught in the pantry.

"I believe he said he was at his club," she said slowly, making her mouth form each word, "although whether he was going on to dine with friends afterwards I don't remember."

"And he didn't tell you?" His enquiry was polite.

Was it extraordinary? Did the careful lie show in her face?

"In view of what we found when we returned home—Charlotte having sent for the police, the distress, our fears—I never thought of it again. It seemed the least important of things."

"Naturally. However, if you don't know, I cannot eliminate the possibility that Mr. Ellison may have passed somewhere near the scene of the crime at the appropriate time." He smiled, showing his teeth, his eyes bright. "And he may have seen something that would help us."

She swallowed hard.

"Yes, of course. I'm afraid I don't know."

"Of course not, Mrs. Ellison. I already know that you passed along Cater Street in a carriage, and in the company of your daughters, and I have spoken to all of you."

"But you have spoken to my husband also. What more can there be to say?" Could she avoid it, persuade him not to see Edward at all? There could be nothing else to ask him, unless he suspected something, already knew somehow that Edward had lied. "Surely, Mr. Pitt, you cannot doubt that if my husband had seen anything at all, he would have told you?"

"*If* he knew it was important, but perhaps he saw an odd thing, a small detail that has slipped his memory. And time is important, you know; the exact time, to the minute, may establish someone's alibi, or break it."

"Alibi?"

"An account of where a person was at the time of a crime, making it impossible for him or her to have been involved."

"I know what the word means, Mr. Pitt; I just had not realized—you were—only eliminating people on—on proof of imposs..." she trailed away, afraid of her conclusion, confused.

"Well, when we have suspects, Mrs. Ellison, it will help to whittle them down, cast the impossible out of the picture."

She wished more than anything that he would leave. He was a policeman, which was almost like a tradesman; it was idiotic to let him dominate her like this. Emily was right; he did have a beautiful voice, resonant and soft. His diction was perfect.

"Quite," she said awkwardly. "But I'm afraid my husband is not at home this morning, and I cannot help you."

He smiled gently.

"I shall come back this evening, if Mr. Ellison is expected home?"

"Yes. He is expected to dinner."

He gave a small bow, and went to the door.

When Edward came home at quarter past six she told him of Pitt's call, and that he would return.

He stood still, staring at her.

"He's coming back this evening?"

"Yes."

"You shouldn't have told him I would be here, Caroline." His face was stiff. "I have to go out again—"

"You said this morning—" she stopped, fear suddenly cutting off her voice. He was avoiding Pitt because he was afraid of lying to him!

"Obviously I have made arrangements since this morning," he snapped. "Anyway, it is quite pointless. I know nothing whatsoever that I have not already told him. You may say that to him, or have Maddock do so."

"Do you think—" she said hesitantly.

"Good heavens, Caroline, he is a policeman, not someone to be socially entertained. Have Maddock tell him I had made previous arrangements, and I know nothing that would fur-

Anne Perry

ther his investigations. If he has found out nothing so far, after all the enquiries he has made and the time he has taken, either it is an insoluble mystery, or the man is incompetent."

But Pitt returned yet again the following evening, and was shown into the withdrawing room where Caroline and Edward were sitting with Charlotte and Grandmama. Everyone else was out at a concert. Maddock opened the door to announce him, and before anyone could reply, Pitt himself moved past him into the room.

"In a gentleman's home, Mr. Pitt," Edward said tartly, "it is customary to wait until you are invited before entering."

Caroline felt herself blush for his rudeness, and go cold for his fear. He must be afraid, to depart so far from his usual good manners. Usual? Did she know him as well as she imagined? Why in God's name had he been in Cater Street?

Pitt did not seem in the least put out. He walked further in and Maddock withdrew.

"Forgive me. Murder doesn't often take me into the homes of gentlemen; but even they have a disinclination to speak to me, which I have to overcome by the best means available. I am sure you are as anxious as I am to identify and apprehend this man."

"Of course." Edward looked at him coldly. "However, I have already told you everything I know—more than once. I have nothing to add. I don't see how repetition will help you."

"You'd be surprised. Details get added, small things remembered."

"I have remembered nothing."

"Where were you that evening, Mr. Ellison?"

Edward frowned. "I have already told you. I was at my club which is nowhere near Cater Street."

"All evening, Mr. Ellison?"

Caroline looked at Edward. His face was pale. She could almost see the struggle in his mind. Could he get away with the lie? Dear God, what was he hiding? She turned to Pitt.

The clever eyes were not watching Edward, but her. Suddenly she was terrified he could see her fear, that her knowledge of the lies was in her face. She looked away, anywhere else, and found Charlotte watching her also. The room suffocated her, terror almost stopped her breathing.

"All evening, Mr. Ellison?" Pitt repeated quietly.

"Er ... no." Edward's voice was tight, the strain rasping.

"Where did you go, then?" Pitt was perfectly polite. If he was at all surprised he hid it.

Had he already known? Caroline's heart tightened. Did he know where Edward had been?

"I went to visit a friend," Edward replied, looking at him.

"Indeed," Pitt smiled. "Which friend, Mr. Ellison?"

Edward hesitated.

Grandmama sat a little more upright.

"Young man!" she said sharply. "Remember your position, both in this house, and in society in general. Mr. Ellison has told you he visited a friend. That is sufficient for your purpose. We appreciate that you have a duty to perform, and an arduous one, necessary for justice, and for public safety. And of course we will assist you as we can, but do not presume upon our goodwill to trespass beyond your duty."

Pitt raised his eyebrows in humour more than annoyance.

"Ma'am, unfortunately murder is no respecter of persons, or of social distinction. This man must be found or one of your granddaughters may be next."

"Nonsense!" Grandmama said furiously. "My granddaughters are women of moral rectitude and decent habits. I appreciate that you may not be familiar with such women, and therefore I will excuse your insult as coming from ignorance rather than ill will."

Pitt took a deep breath and let it out.

"Ma'am, we have no reason to suppose this man has any exclusive hatred of immoral women, or even any predilection for them. Miss Abernathy was a little frivolous, but no worse; Lily Mitchell had a stainless reputation, and we have yet to fault it. Even her behaviour with Brody appears so far to have been perfectly correct."

Grandmama looked at him with a slight flaring of her nostrils.

"What is correct for a serving maid or a policeman may be quite beneath a gentlewoman," she said damningly.

Pitt bowed very slightly.

"I beg to differ, ma'am. I believe morality is universal. Circumstances may alter the degree of blame, but not that an act is wrong."

Grandmama drew breath to condemn his temerity, then considered his argument instead, and let it out without speaking.

Caroline looked at Edward, who was still silent, then at Charlotte. She was watching Pitt with surprise, and some respect.

Pitt looked back at Edward.

"Mr. Ellison, the name and address of your friend, if you please? I assure you, it is necessary. Also, as near as you know it, the exact time of your departure from his house?"

Again there was a moment's silence. To Caroline it was an eternity, like waiting while you tear open a message which you know will be news of disaster.

"I'm afraid I don't know what time I left," Edward replied. "At the time, of course, I had no idea it would be of the least importance."

"Possibly your friend will know," Pitt seemed unperturbed.

"No," Edward said quickly. "My friend—is ill. That is why I called. Er—he was already drifting to sleep when I left— that is why I departed when I did. I'm afraid we can neither of us be of any very precise assistance. I'm sorry."

"But you did come home from the far end of Cater Street?" Pitt was not easily discouraged.

"I've already said so," Edward was also regaining his composure.

"Did you see anyone else at all?"

"Not that I recall, but I was thinking of getting home, not of observing the street."

"Naturally. But no doubt you would have noticed a man running, or two people struggling; or if you had heard a cry of alarm or any kind of scream?"

"Of course I would. If there was anything at all, it must have been relatively inconspicuous, a late traveller like myself, or something of that sort. Actually, I don't remember anyone at all."

"And the address?"

"I beg your pardon?"

"The address from which you came?"

"I see no reason why that is relevant. My friend is ill, and in some distress. I would prefer you did not call on them. It would cause them considerable anxiety, and only increase their illness."

"I see." Pitt stood still. "All the same, I would like to know it. They just might remember the time."

"What good would that do?"

"Establish at least one time at which the crime did not happen. By process of elimination we might pin it down very nicely."

Without thinking, Caroline jumped in.

"That can easily be known." She demanded Pitt's attention. "He arrived here a few minutes after we did, less than five minutes. If you walk from here to Cater Street, you will have the time precisely." She waited with heart lurching to see if he accepted it.

Pitt gave a small smile.

"Quite. Thank you." He glanced at Charlotte, then inclined his head in a gesture of resignation. "I wish you good day." He opened the door for himself and went out. They heard Maddock in the hall, and then the front door close also.

"Well!" Grandmama let out her breath. "What a vulgar young man."

"Persistent," Caroline said before thinking. "But not vul-

129

gar. If he were to be put off by equivocation he would never solve his cases."

"I have never considered you a competent judge of vulgarity, Caroline," Grandmama said with mounting anger. "But I am shocked that you can even entertain the possibility that Edward would know anything about a crime. You appear to doubt him!"

"Of course I don't!" Caroline lied, her face flushing hotly. "I was speaking of the police, not myself. You cannot expect Mr. Pitt to take the same view as I!"

"I do not. But neither did I, until now, expect you to take the same view as Mr. Pitt!"

"She wasn't, Grandmama," Charlotte interrupted. "She was merely pointing out that—"

"Be silent, Charlotte," Edward said crossly. "I forbid anyone to discuss the matter further. It is sordid and has no part in our life beyond the assistance we have already given. If you cannot control yourself, Charlotte, then you may retire to your room."

Charlotte said nothing at all. Grandmama started off again to bemoan the general decline of good manners and the increase of immorality and crime.

Caroline sat staring at a rather ugly photograph of her wedding, and wondering with mounting fear why Edward would not tell Pitt where he had been.

Nothing more was said that day, but the following morning Caroline was going through household accounts at her desk in the back sitting room when Grandmama came in.

"Caroline, I have to ask you what you mean by it, although I fear I know. I think I have a right."

Caroline lied immediately, in defence.

"I'm afraid I don't know what you're talking about, Grandmama." She had been thinking of little else herself, but she pretended now to have her mind on the fishmonger's bill in front of her.

"Then you are more callous even than I presumed. I am

talking about that policeman, and his extraordinary behaviour last night. In my day policemen knew their place."

"A policeman's place is wherever there is crime," Caroline said wearily. She knew she was not going to be able to avoid the confrontation, but she instinctively delayed it, as one recoils from all pain.

"There is no crime in his house, Caroline, except your betrayal of your husband's good name."

"That is a malicious and totally false thing to say!" Caroline swung round from the desk, the pen still in her hand, but held like a knife now. "And you would not dare say it if we were not alone, and if you did not imagine I would not wish to quarrel with you. Well, you mistake me this time! I most certainly shall quarrel, if you say such a mischievous thing again. Do you hear me?"

"It is your conscience that makes you so angry," Grandmama said with evil delight. "And I certainly dare say it again, and I shall, in front of Edward. Then we'll see who will quarrel, and who will not."

"You'd love that, wouldn't you!" Caroline leaned forward. "You'd like to upset Edward and set his house on its head! Well, for once I'm not yielding to your blackmail. You tell Edward anything you want to. But I observe it was not you who defended him when he did not wish to tell the police where he was! You did nothing but antagonize Pitt by being insufferably rude. What did you think that would do? Frighten him off? Then you are living in a dream! It only made him the more suspicious."

"Suspicious of what?" Grandmama was still standing, her body rocking back and forth with rage. "What do you think Edward has done, Caroline? Do you think he trailed out after his housemaid and strangled her? Is that what you think? Does Edward know this is what you think of him?"

"Not unless you've told him! Which would not surprise me. It would certainly cause the kind of unhappiness you feed on! Isn't Lily's death enough for you?"

"Enough for me! Me? What do you think I gain from the

death of some wretched housemaid? I have always hated immorality, but it is not for me to bring down the judgment of
God on her."

"You old hypocrite!" Caroline exploded. "There is nothing
in the world more immoral than pleasure in the pain and
misfortune of others!"

"You have brought your misfortune on yourself, Caroline.
I, for one, cannot get you out of it, whether I wished to or
not," and with a lift of her head Grandmama swept out of
the room before Caroline could reply; although she could
think of nothing to say anyway.

She sat at the desk and stared through tears at the fishmonger's account. She hated quarrels, but this one had been
brewing for years. This had only been an eruption of hatreds
that had simmered in both of them and, but for Lily's death
and its terrors, might have lain dormant forever. Now things
had been said which would never be forgotten, and certainly
could not be forgiven—not by Grandmama, even if she herself
chose to.

The worst of it was that Grandmama would draw in the
whole house; she would compel them all to take sides. There
would be meaningful glances, silences, cryptic remarks, until
curiosity drove someone to ask what it was all about. Edward
would hate it. He loved them both and wished above all
things that there should be peace in his house. Like most
men, he loathed family rows. He would pay a considerable
price for tranquillity. He would pretend to be unaware of it
as long as possible. Dominic would probably be the catalyst,
quite unintentionally. He had not known Grandmama long
enough to read the undercurrents, and ignore them.

It would be awful! And the worst part was that Grandmama was right. She did suspect, with sick fear, that Edward
had done something dishonourable. She could feel her throat
ache with the effort not to weep, and if she looked down the
tears would spill over.

"Mama?"

It was Charlotte. She had not even heard her come in.

She sniffed. "Yes, what is it? I'm busy with accounts."

Charlotte slid her arms round her and kissed her.

"I know, I heard you."

It was welcome, almost unbearable in its relief after she had been feeling so alone. It was harder than ever to control herself, but she had had years of practice.

"Oh. I'm sorry. I had not realized we had raised our voices."

Charlotte adjusted a hairpin for her and stepped away, tactfully leaving her to compose herself. Odd what sensitivity Charlotte had sometimes, while at other times she was so outspoken.

Charlotte was staring through the window.

"Don't worry about Grandmama. If she says anything to Papa he will be very angry with her, and she will come off the worse for it."

Caroline was too surprised to hide it. She swung round in the chair to stare at Charlotte's back.

"Whyever do you think that?"

Charlotte still looked out of the window.

"Because Papa was somewhere he does not wish to speak of. We must face that. Therefore he will be angry with whoever mentions it again."

"What on earth do you mean?" Caroline could hear her own voice shaking now. "What are you saying, Charlotte? You cannot suspect your father—of—of—"

"I don't know. Perhaps he was gambling, or drunk, or associating with people we would not like. But he does not wish Mr. Pitt or us to know of it. It is no use pretending to each other. We cannot pretend to ourselves. But don't worry, Mama, he cannot have had anything to do with Lily, if that's what you're afraid of."

"Charlotte—," she could think of nothing else to say. How could she stand there so calmly, speaking those words?

"I think it may be very foolish," Charlotte went on—and this time Caroline heard the catch in her voice and knew she was only keeping control of herself with the greatest effort—"because I think Mr. Pitt will find out anyway."

"Do you?"

"Yes. And it will seem the worse for not being revealed of one's own free will."

"Then, if we could persuade him—," but she knew she lacked the courage. Edward would be angry, go into that cold bitter retreat she had experienced only a few times—like the occasion she had defied him over Gerald Hapwith. That was years ago, and all so silly now. But the pain of the estrangement was easy to remember.

And more than that, she was afraid to know what it was he wanted to hide. Perhaps Pitt would not find out?

But he did. Mr. Pitt returned two days later, in the evening and—perhaps to be sure of catching Edward—by surprise, not having called in the morning to forewarn them. They were all at home.

"This is not very convenient, Mr. Pitt," Edward said coolly. "What is it this time?"

"We have established that you must have walked back along Cater Street, from approximately five minutes to eleven, until a few minutes past the hour."

"You had no need to come to tell me that," Edward was sharp. "Since I arrived home at about quarter after, that much is obvious."

Nothing seemed to discompose Pitt.

"To you, sir, who know what you did. To us, who have to accept your word, it is satisfying to obtain proof. If murderers could be caught merely by asking them, our job would hardly be worth doing."

Edward's face froze.

"What are you implying, Mr. Pitt?"

"That we have established that you left Mrs. Attwood at quarter to eleven. It would take you about half an hour of comfortable walking to reach your home here, and you would pass along Cater Street between five to eleven, and about five past."

Edward was white-faced.

"You had no right—!"

"It would have been a great deal easier, and have saved much time, sir, if you had given us Mrs. Attwood's address earlier. Now perhaps you would be kind enough to tell me where you were on the night Chloe Abernathy met her death?"

"If you know where I was on the night Lily was killed, you know I can have had nothing to do with it," Edward said between his teeth. For the first time he looked really frightened. "What do you imagine I can tell you about Chloe Abernathy?"

"Only where you were," Pitt smiled broadly. "And if possible, with whom?"

"I was with Alan Cuthbertson, discussing business in his rooms."

Pitt's smile became wider, if anything.

"Good, that is what he says, but since he was acquainted with Miss Abernathy fairly well, it was necessary to check that he was being precisely honest. Thank you, Mr. Ellison. You have done Mr. Cuthbertson and the police a service. I'm obliged. Ma'am," he inclined his head in a small bow. "Good night."

"Who is Mrs. Attwood, Papa?" Sarah said immediately. "I don't recall your having mentioned her?"

"I doubt I did," Edward said, looking away. "She is a rather tiresome woman who is a dependent of a man who once did me a favour, and is now dead himself. She has become ill, and I occasionally render her some small, practical assistance. She is not bedridden, but close to it. She seldom leaves the house. You might visit her yourself, if you wish, but I warn you she is most tiresome, and wandering somewhat in her mind. She confuses reminiscences with fantasy on occasion, although at other times she is lucid enough. No doubt it comes from spending a great deal of time alone, and reading romantic novels of the cheapest kind."

The relief was immense, but later that night in bed, Caroline woke and began to think. At first she worried about the fact that Edward had been so concerned about hiding his visit to this Mrs. Attwood. Was it really to protect a sick woman? Or because she was perhaps a little common, a little loud, someone he did not wish to be associated with?

Then the deeper worry came to the surface and would not be ignored. She had questioned in her mind, had feared for a moment that he had had something to do with Lily. He was lying beside her now, asleep. She had been married to him for more than thirty years. How could it even have crossed her mind that he had murdered a girl in the street? What kind of a woman was she to have considered such a thing, even for a second? She had always believed she loved him, not passionately of course, but adequately. She knew him well—or she had believed so until this week. Now she realized there were things about him she did not know at all.

She had lived in the same house with him, the same bed, for over thirty years, and borne him three children, four counting the son who had died when only a few days old. And yet she had actually considered he might have garotted Lily.

What was her relationship worth? What would Edward think or feel if he knew what had been in her mind? She was confused, and ashamed, and deeply afraid.

*Chapter
Seven*

It was the following week, the beginning of September and hot and still, when Millie came to Charlotte in the garden. Her face was pink and she looked flustered. She had a piece of paper in her hand.

Charlotte put down the hoe she was using to poke around the soil between the flowers. It was a pastime rather than a job, an excuse to be outside instead of attending to the preserves she should have been stewing for Sarah to bottle. But Sarah was out with Dominic on some social affair, while Emily was at a tennis party with a whole group of people, including George Ashworth, and Mama was visiting Susannah.

"What is it, Millie?"

"Please, Miss Charlotte, I found this letter this morning. I've been trying to decide all day what I should do about it." She held out the piece of paper.

Charlotte took it from her and read:

Deer Lily,

This is to tel yu that I ant warnin yu any mor. Ither yu dus as yur told or itll be the wors for yu.

It was unsigned.

"Where did you get this?" Charlotte asked.

"I found it in one of the drawers in my room, Miss. Where Lily used to be."

"I see."

"Did I do the right thing, Miss?"

"Yes, Millie, you did. Most certainly. It would have been very wrong not to have brought it to me. It—it might be important."

"You think the murderer wrote her that, Miss?"

"I don't know, Millie, probably not. But we should let the police have it."

"Yes, ma'am. But Mr. Maddock is busy unpacking the next cases of wine this afternoon, and the master said it had to be done straight away."

"That's all right, Millie. I'll take it myself."

"But, Miss Charlotte, you aren't going out by yourself, are you?"

Charlotte stared at her for a moment. "No, Millie, you'll have to come with me."

"Me, Miss Charlotte?" She froze, her eyes wide.

"Yes, you, Millie. Go and get your coat on. Tell Mrs. Dunphy I need you to come with me on an urgent errand. Now go on."

Three quarters of an hour later Millie was in the outer waiting room of the police station, and Charlotte was shown into Inspector Pitt's small room to await his return. It was drab, functional, and a little dusty. There were three chairs, one of them on a swivel, a table with locked drawers in it, a rolltop desk, also locked, and a brown linoleum floor, worn patchy where feet had trodden from door to desk and back again.

She had been there for only ten minutes when the door opened and a sharp-nosed little man in overly smart clothes came in. His face dropped in surprise.

"'Allo, Miss! You sure you're in the right place?"

"I believe so. I'm waiting for Mr. Pitt."

He looked her up and down carefully. "You don't look like a nose."

"I beg your pardon?"

"You don't look like a nose." He came in and closed the door behind him. "An informer, a spy for the crushers."

"For whom?" she frowned, trying to understand him.

"The police! You did say you wanted to see Mr. Pitt?"

"Yes."

He grinned suddenly, showing broken teeth.

"You a friend of his?"

"I have come on a matter of business which, forgive me for frankness, is not your concern." She had no wish to be rude. He was a harmless enough little man, and apparently friendly.

"Business? You don't look like you have business with the crushers." He sat down on the chair opposite, still looking at her in amiable curiosity.

"Do you belong here?" she said doubtfully.

"Oh, yes," he grinned. "I got business too."

"Indeed?"

"Important," he nodded, his eyes bright. "Do a lot for Mr. Pitt, I do. Don't know how he'd manage without me."

"I dare say he'd survive somehow," Charlotte said with a smile.

He was unoffended.

"Ah, Miss, that's 'cos you don't know anything about it, begging your pardon."

"About what?"

"About the workings, Miss: the way things is done. I'll

139

wager you don't even know how to break a drum or to christen the stuff and fence it afterwards."

Charlotte was completely lost but, in spite of herself, interested.

"No," she admitted. "I don't even know what you're talking about."

"Ah," he settled himself more comfortably. "But you see I knows everything. Born to it. Born in the rookeries, I was. Grew up there. Mother died when I was about three, so they say. And I was very small. Lucky that—"

"Lucky? You mean someone took pity on you?"

He gave her a look of friendly contempt. "I mean they saw my possibilities—that if I stayed little I could be of use."

Memories of things that Pitt had told her about small boys up chimneys came back, and she shivered.

"Had you no family? What about your father, or grandparents?"

"Me father was crapped in forty-two, year I was born, and me grandfather got the boat, so they said. Me ma had a brother who was a fine wirer, but he didn't want nothing to do with kids, did he? Not one that was too young to be any use. Besides, fine wiring ain't an art as needs kids."

"What is 'crapped'?" she asked.

He drew a hand across his throat, then held it up behind him to imitate a rope.

She blushed with embarrassment.

"Oh, I'm sorry—I—"

"Don't matter," he dismissed it. "Weren't no good to me anyway."

"And your grandfather went to sea? Didn't he return?"

"Bless you, Miss. You really is from another world, ain't you? Not went to sea, Miss, but got sent to Australia."

"Oh." She could think of nothing else to say to that. "And your uncle?"

"Fine wiring is the picking of ladies' pockets, Miss. Very delicate art, that is. Don't use kids, like some does. No use for me, see? So they gave me to a kidsman who taught me a bit o' oly fakin'—that's pickin' silk handkerchiefs out o' pockets to you, Miss, to earn me keep, so to speak. Then when I got older, but not much bigger, he sole me to a first-class cracksman. Climb through any set o' bars, I could. Ease myself through them like a snake. Many's the toffken I bin in and out of, and opened the door for 'em."

"What's a toffken?" She felt her father would be furious if he knew of this extraordinary conversation, but it was a world which appalled her too much to turn her back on it. She was fascinated as a child is by a scab that he must keep picking at.

"A swell house, like maybe you lives in." He seemed to bear her no resentment, but rather to find her the more interesting for it.

"I don't think we have a great deal worth taking," she said honestly. "What happened to you then?"

"Well, come the time I got too big, of course. But before that, he got caught and I never seen him again. But he'd taught me a lot o' things, like how to use all 'is tools, how to do a spot of star glazing—"

"Star gazing?" she said incredulously.

He burst out with rich, dry laughter.

"Bless you. You are a caution. Star *glazing*. Look." He got off his seat and went to the window. "Say you wanted to get through that piece of glass. Well, you lean up against it," he demonstrated. "Put your knife here, near the edge, and press hard but gentle, till the glass cracks. Not so hard it falls out, mind. Then you put brown paper plaster over it so it all sticks, and presto—you can pull the glass out without a whole lot o' noise. Put your hand in and undo the latch." He looked back at her in obvious triumph.

"I see. Didn't you ever get caught?"

"Of course I did! But you expects that, don't you, occasional like?"

"You didn't consider taking—a—a—regular job?" She did not want to say an *honest* job. For some incomprehensible reason, she did not want to hurt his feelings.

"I'd got a ready-made team, 'adn't I? Got me tools, a good crow, the 'andsomest canary in London, and a good fence as lived in a flash house, nice and comfortable for us, and a few dolly-shops if we hit hard times. What else did I need? What did I want to go and break me back for in some factory or sweatshop for a few pence a day?"

"What are the birds for?"

"Birds?" his face puckered up. "What birds?"

"The crow and the canary?"

He chuckled in genuine delight.

"Oh, I do like talking to you, Miss. You're a refreshment, you are. A crow is either a quack, a medical man, or in this case, a feller what stands around and gives the warning if anyone comes along as is dangerous, like a jack, or the crushers, or whatever. And a canary is the one who brings your tools for you. If you've got any class, you don't bring your own tools. You goes to the place, takes a good look around, and then your canary brings them when all's clear. She's usually a woman. Works better that way. And Bessie was as 'andsome as a summer day, she was."

"What happened to her?"

"Died of cholera, she did, in 'sixty, the year before the American war. Poor Bessie."

"How old was she?"

"Eighteen, same as me."

Younger than Emily, younger than Lily Mitchell. She had lived in the slums, been a carrier of burglar's tools, and died of disease at age eighteen. It was an existence which mocked Charlotte's tidy life, with its small difficulties. The only big thing that had ever happened to her was her love of Dominic, and Lily's death. Everything else was comfortable. Have we mended all the linen? Shall we preserve peaches or apricots? Is the fishmonger's bill too high? What shall I wear to the party on Friday? Do I really have to be civil to the vicar? And all the while there were people like this funny little man here fighting just to eat. And some of them lost: the smallest and the weakest, the most easily frightened.

"I'm sorry," was all she could say.

He looked at her closely. "You're a funny creature," he said at last.

Before she could react to that, the doors swung open and Pitt came in. His face dropped in surprise when he saw her. Apparently whoever was outside had failed to forewarn him.

"Miss Ellison! What are you doing here?"

"She's waiting for you." The little man shot to his feet with excitement. "She's been here sittin' this past half hour." He pulled an exceedingly elegant gold watch out of his pocket.

Pitt stared at it. "Where did you get that, Willie?"

"You got a nasty mind, Mr. Pitt."

"I've got a nasty temper, too. Where did you get it, Willie?"

"I bought it, Mr. Pitt!" His outrage carried no anger, only ringing innocence.

"From whom? One of your dolly-shops?"

"Mr. Pitt! That's real gold, that is. It's quality."

"Pawnshop then?"

"That's not nice, Mr. Pitt! I bought it respectable."

"All right, Willie. Go out and convince the sergeant while I talk to Miss Ellison."

Willie lifted his hat and bowed elaborately.

"Out, Willie!"

"Yes, sir, Mr. Pitt. Good afternoon, ma'am."

Pitt closed the door behind him and indicated a chair for Charlotte. Now that he was alone with her he seemed less assured, conscious of the shabby surroundings. Charlotte found herself wishing to put him at ease. She pulled out the letter straight away.

"Our new maid, Millie, handed this to me a little over an hour ago. She found it this morning in her room. I should explain that the room used to be Lily's."

He took the letter and unfolded it. He read it, and then held it up to the light.

"It doesn't look old, and hardly the type of letter one would wish to keep. I think we may presume she received it shortly before she was killed."

"It's a threat?" She moved a little closer to look at it herself.

"It would be difficult to read it as anything else. Although, of course, it may not be a threat of death, by any means."

A world of fear opened up to Charlotte's imagination. Poor Lily! Who had threatened her, and why had she not felt she could turn to any of them to help her? What isolated struggle had been going on in their house under the smooth exterior of housemaid's black and white?

"What do you suppose they wanted her to do?" she asked. "Whoever wrote that letter? Do you think you can find them, and punish them?"

"They may not have killed her."

"I don't care! They frightened her! They tried to force her to do something she obviously did not want to! Isn't that a crime?"

He was looking at her with surprise, taking in her anger, her sense of outrage and pity, and perhaps guilt because it had all happened in her house and she had not seen it.

"Yes, it is a crime, if we could prove it. But we don't know who wrote it, or what he wanted her to do. And the poor little creature isn't alive to complain now."

"Aren't you going to find out!" she demanded.

He put out a hand, as if to touch her, then remembered himself and withdrew it.

"We'll try. But I doubt that the person who wrote this killed her. She was garotted exactly the same way, with a wire from behind, as Chloe Abernathy and the Hiltons' maid. A cracksman might have threatened two maids, but he would never have tried it with a girl like Chloe." His eyes opened wider with a new thought. "Unless, of course, he mistook her for Lily. They were of a similar height and colouring. I suppose in the dark—"

"What would he threaten them for? Two maids, I mean?"

"What? Oh, burglars often use housemaids to let them in and tell them where all the valuables are in the house. Perhaps if she refused—," he sighed. "But it seems a rather extreme way of going about business, and largely unnecessary. A burglar could find enough indoor servants who are willing, or loose-tongued, not to need to resort to this kind of thing."

"Why didn't she come to us?"

"Probably because it wasn't a burglar at all, but some kind of romantic involvement," he replied. "Something she preferred that you not be aware of, that she thought you wouldn't approve of. I expect we shall never know."

"But you will try?"

"Yes, we'll try. And you did the right thing to bring it. Thank you."

She found herself uncomfortable under his gaze, and she was conscious of the shabby room again. What had made him become a policeman? She realized how little she knew about him. As so often happened, her thoughts spilled into words.

"Have you always been a policeman, Mr. Pitt?" she asked.

He was surprised, but there was a flicker of amusement in his eyes which at any other time she might have found irritating.

"Yes, since I was seventeen."

"Why? Why did you want to be a policeman! You must see so much—" She could not find the exact words for all the misery and squalor she imagined.

"I grew up in the country. My parents were in service; my mother was cook and my father gamekeeper." He gave a wry little smile, conscious of their difference in station. "They were with a gentleman of considerable means. He had children of his own, a son about my age. I was allowed to sit in the schoolroom. And we used to play together. I knew rather more about the country than he did. I had friends among the poachers and gypsies. Very exciting for a small boy, son of the manor house, with too many sisters and too much time spent with lessons.

"Pheasants were stolen from the estate and sold. My father was blamed. He was charged at the assizes, and found guilty. He was sent to Australia for ten years. In my own mind, I was convinced he didn't do it—naturally, I suppose. I spent a long time trying to prove it. I never succeeded, but that was when it started."

She imagined the child, caring desperately, burning with confusion and injustice. She felt a tenderness for him which appalled her. She stood up quickly and swallowed.

"I see. And you came to London. How interesting. Thank you for telling me. Now I must return home, or they will be anxious for me."

"You shouldn't have come alone," he frowned. "I'll send a sergeant back with you."

"That's not necessary. I thought you might want to speak to Millie, and so I brought her with me."

"No, I see no reason to speak with her now. But I'm glad you were wise enough to have her come with you." He smiled with a tiny, downward gesture. "And I apologize for doubting your good sense."

"Good day, Mr. Pitt." She went out of the door.

"Good day, Miss Ellison."

She knew he was standing in the doorway watching her, and she was idiotically self-conscious. She all but fell over the step on the way out, having to catch Millie's arm to steady herself. Why on earth should a very plain policeman make her feel so—so conspicuous?

Three days later Charlotte was visiting the Abernathys'. She was there alone only because Sarah and Mama were but a hundred yards away round the corner at the vicar's.

"Do have some more tea, Miss Ellison. It is so kind of you to visit us."

"Thank you," Charlotte pushed her cup forward a little. "It's a pleasure to see you looking so much better."

Mrs. Abernathy smiled gently. "Having young people in the house again helps. After Chloe died, no one came for such a long time. At least it seemed so. I suppose one cannot blame them. No one, least of all the young, wishes to visit a house in mourning. It is too much of a reminder of death, when one wishes to think of life."

Charlotte wanted to comfort her, to prevent her feeling that Chloe's friends were callous, thinking more of their own pleasure than her grief.

She leaned forward a little. "Perhaps they did not wish to intrude? When one is deeply shocked, one doesn't know what to say. Nothing can make it better, and one is afraid to be clumsy and make it worse by saying something stupid."

"You are very gentle, my dear Charlotte. I wish poor Chloe could have sought more friends like you, and not some of the foolish ones she did. It all began with that wretched George Ashworth—"

"What?" Charlotte so far forgot herself as to abandon all courtesy.

Mrs. Abernathy looked at her with slight surprise.

"I wish Chloe had not been quite so friendly with Lord Ashworth. I know he is a gentleman, but sometimes the real quality have some strange tastes and habits we wouldn't approve of."

"I didn't know Chloe knew Lord Ashworth." Charlotte was troubled now. Emily's determined little face kept coming into her mind. "Did she know him well?"

"A great deal better than her father and I would have wished. But he was charming, and titled. You can't tell young girls." She blinked several times.

Charlotte would have liked to leave the subject—she knew it could only cause pain where the wound was already deep—but for Emily's sake she had to know.

"Do you think he treated Chloe badly, that he was less than frank with her affections?"

"Mr. Abernathy gets very angry with me for saying this," her face pinched, "but I believe that if Chloe had not known that man she would be alive today."

Charlotte felt as if she were entering a dark corridor, as if its shadows were closing in on her.

"Why do you say that, Mrs. Abernathy?"

Mrs. Abernathy leaned forward, clutching at Charlotte's arm.

"Oh, please don't repeat it, Charlotte! Mr. Abernathy says I could end up in the most terrible trouble if I say too much!"

Charlotte closed her other hand over Mrs. Abernathy's, gripping her firmly. "Of course I won't. But I would like to know why you consider George Ashworth such a bad influence. I have met him, and although I didn't care for him, I would not have judged him as ill as you seem to."

"He flattered Chloe into believing all sorts of things that could not come true, that were not true of her station in life. He took her to places where there were women of low morals."

"How do you know? Did Chloe say so?"

"She told us a little. But I heard it from others who saw them there. A gentleman friend of Mr. Abernathy's told him he had seen Chloe where he did not expect to see any daughter of a respectable family."

"And this friend is truthful? Not given to misunderstanding or exaggeration? And has no cause for spite, no wish to damage Chloe's reputation?"

"Oh, none at all. The most upright of men! Good gracious!"

"Then forgive me, but what was he doing in such a place as you describe?"

Mrs. Abernathy looked confused for a moment.

"My dear Charlotte, it is quite different for men! It is perfectly—acceptable for a gentleman to frequent places that a woman of good moral character would not go to. We all have to accept these things."

Charlotte was loath to accept any such thing at all, but there was no proper way of arguing it now.

"I see. And you feel Lord Ashworth may have led Chloe into unfortunate company, and even tempted her to practices not acceptable to her, or to anyone of decent upbringing?"

"Yes, I do. Chloe was not really part of his world. And I think she died because he tried to make her part of it."

"Let me not misunderstand you, Mrs. Abernathy. Are you

saying that you think either Lord Ashworth, or someone in his circle, killed Chloe?"

"Yes, Charlotte, I believe it. But you have promised not to say that I said so! Nothing can bring Chloe back, and we cannot be revenged against such people."

"One can prevent them from doing it again!" Charlotte said angrily. "And, in fact, one has a duty!"

"Oh, but, Charlotte, please, I do not know anything. It is just my foolish feeling. Perhaps I am quite wrong, and I should be doing a great injustice!" She was on her feet now, anxious, flapping her hands. "You gave me your promise!"

"Mrs. Abernathy, my own sister Emily is currently in acquaintance with Lord Ashworth. If what you say is true, how can I take no interest in your feelings, whether they are accurate or not? I promise you I will say nothing, unless I feel Emily to be in danger. Then I cannot keep silent."

"Oh, my dear," Mrs. Abernathy sat down sharply. "Oh, my dear Charlotte! What can we do?"

"I don't know," Charlotte said frankly. "Have you told me everything you know, that you either know for sure or have reason to suspect?"

"I know that he drinks too much, but then gentlemen often do. I know that he gambles, but I imagine he can afford to. I know that poor Chloe was enamoured of him, that he swept her off her feet and she saw in him all sorts of romantic dreams. I know he took her with him into his social world where standards are quite different from ours, and where they do all kinds of terrible things for amusement. And I believe if she had stayed among her own kind, gentlemen of moderate means and respectable family, she would not now be dead." The tears were running down her face as she stopped at last. "Forgive me." She reached for her handkerchief and began to cry quietly.

Charlotte put her arms round her and held her tightly. She felt a terrible pity for her because there was nothing she could do, and guilt because she had raked it all up again and made her talk of it. Charlotte held on to her, rocking a little, as if Mrs. Abernathy were a child, not a woman her mother's age.

On the way home she could think of nothing to say to her mother or to Sarah, but they were too busy with their own concerns to notice. All evening she sat almost silent, replying only when necessary, and then somewhat at random. Dominic made one or two comments on her absentmindedness, but even for him she could not abandon her anxiety.

If Mrs. Abernathy were right, then George Ashworth was not merely reprobate but positively dangerous, and might even be implicated in murder. It seemed stretching reason too far to suppose the existence of more than one murderer in Cater Street; therefore, he must have also killed Lily and the Hiltons' maid, if indeed he were actually involved. Perhaps several of his friends in drunken madness had waylaid.... The thought was appalling.

But the worst consideration was Emily. Might not Emily, however much she wished not to, somehow become aware of his guilt? And if she did, and betrayed her knowledge in his presence, perhaps she too would be found dead in the street?

But Charlotte had no proof. Perhaps it was all in the imagination of Mrs. Abernathy, distorted by grief, desperately needing someone to blame, preferring any answer to the unknown. And if Charlotte told Emily her suspicions, without proof, Emily would surely disbelieve them, and with some heat. She might even, in defiance, tell George Ashworth, just to prove her trust in him, and thus provoke her own death.

What was the right thing to do? She looked round their faces as they all sat in the withdrawing room after dinner. Whose advice could she ask? Papa was looking at the newspaper, his face grim. He was very probably reading about the stock market. He would be ill-disposed to interruptions at the moment, and he had appeared to approve of Ashworth.

Mama was embroidering. She looked pale. Grandmama had not yet forgiven her for her fears over Papa and his visit to Mrs.—whatever her name was. Grandmama had been dropping small, barbed remarks for days. And there was no use asking Grandmama anyway; she would immediately either tell everyone directly or else drive them mad with innuendos until someone dragged it from her.

Emily was playing the piano. Next to her Sarah was playing bezique with Dominic. Could she ask Sarah? Part of her longed to ask Dominic, to have something to share with him, to ask his advice. And yet within her there was also a growing resistance, a fear that Dominic would not meet the standard of wisdom she needed, that he would give her an answer that was not decisive, did not commit him.

She had no deep confidence in Sarah either, but there was no one else. She found an opportunity to approach her on the landing before retiring.

"Sarah?"

Sarah stopped in surprise. "I thought you had gone to bed."

"I want to speak to you."

"It cannot wait until morning?"

"No. Please come into my bedroom."

When the door was closed Charlotte stood against it, and Sarah sat on the bed.

"I went to see Mrs. Abernathy today."

"I know."

"Did you know that George Ashworth was closely acquainted with Chloe just before she was killed?"

Sarah frowned.

"No, I didn't. I'm sure Emily doesn't know either."

"So am I. And Mrs. Abernathy believes that he took Chloe to places very unsuitable for a decent woman, and that it was through him that she may well have met whoever killed her, at least that the association was in part responsible—"

"Are you quite sure of what you're saying, Charlotte? I know you don't care for Lord Ashworth. Are you not perhaps letting your prejudices run away with you?"

"I don't believe so. What should I say to Emily?"

"Nothing. She wouldn't believe you anyway."

"But I must warn her!"

"Of what? All you can tell her is that Ashworth admired Chloe before he met her. That will help no one. And why shouldn't he? Chloe was very pretty, poor little thing. I don't doubt he has admired a great many girls, and will admire a great many more."

"But what about Emily?" Charlotte demanded. "What if he really did have something to do with Chloe's death? Emily could find out. She could even be next!"

"Don't be hysterical, Charlotte!" Sarah said sharply. "Mrs. Abernathy is very old-fashioned and very narrow in her background. I daresay what appears very daring and immoral to her would be no more than ordinary high spirits to us. I have heard her express disapproval of the waltz! How stuffy is it possible to be? Even the queen waltzes, or she used to before she became old."

"Mrs. Abernathy was talking about murder, not waltzing."

"To us they are opposite ends of the pole, but to her they are not so far apart. In her mind a person capable of one may very well contemplate the other."

"I didn't know you had such a sense of humour," Charlotte said bitterly. "But this is not the time to show it. What should I say to Emily? I cannot merely do nothing."

"At least you haven't told your dreadful policeman yet!"

"Of course I haven't! And that observation is hardly helpful!"

"Sorry. Perhaps we had better have Emily in here and tell her—I don't know precisely what. I suppose the truth?" As she spoke she stood up and came to the door.

Charlotte agreed. It was the best idea, and she was grateful for Sarah's support. She stood aside for Sarah to leave.

A few moments later they were all in Charlotte's bedroom, the door closed.

"Well?" Emily asked.

"Charlotte heard something today which we think you ought to know," Sarah replied. "It's in your own interest."

"When people say that, it always means something unpleasant." Emily looked at Charlotte. "All right, what is it?"

Charlotte took a deep breath. She knew Emily was going to be angry.

"George Ashworth was very well-acquainted with Chloe just before she was murdered. He took her to a great many places."

Emily's eyebrows rose. "Did you imagine I did not know that?"

Charlotte was surprised. "Yes, I did. But perhaps you do not know what kinds of places? Apparently they were places where moral women do not go."

"You mean whorehouses?"

"Emily, please!" Sarah said sharply. "I appreciate you are angry, but there is no need to be coarse."

"No, I do not mean—whorehouses!" Charlotte said sharply. "At least I don't think I do. But this is not a matter to be taken lightly. Remember that Chloe is dead, and remember how she died. Mrs. Abernathy believes that it was her association with George Ashworth that led to her death, either directly or indirectly."

Emily's face was white. "You have not left me unaware that you dislike George, even perhaps that you are jealous, but this is spiteful and quite beneath you! Goodness knows, I am sorry enough for Chloe's death, but it had nothing to do with George!"

"How do you know?"

"Because it is only your prudish spite that imagines it might have! I know George and you do not. Why on earth should he do such a thing?"

"I don't know! But I am not telling you for spite, and it is very wrong of you to say so! I am telling you because I could not bear it if the same thing were to happen to you, if through George Ashworth you met someone who—"

Emily let out a sigh of impatience. "If Chloe mixed in bad company then it was because she had not the wit to recognize it. I hope you do not put me in the same category?"

"I really don't know, Emily," Charlotte said honestly. "Sometimes I wonder."

Emily was defensive again. "So what are you going to do? Tell Papa?"

"What for? He could forbid you to see George Ashworth but you would still do whatever you wished—only secretly, which would be even worse. Just—just be careful!"

Emily's face softened. "Of course I shall be careful. I suppose you mean well. But really sometimes you are—so pompous and such a prude I despair of you! Well, I'm too tired to stand here any longer. Good night."

Charlotte stared at Sarah when Emily had gone.

"You can't do any more," Sarah said quietly. "And honestly, I don't think Ashworth had anything to do with it. It's just Mrs. Abernathy's imagination. Don't worry about it. Good night."

"Good night, Sarah. And thank you."

Chapter
Eight

On the second of October, autumn rain cooling the streets, Maddock knocked on the withdrawing room door after dinner and came in immediately. His trousers were splattered with rain, and his face was gray.

Edward looked up, opened his mouth to question his behaviour, and then saw him. He stood up sharply.

"Maddock! What's the matter, man? Are you ill?"

Maddock stiffened and swayed a little on his feet. "No, sir. If I might speak to you outside, sir?"

"What is it, Maddock?" Edward obviously was afraid now, too. The room was silent.

Charlotte stared at them, cold knotting up·inside her.

"If I might speak to you in confidence, sir?" Maddock asked again.

"Edward," Caroline said very quietly, "if something has happened, we shall have to know. Maddock had as well tell us all as leave us in suspense."

Maddock looked to Edward.

"Very well," Edward nodded. "What is it, Maddock?"

"There has been another murder, sir, in an alley off Cater Street."

"Oh, my God!" Edward went sheet-white and sat down hard on the chair behind him. There was a low moan from Sarah.

"Who was it?" Caroline said so quietly she could barely be heard.

"Verity Lessing, ma'am, the sexton's daughter," Maddock answered her. "A constable has just come from the police to tell us, and warn us all to stay in the house, and not to let the maids out, even into the areaway."

"No, of course not," Edward looked stunned, staring into the room blindly. "Was it the same—?"

"Yes, sir, with a garotting wire, like the others."

"Oh, my God."

"Perhaps I had better go and check all the doors again, sir? And close the shutters on the windows. It would reassure the women."

"Yes," Edward agreed absently. "Yes, do that, please."

"Maddock?" Caroline called as he turned to leave.

"Yes, ma'am?"

"Before you do, please bring us a bottle of brandy and some glasses. I think we could do with a little—help."

"Yes, ma'am, certainly."

A moment after he had brought them in and left there was another clatter outside as Dominic came in, shaking the rain off his jacket.

"Should have taken a coat," he said, looking at his wet hands. "Didn't expect the change." His eyes moved from their faces to the brandy and back again. "What's the matter? You look awful! Come to think of it, there were people all over the street. Mama?" He frowned, peering at her. "Grand-mama's not ill, is she?"

"No," Edward answered for Caroline. "There's been another murder. You'd better sit down and have some brandy, too."

Dominic stared at him, his face blanching. "Oh God!" He drew in his breath and let it out. "Who?"

"Verity Lessing."

Dominic sat down. "The sexton's daughter?"

"Yes." Edward poured him some brandy and passed the glass.

"What's happening?" Dominic said bewilderedly. "Was this in Cater Street, too?"

"In an alley just off it," Edward replied. "I suppose we must face it; whoever this madman is, he is someone who lives here, near Cater Street; or else he has business here, some reason to come here regularly."

No one answered him. Charlotte watched his face. All she could think of was her overwhelming relief that he had been home all evening, that this time when Pitt came—as she did not doubt he would—there would be no questions for Papa.

"I'm sorry," Edward went on. "We can no longer pretend it is some creature from the criminal slums invading us by mischance."

"Papa?" Emily said tremulously. "You don't imagine it could be—could actually be someone we know, do you?"

"Of course not!" Sarah said sharply. "It must be someone quite deranged!"

"That doesn't mean it isn't someone we know." Charlotte painfully gave expression to the thoughts that had been forming in her mind. "After all, *someone* must know him!"

"I don't know what you mean?" Sarah frowned at her. "I don't know anyone deranged."

"How do you know that you don't?"

"Of course I don't!"

Dominic turned to her. "What are you trying to say, Charlotte? That we wouldn't know if someone were as mad as this?"

"Well, would you?" Charlotte looked back at him. "If it were so easy to see, wouldn't those who do know him have

157

said something, done something by now? After all, someone
must know him—tradesmen, servants, neighbours—even if
he doesn't have a family!"

"Oh, but how awful." Emily stared at her. "Imagine being
servant to someone, or neighbour, and knowing they were—
mad like that, that they killed women—"

"That's what I'm trying to say!" Charlotte turned from
one to another of them urgently. "I don't think you *would*
know, or he would have been captured long ago. The police
have talked to all sorts of people. If someone knew, it would
have come out by now."

"Well, there are several people I can think of who are not
all they seem to be on the surface," Grandmama spoke for
the first time. "I've always said you can't tell what wicked-
ness lies underneath the smooth face people show to the
world. Some that appear saints are devils underneath."

"And some that appear devils are still devils, no matter
how far underneath you look," Charlotte said instinctively.

"Is that remark supposed to mean anything?" Grandmama asked very tartly. "It's time, young woman, that you
learned to control your tongue! In my young day a girl your
age knew how to behave herself!"

"In your day you were not faced with four murders in the
streets where you lived." Caroline came to Charlotte's defence, and obliquely her own. "Or so you frequently inform
us."

"Perhaps that is why!" Grandmama returned.

"Why what?" Sarah asked. "We all know that Charlotte's
tongue runs away with her, but are you suggesting that it is
responsible for Verity Lessing's murder off Cater Street this
evening?"

"You are impertinent, Sarah!" Grandmama snapped.
"And it is quite unlike you."

"I think you are being unfair, Grandmama," Dominic
smiled at her. He could usually charm her—he knew it, and
used it. "We are rather badly shocked, both by the loss of

someone we know, and the thought that the murderer may also be someone we know, or at least have seen."

"Yes, mama." Edward stood up. "Perhaps you should retire. Caroline will see that you are brought something to drink before you sleep."

Grandmama stared at him belligerently.

"I do not wish to go to bed. I will not be dismissed!"

"I think it is better," Edward said firmly.

Grandmama sat where she was, but she had met her match, and a few minutes later she allowed him to help her up and, with considerable ill grace, went to bed.

"Thank God," Caroline said wearily. "It really is too much."

"Nevertheless," Dominic scowled, "we cannot avoid the truth that, as Charlotte said, it could be anyone—even someone we speak to, someone we have always felt perfectly at ease with—"

"Stop it, Dominic!" Sarah sat upright. "You will have us suspecting our neighbours, even our friends. We will become unable to conduct a proper conversation with anyone without wondering in our hearts if they could be the one!"

"Perhaps it would be as well," Emily said thoughtfully, "until he is found."

"Emily! How can you say such a thing, even in jest? And it is a bad enough time for humour of any sort."

"Emily is not being humorous," Dominic put in for her. "She is being eminently practical, as always. And to an extent she is right. Perhaps if Verity Lessing had been more suspicious, she would now be alive."

A new thought occurred to Charlotte. "Do you think so, Dominic? Do you think that is why no one has heard screams—because whoever did it was known to each victim, and they were not afraid until it was too late?"

Dominic paled. Obviously he had not thought of it: his mind had been following his words, not leading them. His imagination was still far behind.

Charlotte was surprised. She thought he had seen the

conclusion before her. "It would explain it," she said unhappily.

"So would being taken by surprise from behind," Sarah pointed out.

"I think this conversation is unprofitable," Edward interrupted. "We cannot protect ourselves by indulging in speculation about all our acquaintances, and we may do them grave injustice. We will only end by frightening ourselves even more than is already unavoidable."

"That is easy to say." Caroline looked at her brandy glass. "But it will be very hard to do. From now on I believe I shall find myself thinking about people in a different way, wondering how much I really know about them, and if they are thinking the same of me, or at least of my family."

Sarah stared at her, eyebrows arched. "You mean they might suspect Papa?"

"Why not? Or Dominic? They do not know them as we do."

Charlotte remembered when it had crossed her mind, hers and Mama's, for a black, shaming hour, and they themselves had considered the possibility of Papa's involvement. She did not look at her mother. If she could forget it, so much the better.

"What I am afraid of," she said honestly, "is that one day I might meet someone, and my suspicions show, as they might concerning anyone—but that *this* time they would be justified. And when he recognized my suspicions I would see in his face they were right. Then we would look at each other, and he would know that I knew, and he would have to kill me, quickly, before I spoke or cried out—"

"Charlotte!" Edward stood up and banged his fist on the piecrust table, knocking it over. "Stop it! You are very foolishly frightening everyone, and quite unnecessarily. None of you is going to be alone with this man, or any other."

"We don't know who he is," Charlotte was not put off. "He could be someone we had considered a friend, as safe as one of us! It could be the vicar, or the butcher's boy, or Mr. Abernathy—"

"Don't be ridiculous! It will be someone with whom we have the barest acquaintance, if indeed any at all. We may not be excellent judges of character, but at least we are not capable of so gross a mistake as that."

"Aren't we?" Charlotte was looking at a blank space on the wall. "I've been wondering how much of a person is on the surface, how much we really know about anyone at all. We don't really know very much about each other, never mind those with whom we have only an acquaintanceship."

Dominic was still staring at her, surprise in his face. "I thought we knew each other very well?"

"Did you?" She looked back at him, meeting the dark, bright eyes, for once seeking only meaning, without her heart leaping. "Do you still?"

"Perhaps not." He looked away and walked to the brandy decanter to pour himself some more. "Anyone else wish for another glass?"

Edward stood up. "I think we had better all have an early night; after sleep we may have composed ourselves and be able to face the problems a little more—practically. I shall think about it, and let you know in the morning what I have decided is best for us to do until this creature is caught."

The following day there were the usual grim offices to perform. A police constable called, in the early morning, to inform them officially of the murder, and to ask them if they had any information. Charlotte wondered if Pitt would come, and was curiously both relieved and disappointed when he did not.

Lunch was a more or less silent affair of cold meat and vegetables. In the afternoon all four of them went to pay their respects to the Lessings, and offered to give any assistance they could—although, of course, there was nothing that would do anything to dissipate the shock or ease the pain. Nevertheless, it was a visit which must be paid, a courtesy that would cause hurt if not observed.

They all wore dark colours. Mama wore black itself. Charlotte regarded herself in the mirror with distaste before leaving. She had a dark green dress with black trim, and a black hat. It was not flattering, especially in the autumn sun.

They walked, since it was only a short distance. The Lessing house had all the blinds drawn and there was a constable outside in the street. He looked solid and unhappy. It crossed Charlotte's mind that perhaps he was used to death, even to violence, but not to the grief of those who had loved the dead. It was embarrassing to be obliged to watch grief one cannot help. She wondered if Pitt felt it, the helplessness, or if he were too busy trying to fit the pieces together: who was where; loves; hates; reasons. She suddenly realized how deeply she would dislike the task, how the responsibility would frighten her. All the neighbourhood looked to him to rescue them from their alarms, to find this creature, to prove it was not someone they loved, each of them with his separate loves, secret suspicions and desperate, unspoken fears. Did they look for miracles from him? He could not alter truth. Perhaps he could not even find it!

They were met at the door by the maid, red-eyed and nervous. Mrs. Lessing was in the front parlour, darkened in respect for the dead, gas lamps hissing on the wall. Mrs. Lessing was dressed in black, her face bleached pale, her hair a little untidy, as if she had not taken it down last night but merely pulled it back with a comb this morning and rearranged a few pins.

Caroline went straight over to her and put her arms round her, kissing her on the cheek. Verity had been an only child.

"My dear, I'm so sorry," she said softly. "Can we help with anything? Would you like one of us to stay with you for a little while, to help with things?"

Mrs. Lessing struggled to speak, her eyes widening with surprise, then hope. Then she burst into tears and hid her face on Caroline's shoulder.

Caroline put both her arms round her tighter and held her, touching her hair, arranging the stray wisps gently, as if it mattered.

Charlotte felt a painful welling up of pity. She remembered the last time she had seen Verity. She had been brusque with her, and had meant to apologize for it. Now there would be no chance.

"I'd like to stay, Mrs. Lessing," she said clearly. "I was very fond of Verity. Please let me help. There will be a lot to do. You shouldn't do it alone. And I know Mr. Lessing still has—duties—that cannot be left."

It was several minutes before Mrs. Lessing gained control of herself. She turned to Charlotte, still struggling to master her tears, but unashamed of her grief.

"Thank you, Charlotte. Please—please do!"

There was little for the rest of them to say. Charlotte remained behind, not wishing to leave Mrs. Lessing alone, and it was arranged that Maddock would bring a box of clothes and toiletries for her within the next hour or two.

It was a very hard day. Since Mr. Lessing was sexton to the church, he had duties to perform which kept him from home the great part of it, and so Charlotte stayed with Mrs. Lessing to receive other callers who came to express their condolences. There was little to say, only a repetition of the same words of shock and sympathy, the same expressions of how well they had liked Verity, and the same fears of what horror might come next.

Naturally the vicar called. It was something Charlotte had dreaded but knew was inevitable. Apparently he had been the previous evening, when the news was first heard, but he came again in the late afternoon, bringing Martha with him. The maid let them in, and Charlotte received them in the parlour, Mrs. Lessing had at last agreed to rest on her bed, and had fallen into a light sleep.

"Ah, Miss Ellison." The vicar looked at her with some surprise. "Are you also calling upon poor Mrs. Lessing? How good of you. Well, you may safely leave now; we will guide and comfort her in this terrible hour. The Lord giveth and the Lord taketh away."

"No, I am not calling upon Mrs. Lessing," Charlotte replied

a little sharply. "I am staying here to help her as I can. There is a great deal to be done—"

"I am sure we can do that." The vicar was clearly annoyed, possibly by her tone. "I am somewhat more used to these types of arrangements than you are, at your tender years. It is my calling in life to comfort the afflicted, and to mourn with those who mourn."

"I doubt you have time to govern a house, Vicar." Charlotte stood her ground. "As you say, you will be busy with funeral arrangements. And since it is your calling to comfort the afflicted, you will have other claims upon your time. I dare say poor Mrs. Abernathy is still in need."

Out of the corner of her eye she saw Martha's white face pale even more till her eyes seemed like depressions in her skull and the fair hair of her eyebrows appeared quite dark in contrast. The poor woman looked ready to faint, in spite of her broad shoulders and solid body. "Please sit down." Charlotte half pushed a chair towards her. "You must be terribly tired. Have you been up all night?"

Martha nodded and sank into the chair.

"It's very good of you," she said a little shakily. "So many practical details to see to, so much cooking, letters to write, black to be prepared, and the house still has to be organized, maids given instructions. Is Mrs. Lessing asleep?"

"Yes, and I am most loath to wake her, unless it is something of real urgency," Charlotte said firmly, meaning it for the vicar, although she was still looking at Martha.

The vicar grunted. "I had hoped to be of some spiritual assistance to the poor woman, but if you say she is asleep, I suppose I shall have to call another time."

"Quite," Charlotte agreed. She did not wish to offer them refreshment, but Martha's haggard face inspired her pity. "May I offer you a dish of tea? It would be no trouble."

Martha opened her mouth as if to accept, then doubt mixed with anxiety crossed her face. Again she hesitated but at last she stood up and definitely declined.

After they had gone Charlotte went to the kitchen to see

that a light meal was being prepared for supper, and that the following day's catering was in hand. She was called from those duties by the parlour maid to announce that the police had arrived. She had been expecting their call, had it in her mind from the beginning, and yet now she was taken by surprise.

It was Pitt, of course. She found herself oddly embarrassed that he should find her here, self-conscious of her wish to help.

"Good evening, Miss Ellison," he said without showing more than a lifted eyebrow of surprise. "Is Mrs. Lessing well enough to speak to me? I am aware that Mr. Lessing is still at the church."

"I imagine that she will have to speak to you," Charlotte said quietly. She meant the softness of her tone to rob it of rudeness. "Perhaps it would be easier to have it done as soon as may be. There is no purpose in avoiding it. If you care to wait, I shall go and awaken her. If I take a little while, please excuse me."

"Of course." He hesitated. "Charlotte?"

She turned.

He was frowning. "If she is ill, distressed, there is nothing I need to ask that cannot wait until tomorrow. It's just that I doubt it will be any easier then. It might even give her a better night to have it past."

She found herself smiling. "I think it would. May I stay, if she wishes?"

"I would prefer that you did."

It took her several minutes to rouse Mrs. Lessing and assure her that her appearance was acceptable and would not disgrace her in front of such a lesser creature as a policeman, and, then, that he was courteous, that she had nothing to fear since she had no guilt, and would rest more easily from having the ordeal accomplished. She did not have the heart to tell her it would very likely be merely the first of many calls. One grief, one fear was enough for today.

Pitt was very gentle with her, but the questions were

165

unavoidable: Who were Verity's friends? With whom had she only recently become acquainted? Who were her male admirers? Had she expressed any fears? How well had she known Chloe Abernathy? Had she visited the Hiltons or the Ellisons so that she might have any knowledge of their servants, or they of her? Had they any information or observations in common?

Mrs. Lessing knew nothing that was of help. She answered with the bewildered meaninglessness of someone still suffering from shock. It was as if she did not understand the purpose of his questions.

Finally he gave up and rose to leave. He watched Mrs. Lessing as she walked slowly into the hallway and closed the door behind her.

"Are you remaining, Charlotte?"

It did not even cross her mind to condemn his impertinence then for the use of her given name.

"Yes. There is a great deal to be done, and Mr. Lessing still has to continue his duties. He is not a very practical man, not used to running an orderly house."

"It might be as well to let her do certain things herself. Work cannot heal, but it can alleviate. Idleness gives one time to think."

"Yes, I...I will. I will find household jobs for her to do that do not require thought. But I shall do the planning myself, the preparations for the funeral, telling people, and so on."

He smiled. "I see a great deal of tragedy in my job, and of ugliness; but I see a great deal of kindness as well. Good evening." He turned at the door. "Oh, don't forget, do not go out alone under any circumstances. Even if you should require a doctor, send someone, send Mr. Lessing, or call for assistance next door. They will understand."

"Mr. Pitt!"

"Yes?"

"Do you know anything further yet? I mean, what manner

of man, from what—what walk of life?" She was thinking of George and Emily.

"Do you know something you have not told me?" He was looking at her again in that way that seemed to probe inside her, as if he knew her well, as an equal, not as a policeman.

"No! Of course not! If I knew anything I should tell you!"

"Would you?" There was gentle disbelief in his voice. "Even if it were no more than a suspicion? Would you not be afraid of wronging someone, perhaps someone you loved?"

It was on the edge of her tongue to say quite angrily that she did not love anyone who could possibly be connected with such crimes; then something in him compelled her to be honest—an intelligence, or an honesty in him.

"Yes, of course I should be afraid of wronging someone, if it were merely a matter of suspicion. But I imagine you do not leap to conclusions just because of something someone tells you?" It was a question, because she wanted reassuring.

"No, or we would catch ourselves ten criminals for every crime." He smiled, showing those strong teeth again. "What is it you do not want me to act upon?"

"You are leaping to conclusions!" she said hotly. "I did not say I knew anything!"

"You did not say so directly, but your evasion makes me believe it."

She turned away from him, making up her mind not to speak of it. "You are mistaken. I wish I knew something that could genuinely help, but I do not. I'm sorry if anything I said gave a wrong impression."

"Charlotte!"

"You are becoming overly familiar, Inspector Pitt," she said quietly.

He came up behind her. She was acutely aware of him. Emily's words about his admiration flashed across her mind and she found her skin burning with embarrassment and a sudden appalling knowledge that it was true. She stood rooted to the spot.

"Charlotte," he said gently. "This man has killed four

women already. There is no reason to suppose he will stop. In all likelihood he cannot help himself. It is better some innocent person should be suspected unjustly for a while— he will be one of many—than that another woman should die. How old was Lily? Nineteen? Verity Lessing was only twenty. Chloe Abernathy was little more. Or the Hiltons' maid? I can't even remember her name! If you doubt the monstrosity of it, go upstairs and look at Mrs. Lessing again—"

"I know!" Charlotte said furiously. "You don't have to remind me! I've been here since last night!"

"Then tell me whatever it is you have thought of, or seen, or heard—whatever it is! If it is wrong I shall find out; no one will be pursued unjustly. He will be caught one day, but better now, before he kills again."

She turned round without thinking, to stare at him. "Do you think he will kill again?"

"Don't you?"

She closed her eyes, to avoid looking at his face. "What has happened here? This used to be a quiet, a good place to live. There was nothing worse than a few broken romances, a little gossip. Now suddenly people are dead; we are all looking at each other and wondering! I am! I'm looking at men I've trusted for years, and wondering if it could be them, thinking thoughts about them that make me blush with shame. And I can see in their faces that they know I am suspicious! That's almost the worst part of it! They know I wonder, that I'm not sure. How must they feel? How must it feel to look at your wife or your daughter and see in their faces, in spite of their words, that they are not absolutely sure that it is not you? That it has actually crossed their minds that it could be! Could you ever feel the same again? Could love live through that? Is not love at least partly trust, faith in someone, and knowing them well enough that you don't even have such thoughts?"

She kept her eyes shut. "I realize I hardly even know people I thought I loved. And I see it in others, too. All the

168

people who have come here. I listen to what they say, because I have to. And they are beginning to look around, to try to find someone to blame where it will upset them least. The gossip and the suspicions are beginning, the little whispered suggestions. It isn't only the dead who are going to suffer, or even only those who loved them."

"Then help me, Charlotte. What is it you know, or think you know?"

"George Ashworth. Lord George Ashworth; he knew Chloe Abernathy quite well just before she died. He took her to some—some very unpleasant places, or so Mrs. Abernathy said. And in spite of what Papa says, Chloe was not immoral, not in the least, just silly!"

"I know."

She opened her eyes. "Ashworth is escorting Emily a lot. Please see he isn't—that he doesn't—"

He gave a bitter little grimace. "I shall look discreetly into the late actions of Lord George Ashworth, I promise you. He is not unknown to us, at least by repute."

"You mean—"

"I mean he is a gentleman whose taste is a little—raucous, and whose pocket and family title allow him to do things that in others would be punished. I suppose speaking to Emily would have no effect?"

"None at all. I have done so, and if it had been received differently, I would not have troubled you."

He smiled. "Of course. Don't worry." He put out his hand, as if to touch her arm, and then withdrew it self-consciously. "I shall have Lord Ashworth observed, discreetly. I shall do all I can to see Emily comes to no harm, although I cannot protect her from a possible serious fright."

"That will do her no harm at all," Charlotte said tersely. She was overwhelmingly relieved. "Thank you, Inspector. I—I am glad—of your help."

He coloured faintly, and turned to leave. "Are you going to remain with Mrs. Lessing until after the funeral?"

"Yes. Why?"

"No reason. Good night...Miss Ellison. Thank you for your assistance."

"Good night, Inspector Pitt."

It was over a week later, after the funeral, when Charlotte returned from the Lessings'. She had been forbidden to travel alone, not only by Pitt, but by Papa. She was more than pleased that it was Dominic who came in the cab to collect her.

Even the memory of the funeral, the finality of it, the pathetic black, Mrs. Lessing's grief, could not drive away the pleasure of seeing Dominic, being alone with him. When he met her eyes it was as if he had touched her. His smile warmed her through, melting the chill of fear and helplessness. She sat in the cab beside him, and for a moment everything else was shut out, no past and no future.

They talked of trivialities, but she did not care. It was being with him that mattered, knowing that all his attention was turned towards her.

The cabdriver unloaded her box and Maddock carried it in. She followed behind on Dominic's arm. It was a marvellous feeling.

It collapsed as soon as she entered the withdrawing room. Sarah looked up from the sofa where she was sitting sewing. Her face darkened as soon as she saw them.

"You are not entering a ballroom, Charlotte," she said tartly. "Nor, unless you are feeling faint, do you need someone to hang on to like that!"

Emily was at the piano and looked downward at her hands with an uncomfortable colour creeping up her face.

Charlotte stopped still, her arm, in spite of the warmth and closeness of Dominic, suddenly feeling dead.

Perhaps she was holding him too closely; she could not deny she had done it consciously. Now she was self-conscious, and guilty. She sought to free her arm, but Dominic was still gripping her, and his grip tightened.

"Sarah?" he said with a frown. "Charlotte has just returned home from a visit of charity. Would you have me allow her to come in alone?"

"I would have you welcome her, naturally," Sarah was annoyed, and her voice was tight and hard. "But not to make an entrance, clinging to each other like that!"

Charlotte deliberately freed herself, her face flaming.

"I'm sorry if you were offended, Sarah, but until you spoke, it was no more than excitement at being home again."

"And now that I have spoken, what is it?" Sarah demanded.

"Well, you have certainly taken much of the pleasure from coming home." Charlotte was beginning to become angry herself. This was unjust. Her foolishness did not warrant this degree of criticism, and not publicly.

"You have only been round the corner!" Sarah snapped. "Not to Australia!"

"She has been staying with Mrs. Lessing to help her through her worst time, which was an act of particular generosity." Dominic was growing sharper himself. "It cannot have been easy or very pleasant, under the circumstances."

Sarah glared at him.

"I know perfectly well where she's been. You don't need to be so sanctimonious about it. It was charitable, certainly, but hardly as saintly as you make it seem."

Charlotte could not understand it. She looked at Sarah's face: there was something almost like hatred in it. She turned from it, feeling sick and shaken. Emily would not meet her eyes. She swivelled back to Dominic.

"That's right!" Sarah stood up. "Look to Dominic! That's just what I would expect, except that you should do it behind my back!"

Charlotte could feel the blood flaming in her cheeks, even her brow, because she loved Dominic, had always loved him— but she was blushing for her thoughts, not her deeds. For her deeds, the accusation was unjust.

She drew her breath in deeply and let it out.

"Sarah, I don't know what it is you think, but if it is

anything improper, or in any way unfair or unjust to you, then you are wrong, and your charge does you no credit. It is not true, and I believe you know me well enough to have known that before you spoke."

"I thought I did! I only discovered how blind I had been while you were away doing your charity turn at Mrs. Lessing's! You are the perfect hypocrite, Charlotte. I never even suspected you."

"And you were right," Charlotte heard her own voice coming from a long way away. "There was nothing to suspect. It is now that you are wrong, not before."

She felt Dominic take her arm again, and moved to loose herself, but he was holding her tightly.

"Sarah," he said quietly. "I don't know what you imagine, and I don't wish to know. But you owe Charlotte an apology for whatever your thoughts are, and for having voiced them."

She looked at him squarely, her lip curled with disgust. "Don't lie to me, Dominic. I know, I am not guessing."

His face went blank with complete surprise. "Know what? There isn't anything to know!"

"I know, Dominic. Emily told me."

It was the first time Charlotte had seen Dominic really angry. Suddenly Emily looked frightened, too frightened to move.

"Emily?"

"There's no point in appealing to Emily, or trying to bully her." Sarah stepped forward.

"Bully Emily?" Dominic raised his eyebrows in harsh amusement. "Nobody ever bullied Emily in her life! It would be an impossibility."

"Don't try to be amusing!" Sarah snapped.

Charlotte disregarded them. She was staring at Emily.

Emily lifted her chin a little. "You told Inspector Pitt about George and Chloe Abernathy," she said with only a slight tremor in her voice.

"Because I was afraid for you!" Charlotte defended herself, and yet felt guilty also. She knew Emily saw it as a betrayal, and however little Charlotte had meant it as such, the guilt remained.

"Afraid of what? That I might marry George, leaving you here alone, the only one of us not married?" She shut her eyes, her face white. "I'm sorry. That was a dreadful thing to say."

"I thought he might have killed Chloe, and you might guess it one day, and that then he would have to kill you," Charlotte said simply. She would have given anything she possessed for Dominic not to have been there, not to have heard this.

"You're wrong," Emily said quietly, her eyes still closed. "George has faults, faults you probably wouldn't put up with, but nothing like that. Do you suppose I should think of marrying anyone who would be capable of murdering like that?"

"No. I think you would find out, and that is why he would kill you, too."

"Do you hate him so much?"

"I don't care about him!" Charlotte said in exasperation, almost shouting. "I was thinking about you!"

Emily said nothing.

Dominic was still angry. "So you made up something vicious about Charlotte, and told Sarah to get your revenge?" he accused.

Emily's face tightened. She looked very young, and now also very ashamed. "I shouldn't have told her," she admitted, looking at Dominic.

"Then apologize and withdraw it," Dominic demanded.

Emily's face set. "I shouldn't have said it, but that does not make it untrue. Charlotte is in love with Dominic. She has been ever since he first came. And Dominic is flattered by it. He enjoys it. I don't know how much?" She left it a question, painful and suggestive.

"Emily!" Charlotte pleaded.

Emily turned to her. "Can you take back what you said to Inspector Pitt? Can you make him forget it? Then why do you expect me to take back? You'll have to live with it—just as I shall." And she pushed past them and went out into the hallway.

Charlotte looked at Sarah.

"If you are waiting for me to apologize, you will wait in vain," Sarah said stiffly. "Now perhaps you would be good enough to go upstairs and unpack. I would prefer to speak to my husband alone. You won't be surprised that I have questions to ask!"

Charlotte hesitated, but there was nothing else to say, nothing that could do anything but make it worse. She disengaged herself from Dominic and turned to leave. Perhaps tomorrow there would be apologies, and perhaps not. But whatever was said, nothing would wipe out the memory of today; feelings could not be the same again. What she had said to Pitt was true. This was all like ripples on a pool, and rhaps the rings would never stop.

Chapter
Nine

The following day Dominic went into the city as usual, and on returning home was due to go out and dine with a retired brigadier and his wife. It was an occasion Sarah had been looking forward to for some time, but when he returned home he found her in a mood that reflected none of the excitement and pleasure he had expected. She seemed remote, not merely preoccupied but positively offended by his presence. He tried all the usual tactics. He complimented her on her gown; he told her all he knew about the brigadier's wife and her social connections; he assured her she would be more than equal to the occasion. He kissed her without disarranging either her hair or her gown. None of it was to any effect; she withdrew from his touch and avoided his eyes.

There was no opportunity to ask her what was annoying her. On two or three occasions during the evening he tried to speak to her without being overheard, but each time either they were interrupted, or she changed the subject and drew some other person's attention to them.

In the carriage on the way home they were alone for the first time.

"Sarah?"

"Yes?" She kept her face away.

"What is it, Sarah? You've been behaving like—like a stranger all evening. No, that's not true, a stranger would have shown better manners."

"I'm sorry you find my manners inadequate."

"Stop playing, Sarah. If there's something wrong, tell me."

"Something wrong!" She turned to face him, her eyes blazing in the flashes of gaslight from the street. "Yes, something is very wrong, and if you are not aware that it is wrong, then you have a sense of morality that is despicable. I really haven't anything to say to you."

"Morality about what? Oh, for God's sake! You're not still making a fuss because I took Charlotte's arm when she came home yesterday? That's ridiculous, and you know it. You're just looking for an excuse for a row. At least be honest."

"Looking! I don't have far to look, do I? You are busy admiring my sister, holding her hand, whispering to her, and heaven knows what else! And you think I have to look for something to quarrel over?" She turned away again, her voice choking.

He put his arm towards her, but she was dead to his touch.

"Sarah! Don't be ridiculous! I have no interest in Charlotte, except that she's your sister. I like her, nothing else. For heaven's sake, I knew Charlotte when I married you. If I'd wanted her, I would have asked for her!"

"That was six years ago! People change," she sniffed, and then was obviously angry with herself for what she considered a vulgarity.

He was sorry, not wanting to hurt her, but the whole thing was preposterous. He could not help being irritated for a whole evening spoiled—and now a silly argument when they were both tired!

"Sarah, that's stupid! I haven't changed, and I don't think you have. And as far as I can see, Charlotte hasn't either. But Charlotte hasn't anything to do with this anyway. Surely you can see Emily just said whatever she did because she's in love with George Ashworth and Charlotte told the police-man—what's his name?—that Ashworth knew Chloe a lot better than he'd said. You've got to have enough wisdom to see that, and discard it for the nonsense it is!"

"Why do you lose your temper if you're not guilty?" she said calmly.

"Because it's so damn silly!" he exploded in exasperation.

"I have just found out that you are in love with my sister, and she with you, and I am silly because it upsets me!"

"Oh, Sarah, for heaven's sake stop it," he said wearily. "That's none of it true, and you know it. I have never been remotely interested in Charlotte, except as a sister-in-law; she's intelligent, has a wit, and a mind of her own—none of them very feminine attributes, which you've been the first to point out—"

"Inspector Pitt doesn't seem to mind!" she said accusingly. "He's in love with her; anyone can see that!"

"For God's sake, Sarah! What have I in common with some wretched policeman! And I should imagine Charlotte is em-barrassed by the whole affair, if indeed it's true. He's—work-ing class! He's not more than a tradesman! And why shouldn't he admire Charlotte, as long as he remembers his place? She's a very handsome woman—"

"You think so!" Again there was accusation in her voice, almost triumph.

"Yes, I do!" His own voice rose in anger. Really she was being very stupid and very tiresome indeed. He was tired, and in no mood for this. He had been patient all evening, but his patience was rapidly coming to an end. "Now please don't pursue it any more. I have done nothing whatsoever that requires apology, or deserves your criticism."

She said nothing, but when they arrived home she went straight upstairs. When Dominic had spoken to Edward in the study and followed her up, she was already in bed, her back turned to him. He considered for a moment approaching her again, but he had no feeling of warmth, no desire. And honestly he was too tired for the effort, the hypocrisy. He undressed and went to sleep without speaking.

The following day he woke having forgotten the whole stupid affair, but he was stiffly reminded. When he returned home in the evening things were no better. There was also a certain coolness between Emily and Charlotte, but no one else seemed to observe it. Conversation was unusually restrained. Caroline spoke of neighbourhood trivialities which Edward did little more than acknowledge. Only Grandmama was voluble; she was full of speculation about what secrets gossip attributed to all the families, especially the men, in the vicinity of Cater Street. At last Edward told her rather testily to be silent.

The day after was no better, and on the following evening Dominic decided he would remain at his club for dinner. Sarah would come out of it sooner or later, but for the present she was being very tedious. He had no idea why she was doing it: he had never entertained any interest other than friendly in Charlotte. Sarah must know that. Women frequently did odd and inexplicable things; it was usually an obscure way of laying claim to attention, and after a little flattery they were back to normal. Whatever Sarah wanted this time, she was making rather too much of an issue of it. He was bored with it, and becoming genuinely angry.

He dined at his club again two evenings later. It was on the third occasion that he fell into conversation with four other men who lived within a mile or two of Cater Street. At first he had done no more than overhear, but his interest was drawn when they began to discuss the murders.

"... wretched police all over the place, and they don't seem to be accomplishing a damn thing!" one complained.

"Poor devils are as lost as we are," someone else argued.

"More lost! Don't even belong in our world, part of a different social class. Don't understand us any more than we understand them."

"Good God! You aren't suggesting this lunatic is a gentleman?" There was amusement, incredulity, and the edge of anger in this voice.

"Why not?"

"Good God!" he was stunned.

"Well, we've got to admit it. If he were a stranger he would have been noticed by now." The man leaned forward. "For the love of heaven, man, the way everyone feels at the moment, do you think any stranger could go unobserved? Everyone is looking over his shoulder; women daren't even go next door alone; the men are all watching and waiting. Delivery boys practically clock in and out; they want themselves timed to prove where they were and when. Even cabbies don't like coming to Cater Street any more. In the past week, two have been stopped by constables, only because they were strange faces."

"You know," the man opposite him frowned, "it's just come to me what that old fool Blenkinsop was talking about the other day! I thought he was rambling at the time, but now I realize he was saying in a roundabout way that he suspected me!"

"Quite! That's the most damnable thing about it: having people looking queerly at you, not precisely saying anything, but you know cursed well what's going on in their minds. Even errand boys are getting above themselves."

"You're not alone, old fellow! Left my carriage for my wife and was out late. Had to get a cab home. Wretched cabbie asked my destination. I told him and the man had the impertinence to refuse me. 'Not going to Cater Street,' he said. I ask you!"

One of them caught Dominic in his peripheral vision.

"Ah, Corde! You'll know what we're talking about. Dreadful business, isn't it? Whole place turned upside down. Creature must be insane, of course."

"Unfortunately it isn't obvious," Dominic replied, sitting down in the proffered chair.

"Not obvious? What d'you mean? I would have thought it could hardly be more obvious than to run around the streets garotting helpless women!"

"I mean it does not show in his demeanour at other times," Dominic explained. "In his face, his actions, or in anything else. He must look exactly like anyone else, most of the time." Charlotte's words came back to him. "For all we know, he could be here now, any one of these extremely respectable gentlemen."

"I don't care for your sense of humour, Corde. Misplaced. Poor taste, if I may say so."

"To make jokes about murder at all is poor taste. But I wasn't joking; I was perfectly serious. Even if you don't believe in the intelligence of the police, with feeling running as it is, if this man were visible for what he is, surely one of us would have spotted him before now?"

The man stared at him, his face turning purple, then paling.

"Bless me! Shockin' thought. Not nice having one's neighbours think—"

"Has it never crossed your mind about someone else?"

"I admit it occurred to me. Gatling behaved a trifle odd. Caught him being overly solicitous to my wife the other day. Hands where they had no business, helping her with a shawl. Said something to him at the time. Never thought of it— perhaps that's why he was so offended—thought I meant— oh well, all past now."

"Damned unpleasant, though. Feel as if no one tells me what they mean anymore. See meanings behind meanings, if you understand me?"

"Thing I can't stand is the maids looking at one as if one were...."

And so it went on. Dominic heard the same views over and over again; the embarrassment, the anger, the bewilderment—and, something worse, the almost inevitable sense that somewhere close, to someone they knew, it would happen again.

He wanted to forget it, to go back for a few hours to the way it was before the first murder.

Dominic was delighted a week later to see George Ashworth, dressed very formally, obviously ready for a night out.

"Ah, Corde!" Ashworth slapped him on the back. "Coming for a night's entertainment? As long as you don't tell Sarah!" he smiled, meaning it as a joke. It was unthinkable, of course, that Dominic would say anything. One did not mention such things to women, *any* women, except bawds.

Dominic made up his mind instantly.

"Exactly what I need. Certainly I'll come. Where are we going?"

Ashworth grinned. "Bessie Mullane's, to end with. Perhaps one or two other places beforehand. Have you eaten yet?"

"No."

"Excellent. I know a place you will like, quite small, but the best food and the most entertaining company."

And so it proved. It was certainly a little bawdy, but Dominic had never eaten a richer, more delicately cooked meal, or enjoyed such free wine. Gradually he forgot Cater Street and all those who lived there—or died there. Even Sarah's present foolishness disappeared from his mind with the good spirits and conviviality of the company.

Bessie Mullane's proved to be a cheerful and extremely comfortable bawdy house where they were lavishly welcomed. Ashworth was obviously not only known, but quite genuinely liked. They had not been there above half an hour when they were joined by a young swell, extravagantly dressed and a little drunk, but not yet objectionable.

"George!" he said with evident pleasure. "Haven't seen you in weeks!" He slid into the seat beside him. "Good evening, sir," he inclined his head towards Dominic. "I say, have you seen Jervis? Thought I'd take him out of himself a bit, but can't find him!"

"What's the matter with him?" Ashworth enquired pleasantly. "By the way," he indicated Dominic, "Dominic Corde, Charles Danley."

Danley nodded.

"Silly fool lost at cards, lost rather a lot."

"Shouldn't play more than you can afford," Ashworth said without sympathy. "Stay with your own level of game."

"Thought he was," Danley curled up the corners of his lips in disgust. "Other fellow cheated. Could have told him he would."

"Thought Jervis was pretty comfortable?" Ashworth opened his eyes indicating it was something of a question. "He'll recover. Have to curtail his entertaining for a while."

"That isn't it! He was stupid enough to accuse the bastard of cheating."

Ashworth grinned. "What happened? Did he call him out for a duel? Should have thought after all that scandal with Churchill and the Prince of Wales five years ago he'd have steered clear of anything like that!"

"No, of course he didn't! Apparently the cheating hadn't been particularly well done, and he was able to expose it without any effort—which he was idiotic enough to do!"

"Why idiotic?" Dominic interrupted from sheer curiosity. "I would have thought if a man were crass enough to cheat, and do it badly, he deserved whatever came to him?"

"Naturally! But this was an extremely ill-tempered fellow, and with some weight of influence. He'll be ruined, of course! Ultimate sin, to cheat badly. Implies you don't even have the respect for your fellows to do it well! But he'll make damned sure he takes poor Jervis with him."

Ashworth frowned. "How? Jervis didn't cheat, did he? Even if he did, he wasn't caught, which is the main thing. After all, everyone cheats. The accusation will look mere spite!"

"Nothing to do with cheating, dear fellow. Man's married to Jervis's cousin, of whom he's very fond—Jervis, I mean."

"So?"

"Seems she has a lover, which is common enough, and nothing in itself. Gave him five children and he's bored with her, and she with him. Understandable. All perfectly all right, as long as it's discreet. Seems she wasn't. Country weekend, didn't lock her door. Someone came in, mistaking it for another lady's room, and found her with some fellow or other. Upshot of it all is that this wretched cheat threatened to divorce her."

Ashworth shut his eyes.

"Oh my God. She'd be ruined!"

"Of course. Upset poor Jervis no end. Very fond of her, apart from the family name and all that. Makes things dashed difficult for him in society, cousin who's divorced."

"And your cheating feller gets away with it scot-free?"

"Quite! Having a deuced good time; he'll marry again, when it suits him. And she, poor creature, an outcast. Teach you to lock your doors."

"Didn't catch her himself?"

"Gracious, no. He was in bed with Dolly Lawton-Smith, oblivious to the world. But that's irrelevant. Different for a man, of course."

"What about Dolly? Wouldn't do her any good."

"Nor harm either. Everyone knows about everyone else; it's what is seen that counts, and the vulgarity of being caught. Instead of being a bit of a fellow, makes one look ridiculous. And divorce is of no great importance to a man, but it ruins a woman. After all, it's one thing to have a little fun oneself, but one is made to look a complete fool if it is seen that one's wife prefers someone else."

"And Dolly's husband?"

"Oh, I believe they have an amicable enough arrangement. He certainly won't divorce her, if that's what you're thinking. Why should he? No one caught *him* cheating at cards!"

"Poor old Jervis," Ashworth sighed. "What a perilous life."

"Talking of peril, what about all the grisly business in Cater Street? Four murders! Man must be mad. Damn glad

I don't live there." He frowned suddenly. "You go there quite often, don't you? That pretty little thing I saw you with at Acton's. Didn't you say she lived there? Liked her. Woman of spirit. Not blue-blooded, but dashed pretty."

Dominic opened his mouth to speak, then decided to listen instead. He liked Emily, but regardless of that, there was a certain loyalty.

"Blue blood gets a bit tedious at times," Ashworth said slowly, disregarding Dominic entirely. "All too strictly brought up, looking for the right marriage. I ought to marry money, I suppose, or at least some expectation of it, but so many rich young women are such utter bores."

Dominic remembered Emily's determined little face. Whatever she was, and sometimes she was uncommonly irritating, she was never a bore. In her own way, she was as wilful as Charlotte, if a good deal more devious.

"Well for heaven's sake, George." Danley leaned back and signalled to one of the women, holding up his empty glass. "Marry a woman of blood and money, by all means, but keep this other one as a mistress! I would have thought the answer sufficiently obvious."

Ashworth glanced sideways at Dominic with a grin. "Dashed good suggestion, Charlie, but not in front of her brother-in-law!"

"What?" Danley's face dropped, then the colour swept up his cheek.

"Don't care for your sense of humour, George." He pulled one of the passing girls onto his knee, disregarding her giggle. "Uncivil of you."

Dominic looked at him. "Miss Ellison *is* my sister-in-law," he said with distinct pleasure. "And I cannot see her settling for mistress to anyone, even someone as distinguished as George. However, you may try, by all means!"

Ashworth was grinning broadly. He was a remarkably handsome man. "The fun is in the chase. For more generous entertainment one can always come here. Emily offers something a good deal more—interesting. Involves the brain, and the skill, don't you see?"

Sarah was always at home when Dominic returned from his nights out. She was no longer cool, nor did she mention the matter of any untoward affection between Charlotte and himself again, but he knew from her manner, and a certain reticence, that she had not forgot it. There was nothing he could do; indeed he did not seriously consider doing anything. But even so, it was unpleasant. It robbed him of a warmth, a happiness that he used to take for granted.

The police were still questioning people. The fear was still there, although the first urgency had gone. Verity Lessing had been buried, and mourners picked up their lives again. Suspicions were presumably still festering under the surface, but the hysteria was decently controlled.

It was October, and rapidly chilling, when Dominic ran into Inspector Pitt quite by chance in a coffeehouse. Dominic was alone. Pitt stopped by his table. Really he was an inelegant creature. No one could possibly have mistaken him for a man of society. There was no concession to fashion in him, and only a passing accommodation to convention.

"Good afternoon, Mr. Corde," Pitt said cheerfully. "Alone?"

"Good afternoon, Mr. Pitt. Yes, my companion has left."

"Then may I join you?" Pitt put his hand out onto the back of the chair opposite.

Dominic was taken by surprise. He was not used to entertaining policemen socially, still less in public. The man seemed to have no sense of his position.

"If you wish," he replied with reluctance.

Pitt smiled broadly and pulled out the chair. He sat comfortably.

"Thank you. Is this coffee fresh?"

"Yes. Please, help yourself. Did you wish to speak to me about something?" Surely the man was not foisting himself on him for purely social reasons? He could not be so insensitive.

"Thank you." Pitt poured from the pot and drank with delicately flared nostrils. "How are you, and your family?"

Presumably he meant Charlotte. Emily was probably exaggerating, but there was no doubt Pitt did admire Charlotte.

"Well enough, I think, thank you. Naturally the tragedies in Cater Street have not left us untouched. I suppose you are no nearer a solution?"

Pitt pulled a face. He had remarkably mobile, expressive features. "Only insofar as we have eliminated more possibilities. I suppose that is some kind of progress?"

"Not much." Dominic was not in a mood to spare his feelings. "Have you given up? I observe you haven't been to bother us any more."

"I haven't thought of anything else to ask you," Pitt said reasonably.

"I had not noticed that's preventing you in the past." Damn the man. If he could not solve the crime he should call in assistance from his superiors. "Why don't you hand over the case to someone higher up, or get help?"

Pitt met his eyes. Dominic was made a little uncomfortable, a little self-conscious by the sheer intelligence in them.

"I have, Mr. Corde. Everyone at Scotland Yard is bending their minds to it, I assure you. But there are other crimes, you know? Robberies, forgeries, embezzlement, corruption, burglaries, and even other murders."

Dominic was stung. Could the man possibly be patronizing him?

"Of course there are! I hadn't imagined ours was the only crime in London. But surely you consider ours to be the most serious?"

Pitt's smile vanished. "Of course. Mass murder is the most dreadful crime of all—the more so since it will almost certainly be repeated. What do you suggest we do?"

Dominic was taken aback by the sheer brazenness of it.

"How on earth would I know? I am not a policeman! But I would have thought if there were more of you, more experienced perhaps—"

"To do what?" Pitt raised his eyebrows. "Ask more questions? We have dug up an incredible number of trivial eccentricities, immoralities, small dishonesties and cruelties, but no clue to murder—at least none that can be recognized as such." His face became very grave. "We are dealing with insanity, Mr. Corde. It's no use looking for reasons or patterns that you or I would recognize."

Dominic stared at him, afraid. This wretched man was speaking about something horrible, something hellish and incomprehensible, and it frightened him.

"What manner of man are we looking for?" Pitt went on. "Does he choose his particular victims for any specific reason? Or is his choice arbitrary? Do they just happen to be at the right place at the right time? Does he even know who they are? What have they in common? They are all young, all pleasing enough to look at, but that is all as far as we know. Two were servants, two daughters of respectable families. The Hiltons' maid was somewhat loose in her morals, but Lily Mitchell was entirely proper. Chloe Abernathy was a little silly, but no more. Verity Lessing mixed in high society. You tell me what they had in common, apart from being young and living in or near Cater Street!"

"He must be a madman!" Dominic said futilely.

Pitt pulled a bitter smile. "We had already got so far."

"Robbery?" Dominic suggested, then knew it was silly as soon as he had said it.

Pitt raised his eyebrows. "Of a maid on her evening off?"

"Were they—?" Dominic did not like to use the word.

Pitt had no such scruples. "Raped? No. Verity Lessing's dress was torn open and her bosom scratched quite deeply, but nothing more."

"Why?" Dominic shouted, oblivious of the heads turning from the other tables. "He must be a raving—! A—a—" He could think of no word. His anger collapsed. "It doesn't make any sense!" he said helplessly.

"No," Pitt agreed. "And while we are trying to understand

it, trying to see some sort of pattern in the evidence, we still have to do something about the other crimes."

"Yes, of course," Dominic stared into his empty coffee cup. "Can't you leave that to your sergeant, or something? The street is in a terrible state, everyone is afraid of everyone else." He thought of Sarah. "It's affecting even the ways we think of each other."

"It will," Pitt agreed. "Nothing strips the soul quite as naked as fear. We see things in ourselves and in others that we would far rather not have known about. But my sergeant is in hospital."

"Was he taken ill?" Dominic was not really interested, but it was something to say.

"No, he was injured. We went into a slum quarter after a forger."

"And he attacked you?"

"No," Pitt said wryly. "Thieves and forgers far more often run than fight. You've never been into the vast warrens where these people live and work, or you wouldn't have asked. Buildings are packed so close together they are indistinguishable: any single row has a dozen entrances and exits. They usually post some sort of watchman—a child or an old woman, a beggar, anyone. And they prepare traps. We're used to the trapdoors that open up beneath you and drop you into a sort of oubliette, a hole perhaps fifteen or twenty feet deep, possibly even into the sewers. But this was different. This fellow went upwards towards the roof, and we chased him up the stairs. I had been set upon by two other villains and was busy fighting them off. Poor Flack charged up the stairway and the forger disappeared ahead of him, dropping a trapdoor downwards, across the stairs. The thing was fitted with great iron spikes. One sliced through Flack's shoulder, another missed his face by inches."

"Oh God!" Dominic was horrified. Pictures swam into his mind of dark and filthy caves and passages smelling of refuse, running with rats; his stomach rose at the thought of entering them. He imagined the ceiling slamming shut in front of him, the iron spikes driving into flesh, the pain and the blood. He thought for a moment he was going to be sick.

Pitt was staring at him. "He'll likely lose the arm, but unless it becomes gangrenous, he'll live," he was saying. He passed over the dish of coffee. "You see, there are other crimes, Mr. Corde."

"Did you catch him?" Dominic found his voice scratchy. "He ought to be hanged!"

"Yes, we caught him a day later. And he'll be transported for twenty-five or thirty years. From what I hear that'll likely be as bad. Maybe he'll be of some use to someone in Australia."

"I still say he should be hanged!"

"It's easy to judge, Mr. Corde, when your father was a gentleman, and you have clothes on your back and food on your plate every day. Williams's father was a resurrectionist—"

"A churchman!" Dominic was shocked.

Pitt smiled sardonically. "No, Mr. Corde, a man who made his living by stealing corpses to sell to the medical schools, before the law was changed in the 'thirties—"

"Sweet God!"

"Oh, there were plenty of unwanted corpses around the rookeries, the slum areas of the old days. It was a crime, of course, and it demanded a good deal of skill and nerve to smuggle them from wherever they were stolen to wherever they were handed over and the money received. Sometimes they were even dressed and propped up to look like live passengers—"

"Stop it!" Dominic stood up. "I take your point that the wretched man may not know better, but I don't want to hear about it. It doesn't excuse him, or help your sergeant. Let the man forge his money. What's a few guineas more or less in the whole of London? But find our hangman!"

Pitt was still seated. "A few guineas more or less is nothing to you, Mr. Corde, but to a woman with a child, it may be the difference between food and starvation. And if you can tell me what else to do to catch your hangman, I'll be only too willing to do it."

Dominic left the coffeehouse feeling miserable, confused, and deeply angry. Pitt had no right to speak to him like that. There was nothing whatsoever he could do about it, and it was unfair he should be forced to listen.

When he arrived home he felt no better. Sarah met him in the hall. He kissed her, putting his arms round her, but she did not relax against him. In irritation he let go of her sharply.

"Sarah, I've had enough of this childish attitude of yours. You are behaving stupidly, and it's time you stopped!"

"Do you know how many nights you have been out this last month?" she countered.

"No, I do not. Do you?"

"Yes, thirteen in the last three weeks."

"Alone. And if you were to behave yourself with dignity and like a grown woman instead of an undisciplined child, I should take you with me."

"I hardly think I should care for the places which you have been frequenting."

He drew breath to say he would change the places, but then his anger hardened and he changed his mind. There was no purpose in arguing with words; it was feelings that mattered, and as long as she felt like this it was pointless. He turned away and went into the withdrawing room. Sarah went back to the kitchen.

Charlotte was in the withdrawing room, standing by the open window painting.

"This is a withdrawing room, Charlotte, not a studio," he said waspishly.

She looked surprised, and a little hurt.

"I'm sorry. Everyone else is either out or busy, and I was not expecting you home so early, or I would have put it away." She did not, however, move to close her box.

"I met your damned policeman."

"Mr. Pitt?"

"Have you another?"

"I haven't any."

"Don't be coy, Charlotte." He sat down irritably. "You know perfectly well he admires you, indeed is enamoured of you. If you haven't observed it for yourself, Emily has certainly told you!"

Charlotte flushed with embarrassment.

"Emily was saying it to annoy. And you of all people should know that Emily can say things merely to cause trouble!"

He turned to look at her properly. He had been unfair. He was taking out his anger with Pitt and with Sarah on Charlotte.

"I'm sorry," he said frankly. "Yes, Emily has an irresponsible tongue, although I think she may well be right about Pitt. After all, why shouldn't he admire you? You are an extremely handsome woman, and have the kind of spirit that might appeal to him."

He was surprised to see Charlotte colour even more deeply. He had meant it to comfort her, not to make her embarrassment worse. She was the most forthright person he had ever met, and yet paradoxically, the hardest for him to understand. Obviously one did not want the attentions of someone like Pitt, but it should be no more than an irritation, to be forgotten.

"Where did you meet him?" she asked, still absently fiddling with her palette.

"In a coffeehouse. Didn't know policemen frequented such places. He had the nerve to just come and sit down at my table!"

His anger rekindled at the memory.

"What did he want?" She looked worried.

He tried to think back, but he could not remember. Pitt had not asked anything pertinent.

"I don't know, perhaps just to talk. Why?"

She lifted a shoulder slightly in a small shrug.

"He went on about forgers, and resurrectionists."

She looked round. "Resurrectionists? What are they—religious charlatans?"

"No. Men who steal corpses to sell to medical students."

"Oh. How pathetic."

"Pathetic? It's disgusting!"

"It's also pathetic, that people should be reduced to such a level."

"Are you sure they haven't reduced themselves?"

"If they have, that's even worse."

What an odd woman she was. Sarah would never have viewed it that way. There was an innocence in Charlotte, a gentleness that was quite misplaced, and yet he was drawn to her because of it. Odd. He had always thought it was Sarah who was gentle, and Charlotte who had a streak of...of resistance in her, something unfeminine. He looked at her now as she stood with the paintbrush in her hand. She was not as pretty as Sarah, and she lacked the small touches—the fine lace, the little earrings, the delicate curls in the nape of the neck—and yet in a way she was also more beautiful. And in thirty years, when Sarah would be plump, her chin line gone, her hair faded, the bones in Charlotte's face would still be beautiful.

"It's a terrible responsibility," she said slowly. "We all expect him to be able to solve the murders for us, put us back to where we were before."

And she would still be saying whatever came into her mind, he thought wryly. She would never learn the small deceits that make women mysterious, feminine—that they survive by.

But Charlotte would not sulk over some imagined slight; Charlotte would have a blazing row. In the long run that might be better, easier to put up with.

"At least he doesn't have to live here. Nobody suspects him," he said, going back to her remark.

"No, but we'll all blame him if he doesn't find the man."

He had not even thought of that. Now that she pointed it

out to him, he felt a surge of sympathy for Pitt. He wished he had not been so patronizing in the coffeehouse.

Charlotte was staring at her picture on the easel. "I wonder if he even knows who he is, or if he's just as afraid as we are?"

"Of course not! If he knew he'd arrest him!"

"Not Pitt! The man, whoever he is. Does he remember, does he know? Or is he as frightened and as puzzled as the rest of us?"

"Oh God! What an unspeakable thought! Whatever put that into your head?"

"I don't know. But it's possible, isn't it!"

"I shouldn't think so; I would very much rather not think so. If that were true, it could be—it could be anyone!"

She looked at him solemnly, her eyes very steady and gray. "It could be anyone now."

"Charlotte, stop it. For heaven's sake let's just pray Pitt finds him. Stop thinking about it. There's nothing we can do except never go out alone, under any circumstances." He shivered. "Only go out if you have to, and then take Maddock, or your father, or I'll come with you."

She smiled—a strange, tight little gesture—and turned back to the painting. "Thank you, Dominic."

He looked at her. Odd, he had always thought her open, obvious; now she seemed enigmatic, more mysterious than Sarah.

Did one ever learn to understand women?

A couple of days later Dominic had yet more cause to ponder the female mind. They were all sitting in the withdrawing room after dinner; even Emily was at home. Grandmama was crocheting, squinting a little when she occasionally glanced at her work; most of the time she worked blind, her fingers and long habit guiding her.

"I called on the vicar this afternoon," Grandmama said a little sharply. There was a hint of criticism in her voice. "Sarah took me."

"Oh?" Caroline looked up. "Did you find them well?"

"Not especially. The vicar was well enough, I suppose, but Martha looked very strained, I thought. A woman should never let herself go like that. She begins to have the look of a drudge."

"She does work very hard," Sarah said in her defence.

"That has nothing to do with it, my dear," Grandmama said disapprovingly. "However hard one works, one should still take care of one's appearance. It matters a great deal."

Emily looked up. "I doubt it matters to the vicar. I should be surprised if he ever notices."

"That is not the point." Grandmama was not to be put off. "A woman owes it to herself. It is a matter of duty."

"I'm sure anything to do with duty would appeal to the vicar," Charlotte observed. "Especially if it were unpleasant."

"Charlotte, we all know that you do not care for the vicar; you have made it abundantly obvious." Grandmama looked a little down her nose. "However, comments like that are of no use at all, and do you no credit. The vicar is a very worthy man, and as suits a man of the cloth, he disapproves of frivolity and paint on the face, and anything that encourages harlotry."

"Not by the wildest stretch of lunacy can I imagine Martha Prebble encouraging harlotry," Charlotte was unabashed. "Except by perverse example."

Caroline dropped her linen pillowcase. "Charlotte! What on earth do you mean?"

"That the sight of Martha's pale face and the thought of living with someone as critical and self-righteous as the vicar would make one entertain the idea of harlotry as a more bearable alternative," Charlotte said with devastating frankness.

"I can only presume," Grandmama said icily, "that you imagine that to be in some fashion amusing. When I consider what manners are coming to these days, I sometimes despair. What passes for wit has become mere vulgarity!"

"I think you are a little unkind, Charlotte," Caroline spoke more mildly. "The vicar is a little difficult, I admit, and not a very likeable man, but he does a great deal of good work. And poor Martha is almost tireless."

"I don't think you realize," Sarah added, "just how much she does. Or that she has suffered deeply with all these murders. She was very fond of both Chloe and Verity, you know?"

Charlotte looked surprised. "No, I didn't know. I knew about Verity, but I didn't know she knew Chloe. I wouldn't have thought they had many interests in common."

"I think she was trying to help Chloe to—to keep her feet on the ground. She was a little silly, but quite kind, you know."

Listening to her, Dominic suddenly felt an appalling sense of pity. He had not cared in the least for Chloe when she was alive; in fact he had found her tiresome. Now he felt something that was as strong as love, and far more painful.

Without thinking, he looked at Charlotte. She was blinking hard, a tear had spilled over onto her cheek. Caroline had picked up her linen again. Emily was doing nothing, and Grandmama was staring at Charlotte with disgust.

What were they thinking?

Grandmama was blaming everyone for the decline in morals. Caroline was concentrating on her sewing. Emily also would be thinking of something practical. Sarah had defended Chloe; and Charlotte had wept for her.

How well did he know any of them?

Dominic continued to go out to his club, and to other places to dine and generally enjoy himself. On several occasions he saw George Ashworth, and found him easy and pleasing company.

He fully expected Sarah to forget the silly affair with Emily and the accusation she had made against Charlotte and himself, but apparently she had not. She said nothing further, but the coolness remained. The distance between them grew greater, if anything.

It was an icy evening in November, fog swirling in the

streets and swathing the gas lamps in wreaths of mist. It was clammy and bitterly cold, and he was glad when his cab turned the corner from Cater Street into his own road and a few moments later stopped and set him down. He paid, and heard the horse's hooves clopping away on the stones, muffled by sound-deadening fog within minutes. He was marooned on a small island of one gas lamp; everything else was impenetrable darkness. The next lamp seemed very far away.

It had been an excellent evening, warm in both wine and companionship. Standing alone in the fog, however, he could think of nothing but women alone in the street, footsteps behind them, perhaps even a face or a voice they knew. Then they would feel a cutting pain in the throat, and darkness, bursting lungs, and death—a limp body to be found on the wet stones in the morning by some passer-by, then examined by the police.

He shivered as the cold cut into his bones and his spirit. He hurried up the steps and knocked sharply on the door. It seemed like an age passed before Maddock opened it and he was able to push beyond him into the warmth and the light. He was even pleased when it was closed behind him, shutting out the street with its fog and darkness and God knew what unspeakable creatures.

"Miss Sarah has retired, sir," Maddock said from behind him. "But not long since. Mr. Ellison is in his study, reading and smoking, but the withdrawing room is empty, if you wish me to bring you something? Would you prefer a hot drink, sir, or brandy?"

"Nothing, thank you, Maddock. I think I'll go to bed myself. It's infernally cold outside, and the fog is coming down pretty thick."

"Most unpleasant, sir. Would you care for me to draw you a hot bath?"

"No, that's all right, thank you. I'll just go to bed. Good night."

"Good night, sir."

Upstairs everything was silent; only a small night-light

burned on the landing. He went into his dressing room and took off his clothes. Ten minutes later he opened the door to the bedroom. "There's no need to creep," she said coldly.

"I thought you might be asleep."

"You mean you hoped I might be!"

He did not understand. "Why should I care one way or the other? I merely did not wish to disturb you if you were."

"Where have you been?"

"At my club." It was not precisely the truth, but near enough. There was no lie in it that mattered.

She raised her eyebrows in sarcasm. "All evening?"

She had never questioned him before. He was too surprised to be annoyed. "No: I went on to a few other clubs. Why?"

"Alone?"

"Well, I certainly wasn't with Charlotte, if that's what you had in mind," he snapped.

"I can't imagine Charlotte being seen in that sort of place, even to be with you." She was staring at him icily.

"What on earth's the matter with you?" His confusion was growing. "I was out with George Ashworth. I thought you approved of him!"

She looked away. "I went to see Mrs. Lessing today."

"Oh," he sat down on the dressing stool. He was not in the least interested in whom she had visited, but obviously she was leading up to something.

"I did not realize until today how well you knew Verity," she went on. "I knew you were well acquainted with Chloe, but Verity was a surprise to me."

"What does it matter? I only spoke with her a few times. I think she liked me. But the poor child's dead. For heaven's sake, Sarah, you can't be jealous of a dead girl. Think where she is now!"

"I hadn't forgotten where she is, Dominic, nor that Chloe is there also."

"And Lily, and Bessie. Or are you jealous of the maids as well?" He was getting really angry. He had not looked at Charlotte, except as a sister, and it was bad enough that

Sarah should have accused him of involvement with her—but *this* was ridiculous, and obscene.

Sarah was sitting upright in the bed.

"Who's Bessie? The Hiltons' maid? I didn't even know her name. How did you know it?"

"I don't know! What the hell does it matter? She's dead!"

"I know that, Dominic. They're all dead."

He looked at her. She was staring at him with wide eyes, as if he were a stranger and she had seen him for the first time, as if he had come out of the fog with a wire in his hands.

Now why did he think of something horrible like that? Because it was in her face. She was afraid of him. She was all knotted up, sitting there on the bed with her shoulders hunched. He could see the strain across her neck, in the muscles of her throat.

"Sarah!"

Her face was frozen, stiff, and unable to speak.

"Sarah! For God's sake!" He moved towards her, sitting on the bed, leaning forward to put his hands on her bare arms. Her flesh was rigid underneath his fingers. "You can't think —Sarah! You know me! You can't think I could have..." he trailed off, his voice dying. There was no response in her.

He let go. Suddenly he did not want to touch her. He was cold inside, as if he had received a wound and could see the horror of it. But shock kept the wound numb. The pain would come later, perhaps tomorrow.

He stood up.

"I'll sleep in the dressing room. Good night, Sarah. Lock the door if it'll make you feel safer."

He heard her speak his name, quietly, hoarsely, but he shut the door behind him without turning. He wanted to be alone, to absorb it, and to sleep.

Chapter
Ten

Of course, Charlotte knew nothing about Dominic's feelings, or what had passed between him and Sarah on his return from the club. But the following day she could not help but be aware that there was a deep strain between them, deeper than anything accountable for by Sarah's standing suspicion about Dominic and herself.

The whole matter was swept violently from her mind in the afternoon, however, when she was alone in the house, copying out a folder of recipes for Mrs. Lessing. She had just turned to the window to look at the clouds massing; everyone else was out visiting and Charlotte was thinking that they would get wet—when there was a timid, urgent rapping at the door.

"Come in," she said absently. It was too early for tea. It must be some problem with the preparations for dinner.

It was Millie, the new maid, and she looked terrified. Charlotte's immediate thought was that she had been outside on some errand, perhaps only as far as the areaway, and had either been molested herself, or seen something or someone that had put the hangman into her mind.

"Come in, Millie," Charlotte said again. "You had better sit down. You look dreadful. What is it?"

"Oh, Miss Charlotte." The poor child was shaking as if she had a fever. "I'm so glad it's you!"

"Sit down, Millie, and tell me what has happened," Charlotte commanded.

Millie's legs seemed locked rigid and her hands were twisting in each other as if of their own volition. Suddenly speech deserted her and she looked as though she was about to run.

"For goodness' sake," Charlotte sighed, taking Millie bodily and pushing her into a chair. "Now what has happened? Were you outside on an errand? Or in the areaway?"

"Oh no, Miss Charlotte!" she looked quite surprised.

"Well, what is it then? Where were you?"

"Upstairs in my room, Miss. Oh, Mrs. Dunphy told me I could go!"

Charlotte stepped back; she was confused herself. She had been sure Millie's pale demeanor had something to do with the hangman. Now it seemed it had not.

"So what's wrong, Millie? Are you sick?"

"No, Miss," Millie stared down at her hands, still twisting in her lap. Charlotte followed her eyes, and realized for the first time that she was holding something.

"What have you got, Millie?"

"Oh," Millie's eyes filled with tears. "I wouldn't have brought it Miss, but I was afraid for my name!" She sniffed violently. "I'm so glad it's you, Miss." She began to cry with quiet hopelessness.

Charlotte was puzzled; she was not only sorry for Millie, but a little frightened herself.

"What is it, Millie?" She put out her hand. "Give it to me."

Slowly Millie's white little fingers uncurled to show a crumpled man's necktie. It meant nothing at all to Charlotte. She could not see any reason why Millie had brought it to her, or why it should inspire any feeling whatever, let alone the paralyzing terror that so obviously had stricken Millie.

Charlotte took it and held it up. Millie stared at her with enormous eyes.

"It's a necktie," Charlotte said blankly. "What's the matter with it?" Then another thought came to her. "Millie, you didn't think anyone was strangled with a necktie, did you?" She felt relief sweep through her, almost weakening her knees. She wanted to laugh. "It wasn't a necktie, Millie! It was a garotting wire. Nothing like this! Take it away, and have Maddock attend to it. It's filthy!"

"Yes, Miss Charlotte," but Millie didn't move. The fear still held her white and motionless.

"Go on, Millie!"

"It's Mr. Dominic's, Miss Charlotte. I know, because I collect the laundry. The master's are made of a different stuff. You can always tell them apart. When I take the laundry back I only have to look, and I know whose it is."

Charlotte felt the sick fear come back, though it was without reason. Why should it matter that Dominic had lost a tie?

"So it's Mr. Dominic's," she said with a quick swallow. "It's filthy. Take it back to the laundry."

Millie stood up very slowly, gripping the tie hard, mangling it in her hands.

"It's nothing to do with me, Miss Charlotte; I swear it isn't. As God is my judge, Miss, I swear it!" She was shaking with the passion of her fear and her need to be believed.

Charlotte could no longer avoid it. Her stomach felt hard and cold inside her. There could be only one question that mattered. She asked it.

"Where did you find it, Millie?"

"In my bedroom, Miss." Her face flushed painfully. "It was under the bed. When I turned the mattress it fell from round the bedstead onto the floor, Miss. That's why it's all creased and dusty. It was there from before I came, Miss. I swear it!"

Charlotte felt as if her world had exploded. A voice whispered inside her that she should have expected it. She hunted in the chaos for something worth saving, to start rebuilding with. That had been Lily's room for years. Sarah had never slept there; there had never been legitimate reason for Dominic to go to it. Could Lily have taken laundry there for some reason? Could Lily have taken it to mend? That possibility was excluded simply enough. There was no tear in it. Could Millie be lying? A glance at her face was enough to dismiss that notion.

"I'm sorry, Miss," Millie whispered desperately. "Did I do wrong?"

Charlotte put out her hand and touched the girl's clenched arm.

"No, Millie, you did the right thing, and there is no need to be afraid. But in case anyone should misunderstand, don't speak of it again unless...." She did not want to say it.

"Unless what, Miss?" Millie stared at her, gratitude in her eyes. "What should I say if I'm asked, Miss Charlotte?"

"I don't see any reason why you should be asked, but if you are then tell the truth, Millie: just exactly what you know, nothing else. Don't make any guesses. Do you understand?"

"Yes, Miss Charlotte. And—thank you, Miss."

"That's all right, Millie. And you'd better get that thing washed, and put it with the rest of the laundry. Please do it yourself. Don't let Miss Sarah know."

Millie's face whitened.

"Miss Charlotte, do you think—"

"I don't think anything, Millie. And I don't want Miss Sarah to think anything either. Now go and do as you're told."

"Yes, Miss." Millie bobbed a little curtsey and almost tripped over her feet going out.

As soon as she had gone, Charlotte collapsed onto the seat behind her, her legs shaking, her fingers stiff with pins and needles.

Dominic and Lily! Dominic on Lily's bed! Dominic taking

his tie off, his shirt, perhaps more, and then putting them on again in such a hurry he forgot his tie. She felt sick. Lily — little Lily Mitchell.

She had loved Dominic with all her heart, not asking anything in return, and he had gone to Lily, the maid. Was there something wrong with Dominic, with all men? Or with her? Was it her tongue? Was she unfeminine? People had liked her, but only that wretched Pitt had ever admired her, been enamoured of her because she was a woman.

This was ridiculous. Self-pity helped no one. She must think of something else. Lily was dead. Had she loved Dominic, too, or was it just — no, don't think about that! Dominic was handsome, charming — her heart lurched. Why shouldn't any woman admire him? Verity had, and she had seen it in Chloe's eyes, too. And they were both dead!

She sat frozen. It could not be! Dominic had seen Papa in Cater Street the night Lily was killed. That meant he had been there himself. They had forgotten that. They had only thought about Papa. It had never even occurred to her that Dominic...?

What was she saying? She loved Dominic; she had always loved him, as long as she had been a woman. How could this even be entering her mind?

What was the love she felt for him, then? What was it worth if she knew him so little she did not even know in her heart whether he could have done such things? Could she really love someone whom she knew so little? Before this afternoon she could not have conceived of his sleeping with Lily! And now in less than an hour she had accepted it. Was her love little more than fascination, love for love itself, love for something she imagined him to be, even love for his face, his smile, his eyes, the way his hair grew? Did she know, or love, anything of the man inside? What did he feel or think that had nothing to do with her, or even Sarah? Was it possible he loved Lily, or Verity — or hated them?

The more she thought about it, the more confused she became, the more she doubted herself and the love she thought she had felt so passionately all these years.

She was still sitting oblivious of the room, of the house, and certainly of time, when there was a knock on the door. It was Dora to say that the vicar's wife had called, and should she bring tea, since it was approaching four o'clock.

Charlotte recalled herself with a massive effort. She had absolutely no desire whatever to see anyone, least of all Martha Prebble.

"Yes, Dora, by all means," she said automatically. "And show Mrs. Prebble in."

Martha Prebble looked less weary than the last time Charlotte had seen her. Some of her spirit seemed to have returned and there was a look of purpose in her face again.

She came forward with her hands out, frowning a little.

"My dear Charlotte, you look very pale. Are you well, my dear?"

"Oh yes, thank you, Mrs. Prebble." Then she thought she had better explain herself, if she looked anything like she felt. "A little tired perhaps. I didn't sleep very well last night. Nothing to be concerned about. Please sit down?" she indicated the overstuffed chair. She knew it was comfortable.

Martha sat. "You must take care of yourself. You have been such a help to poor Mrs. Lessing. Don't now wear yourself out."

Charlotte forced a smile. "You should be the last person to offer such advice. You seem to be everywhere, helping everyone." A thought occurred to her. "And now you are here alone! Did you walk through the streets alone? You really shouldn't do that! I shall send Maddock back with you. It will be growing darker by the time you leave. It could be quite dangerous!"

"That is most kind of you, but I fear I cannot become accustomed to having an escort wherever I go."

"Then you must stay at home, at least . . . at least as long—"

Martha leaned forward, a faint smile on her strong face. "As long as what, my dear? Until the police catch this man?

And how long do you imagine that will be? I cannot stop my parish work. There are many who need me. We are not all equally fortunate, you know. There are those who are alone, old, perhaps sick. Women whose husbands are dead or have abandoned them, women who have children to bring up without any help. The comfortable in the parish do not wish to know about them, but they are here."

"In this area?" Charlotte was surprised. She thought everyone near Cater Street was at least satisfactorily placed, had the necessities of life, even a few comforts. She had never seen any poor, not that lived here.

"Oh, very respectable." Martha's eyes looked out of the window. "The poverty is underneath; the clothes are patched, sewed over and over. Perhaps there is only one pair of shoes, perhaps only one meal a day. Appearance, self-respect are everything."

"Oh, how dreadful," Charlotte did not mean it as tritely as it sounded. It was dreadful. It hurt. It was not like the grinding, starving poverty Inspector Pitt had told her about, but it was still painful, a constant, wearing pain. She had never in her life been hungry, or even had to wonder if something could be afforded. True, she had admired clothes she knew she could not have, but she had more than she could possibly claim to need.

"I'm sorry. Can I help?"

Martha smiled, putting her hand out to touch Charlotte's knee.

"You are a very good girl, Charlotte. You take after your mother. I'm sure there will be things you can do, things you already have done. It is a great tragedy not all the young women in the parish conduct themselves as you do."

She was interrupted by Dora bringing in tea. After Dora had gone, and Charlotte had poured and handed her her cup, she continued.

"There is so much lightmindedness, seeking one's own pleasure."

Charlotte reluctantly thought of Emily. Dearly as she

Anne Perry

loved her, she could not recall Emily ever having pursued any ends but her own.

"I'm afraid so," she agreed. "Perhaps it is only lack of understanding?"

"Ignorance is something of an excuse, but not entirely. So often we do not look because if we looked we should feel obliged to do something."

It was undeniably true, and it struck a note of guilt in Charlotte. Inadvertently she thought of Pitt. He had obliged her to see things she would have preferred not to, things that disturbed her, destroyed her peace of mind, her comfort. And she had disliked him intensely for it.

"I tried to make Verity see it the same way," Martha was saying, her eyes on Charlotte's face. "She had so many good qualities, poor Verity."

"And I understand you knew Chloe fairly well, too." The minute Charlotte had said it she wished she had not. It was a cruel reminder, a wakening of pain. She saw Martha's face tighten and a spasm pass through the muscles round her mouth.

"Poor Chloe," she said with a tone Charlotte could not understand. "So frivolous, so light. Laughing when she should not have. Pursuing society. I'm afraid there were sometimes sinful things on her mind, things of the—," she caught her breath. "But let us not speak ill of the dead. She has paid for her sin and everything that was corrupting and corruptible in her is gone."

Charlotte stared at her. The strong, fair face was full of confusion and unhappiness.

"Let us talk of something else," Charlotte said firmly. "I have been copying out some recipes. I am sure you would be interested in at least one of them, because I remember Sarah saying you had enquired after a recipe for fricandeau of veal with spinach. I hear Mrs. Hilton has an extremely good cook? Or so Mrs. Dunphy was saying to Mama."

"Yes, indeed. And so willing," Martha agreed. "She does so much for church fetes and so forth, an excellent hand with

206

pastry. It is not every cook who can make a good puff pastry, you know. Put their fingers in it too much. Light and quick, one needs to be. And also very clever with preserves and candied fruits. She was always sending her maid round with—" she stopped, her face pale, eyes distressed again.

Charlotte put out her hand instinctively.

"I know. Let us not think of it. We cannot alter it now. I'll find you the recipe for the fricandeau." She pulled her hand away quickly and stood up. Martha followed her and Charlotte moved round the other side of the table. She wanted the interview to end. It was embarrassing. She had handled it badly. She was deeply sorry for Martha, both particularly because of her distress for the dead girls, and generally because of her life with the vicar, a fate which right now seemed quite as bad as anything Pitt had spoken of.

"Here," she held out a slip of paper. "I have already copied the fricandeau. I can easily do another one. Please? And I insist that Maddock walk home with you."

"It's not necessary." Martha took the recipe without looking at it. "I assure you!"

"I refuse to permit you to leave my house alone," Charlotte said firmly. She reached for the bell rope. "I should be guilty all evening. I should worry myself sick!"

And so Martha had no choice but to accept, and ten minutes later she took her departure with Maddock trailing dutifully behind.

Charlotte was not permitted to have a peaceful evening in which to sort out her chaotic feelings. Emily arrived home from visiting with the bombshell that she had invited Lord George Ashworth to dinner, and would be expecting him a little after seven o'clock.

Emily's news drove the entire household into immediate panic. Only Grandmama seemed to derive any unalloyed pleasure from it. She was delighted to observe the frenzy, and gave a running monologue on the proper way to order a house in such a fashion that even an unexpected visit from royalty itself could be managed with dignity and at least an adequate table. Emily was too excited and Caroline too worried—and Charlotte too overwhelmed by her own problems to reply to her. It was eventually Sarah who told her sharply to hold her tongue, and thus sent Grandmama into a paroxysm of righteous rage so severe she had to go upstairs and lie down.

"Well done," Charlotte said laconically. Sarah gave her the first real smile she had offered in weeks.

Everything was calm, at least on the surface, a full five minutes before George Ashworth arrived. They were all sitting in the withdrawing room, Emily dressed in rose pink which suited her very well, even if the extravagance of another new gown had not suited Papa. Sarah was dressed in green, also very becoming, and Charlotte in dull slate blue, a colour she had disliked until she caught sight of herself in the glass and saw how it flattered her eyes and the warm tones of her skin and hair.

She blushed uncomfortably when Ashworth bowed over her hand and his eyes lingered on her with approval. She disliked him, and thought him to be trifling with Emily. She replied to him formally with no more warmth than courtesy demanded.

Throughout the evening, however, she was obliged to revise her opinion to some extent. He behaved without appreciable fault; in fact, if he had not been in danger of hurting Emily, both publicly and privately, she could have quite sincerely liked him. He had wit and a certain outspokenness, although, no doubt, in his social position he could afford to say what he chose without fearing the consequences. He even flattered Grandmama, which was not difficult since she loved a handsome man, and loved a title even more.

Charlotte looked across and saw Emily's face pucker in a little smile. Apparently she knew perfectly well what he was doing, and it suited her. Once again Charlotte's anger rose. Damn the man for hurting Emily. She was a child in the ways of the world, compared to him!

The next time Charlotte spoke to him it was with a considerable chill in her voice. She saw Dominic staring at her in bewilderment, but she was too angry to care. And then all her old confusion about Dominic returned. She had loved him so much, and now all she could feel was a heart-sickening urge to protect him from—from what? From Pitt, the police—or himself?

It seemed as if the evening stretched forever. It was only eleven however, when George Ashworth took his leave and Charlotte excused herself and gratefully escaped to bed. She had expected to lie awake in a fever of thought all night, but she was hardly aware of lying down before the sleep of exhaustion overtook her.

The following day something infinitely worse awaited her. It was no more than ten o'clock in the morning when Maddock came to say that Inspector Pitt was in the hall and wished to see her.

"Me?" She tried to fend it off, hoping he would see someone else, perhaps that he had even come to see Papa, and was here now only to ensure that Papa would be in that evening.

"Yes, ma'am," Maddock said firmly. "He especially asked for you."

"Make sure it isn't really the master he wants to see, this evening, will you, Maddock?"

"Yes, ma'am." Maddock turned to leave, and as he was at the door, Pitt himself opened it and came in.

"Inspector Pitt!" Charlotte said sharply, intending to embarrass him into withdrawing. He was the last person in the world she wanted to see. Dominic's tie loomed so large in her mind, it seemed as if Pitt would only have to speak to Millie, go into any part of the kitchen or laundry, and it would stare him in the face with all its appalling implications. She was even more afraid of what she herself might say. The sheer concentration on not mentioning it, the fear, kept it in the forefront of her mind.

"Good morning, Miss Ellison." He watched Maddock disappear into the hall and closed the door behind him. "Charlotte, I came to tell you about George Ashworth."

Relief flooded through her. It was nothing to do with Dominic.

"You know?" he said with surprise. What an extraordinary face he had; his feelings were so easily reflected, almost magnified in it.

She was confused.

"No? What about him? Did you discover something?" Again she was afraid, thinking of Emily. Was it Ashworth after all? That would at least mean he would not be able to hurt Emily any more, humiliate her by leaving her for someone else. The thought was touched with deep regret, which was ridiculous. It was only a very small part of her that had liked him.

Pitt was watching her. "You like him," he observed with a smile. His eyes were gentle.

"I dislike him intensely," she said with considerable sharpness.

"Why? Because you are afraid for Emily? Afraid he would kill her, or afraid he will eventually get bored with her and move on to someone else, perhaps someone with money, or a title?"

She resented his accuracy, his intrusion. Emily's humiliation and hurt were none of his business.

"Afraid he might kill her, of course! What is it you came to tell me, Mr. Pitt?"

He ignored her terseness, still smiling. "That he probably did not even know the Hiltons' maid, and he certainly did not kill Lily Mitchell. His actions are very fully accounted for all that day and night."

She was pleased, very pleased, which made no sense. It meant Ashworth would remain free to humiliate Emily, and she cared very much that that should not happen.

"So you have eliminated one more person," she said, looking for words, anything to say to him to banish the silence and avoid his eyes watching her, smiling, seeing every expression, every thought in her face.

"Yes," he agreed. "Not a very satisfactory method of detection."

"Is that all you can do?" She meant it as a genuine question, not a criticism.

He smiled a littly wryly, a self-deprecating gesture. "Not quite. I'm trying to build up in my mind a picture of the kind of person we're looking for, of the sort of man driven to do such things."

Involuntarily she voiced the same thought that had so horrified Dominic. "Do you think perhaps he's a man—who—doesn't know *himself* what he's done, doesn't know why, doesn't even remember afterwards? Then he would be just as ignorant and as afraid as the rest of us?"

"Yes," he said simply.

It was no comfort. She wished he had said no. It brought the person, the hangman, closer; it removed the gulf between them. He could be any one of them. Only God could know how he would feel when he discovered himself!

"I'm sorry, Charlotte," he said quietly. "It frightens me, too. He must be found, but I am not looking forward to doing it."

She could think of nothing to say. Her mind's eye could see only Dominic's black tie, big enough to strangle the world. She wished Pitt would go away, before the very dominance of it in her mind made her tongue slip.

"I saw your brother-in-law the other day," he went on.

She felt herself tighten. Fortunately she had her back to him and he could not see the spasm in her throat, the terror. She tried to speak, to sound casual, but nothing came. Was that what he had really come for, because he knew or guessed already?

"In a coffeeshop," he continued.

"Indeed?" she managed to speak at last.

He did not reply. She knew he was looking at her. She

211

could not bear the silence. "I cannot imagine you had a great deal to discuss."

"The hangman, of course, but not much else, except a few other crimes. He seemed to feel this was the most important."

"Isn't it?" She turned back to look at him, to judge from his face what he meant.

"Yes, of course it is, but there are many others. My sergeant lost his arm a week ago."

"Lost his arm!" she was horrified. "How? What happened?" She remembered the little man vividly. How could he have had such an appalling accident?

"Gangrene," he said simply, but she saw the anger in his eyes. For a moment she actually forgot about Dominic. "He got an iron spike through it," he went on, "when we went into the rookeries after a forger." He told her what had happened.

"That's horrible," she said fiercely. "Does that sort of thing happen to—to many of you?"

She saw the flicker of hope in his face, then self-mockery as he derided his own feelings. Emily was at least partially right. He did care what she thought of him.

"No, not many," he answered. "It's as often tragic, pitiful, or even funny, as it is violent. Most people would prefer to serve their sentences and stay alive. The punishments for violence are too savage to be taken lightly. Murder is a hanging offence."

"Funny?" she said incredulously.

He sat sideways on the arm of one of the chairs. "How do you suppose people stay alive, in the rookeries, without a sense of humour? Without a rather bitter notion of the ludicrous, without wit, one could drown in it. You wouldn't understand the costermonger, the prostitutes, the dolly-shop owners, but if you did, you'd find them funny sometimes: savage, giving no quarter and expecting none, inventive, greedy, but often funny as well. That's the sort of world they live in. The weak and the disloyal die."

"What about the sick, the orphaned, the old?" she demanded. "How can you regard that with humour!"

"They die, just as they often do even at your end of society," he replied. "Their deaths are different, that's all. But what happens to a divorced woman in your world, or one who has an illegitimate child, or a woman whose husband dies or can't meet the bills? He's politely driven to ruin, and often suicide. As far as you're concerned, he or she is ruined from the day of their disgrace. You no longer see them in the street. You no longer call on them in the afternoons. There is no possibility of work, of marriage for the daughters, no credit with tradesmen. It's a different kind of death, but we usually see the end of it, all the same."

There was nothing to say to him. She would like to have hated him, to have denied it all, or justified it, but she knew inside her it was true. Little bits of memory returned, people whose names were not to be mentioned anymore, people one suddenly did not see again.

He put his hand out and touched her arm gently. She could feel the warmth of him.

"I'm sorry, Charlotte. I had no right to say that as if it were your fault, as if you were part of it willingly or consciously."

"That doesn't alter it though, does it?" she said bleakly.

"No."

"Tell me about some of the things that are funny. I think I need to know."

He leaned back, taking his hand away. She felt a coldness from the move. She would have expected to find his touch offensive; it surprised her that she did not.

He smiled a little wryly. "You met Willie at the police station?"

Involuntarily she smiled also. She recalled the thin face, the friendly mixture of interest and contempt for her ignorance.

"Yes; yes, I imagine he could tell a few colourful stories."

"Hundreds, some of them even true. I remember one he

told me about a costermonger family, and a long and picturesque revenge against a shofulman—"

"A what?"

"A passer of forged money. And Belle—I was going to say you would like Belle, but she's a prostitute—"

"I might still be capable of liking her," Charlotte replied, then wondered if she had committed herself too rashly. "Perhaps...."

His face softened in amusement. "Belle came from Bournemouth. Her parents were respectable but extremely poor, in service in a middle-class house. Belle was seduced—I understand with more force than charm—by the son of the house, and as a result turned out. She was henceforth marked as soiled. Naturally it was never considered that he should marry her. She came to London and discovered she was pregnant. To begin with she worked as a seamstress, sewing shirts—collars and wristbands stitched, six buttonholes, four rows of stitching down the front, for two and a half pence each. Do you sew, Charlotte? Do you know how long it takes to make a shirt? Do you do household accounts? Do you know what two and a half pence will buy?

"She tried the workhouse, but was turned away because she did not have an official admittance order. At that point she was propositioned by a gentleman not old enough to be rich enough to make an advantageous marriage, but with plenty of natural appetite. It earned her enough to feed her child and buy him a blanket to sleep in.

"And it opened a whole new world to her. She wrote to her parents every week; she still does, and sends them money. They think she earns it dressmaking. And what good would it serve to let them discover otherwise? They don't know what dressmakers earn in London.

"She found a landlord who protected her, but then he started taking more and more of her money. But this time she had friends—of many sorts, not just customers. She's a handsome girl, shrewd, but not unkind, and I've seldom seen her when she couldn't smile about something."

"What did she do?" Charlotte cared.

"She had a steady lover who was a screever, a writer of letters, a forger of certificates, false testimonials and so forth. He had an uncle who was a kidsman. He organized all his little protégés to plague the landlord every time he went out of the door. His watch was stolen, his seals, his money. But worse than that, they jeered at him, pinned notes to him, and made him a laughingstock."

"If he was robbed, why didn't he call the police?" she felt compelled to ask. "Especially if he saw who did it, and it continued?"

"Oh he did! That's how I came to know of it."

"You arrested them?" she was horrified and angry.

He smiled at her, meeting her eyes squarely.

"Unfortunately I had a stiff leg that day, and I was unable to run fast enough to catch any of them. Sergeant Flack got something in his eye, was obliged to stop and get it out, and by the time he could see again, they had gone."

She felt a wave of relief. "And Belle?"

"She got a reasonable rent, and kept the rest of the earnings."

"And did she continue—as—as a prostitute?"

"What else? Go back to stitching shirts at two and a half pence each?"

"No, of course not. I suppose it was a silly question. It makes me realize a little how lucky I am to be born as I was. I always used to think it was unjust, that saying about the sins of the fathers being visited on the children to the third and fourth generations. But it isn't, is it? It's just a fact of life. We reap what our parents have sown."

She looked up and found Pitt's eyes on her. The softness in them embarrassed her, and she turned away.

"What about the hangman? Do you think he—can't help it?"

"I think it's possible he doesn't even entirely know it. Which is perhaps why even those closest to him don't know it either," he answered.

The black tie came back to her mind with cold horror. For a while she had forgotten it, forgotten Pitt as a threat and thought of him only as—no, that was ridiculous!

She stood up a little stiffly. "Thank you for coming to tell me about Lord Ashworth. It was extremely courteous of you, and has set my mind at rest, at least from the worst fear."

He stood up also, accepting the dismissal, but there was disappointment in his face. She was sorry for it; he did not deserve it. But she was too afraid of him to let him stay. He had an ability to anticipate her, to understand her thoughts too well. His quick sympathy, his intelligence, would lead her into betraying herself, and Dominic.

He was still looking at her, damn him!

Oh God! Had she dismissed him so hastily he sensed her fear? Had she dismissed him so soon after their mention of the hangman and his possible ignorance of his own actions, that he guessed she knew something? She must make amends.

"I'm sorry, Mr. Pitt. I did not mean to appear rude. I have not even offered you any refreshment." She forced herself to meet his eyes. She smiled, her face stiff. She must look ghastly. "May I ring for something for you?"

"No, thank you." he walked to the door, then turned, frowning a little. "Charlotte, what are you afraid of?"

She drew a deep breath, her throat tight. A moment passed before she could make any sound come.

"Why, the hangman, of course. Isn't everyone?"

"Yes," he said quietly. "Possibly even the hangman himself."

The room swung round her. An earthquake must feel like this. It was ridiculous. She must not faint. Dominic might be weak, give way to his appetites, but then one must accept that all gentlemen were like that. But Dominic could have had nothing to do with murder, wires round choking white necks in the street! She must have been insane, weak, and treacherous to have let such suspicions come into her mind.

"Yes," Charlotte agreed. "I imagine so. But you must catch

him all the same, for everyone's sake." She deliberately put a lift into her voice, a positive sound as if it were all only peripherally to do with her, a social concern and not a personal one.

His mouth curled a little at the corner and with a tiny gesture like a bow, he turned and went out of the room. She heard Maddock opening and closing the front door for him.

Her knees gave way and she collapsed onto the sofa, tears running down her face.

When Dominic returned in the evening she could not meet his eyes. Sarah also sat through dinner in silence. Emily was out with George Ashworth and a group of his friends. Grandmama delivered a monologue on the decline of social manners. Edward and Caroline maintained the rudiments of a conversation that no one else listened to.

Afterwards Sarah said a little stiffly that she had a headache, and retired to bed. Mama accompanied Grandmama up to her sitting room to read to her for an hour or so, and Papa went into the study to smoke and write some letters.

Dominic and Charlotte were left alone in the withdrawing room. It was a situation Charlotte had dreaded, and yet it was almost a relief to face it. The reality might not be as bad as her fears had become.

She waited for a few minutes after the others had gone; then she looked up, afraid that if she did not speak soon, he might also leave.

"Dominic?"

He turned to face her.

She was alone with him; she had his entire attention. The dark eyes were fully on her, a little worried. It should have turned her heart over. But all she could think of was Lily Mitchell, and Sarah upstairs unhappy over a trifle, when there was so much more Sarah did not even guess—or did she? And Pitt. She could see Pitt's face in her mind, the light, probing eyes that made her feel so close. She shook herself hard. The thought was ridiculous.

"Yes?" Dominic prompted.

She had never been gifted with tact, never been able to approach things obliquely. Mama would have been so much better at this.

"Did you like Lily?" she asked.

His face puckered in surprise. "The maid Lily, Lily Mitchell?"

"Yes."

"Did I like her?" he repeated incredulously.

"Yes, did you? Please answer me honestly. It matters." It did matter, although she was not sure what she wanted the answer to be. The thought that he had cared for her was sharply painful, and yet the thought that he had used her without caring was worse; it was shabbier, dirtier, wider in its meaning.

There was a faint colour in his face.

"Yes, I liked her well enough. She was a funny little thing. Used to talk about the country, where she grew up. Why? Do you want to do something about her? She was an orphan, you know, actually illegitimate, I think. There's no family to speak of."

"No, I wasn't thinking of doing anything," she said a little sharply. She had not known Lily was an orphan. She had lived in the same house with her all those years, and for all the interest she had shown, Lily might as well not have existed. Was Dominic really any worse? "I wanted to know because of you."

"Me?"

Was she mistaken, or had the colour deepened in his face?

"Yes." There was no point in lying, in trying to be evasive. He was staring at her. Why on earth should she want so much to touch him now? To reassure herself he was still the same person, the Dominic she had loved all her womanhood? Or was she feeling something like pity?

"I don't understand you," he said slowly.

She met his eyes with an honesty she could not have imagined a month ago. For the first time she looked deep into him, without fluttering heart or beating pulse. She looked at the person, and forgot the man, the beauty, the excitement.

"Yes, you do. Millie brought me the necktie she found at the back of the bed when she turned the mattress. It was yours."

It seemed not to occur to him to lie. The colour came to his face painfully now, but he did not look away.

"Yes, I liked her. She was very—uncomplicated. Sarah can be desperately stuffy sometimes."

"So can you," she said brutally, and to her own surprise. A new, angry thought occurred to her, and as soon as it was in her head, it, too, was on her tongue. "How would you feel if Sarah went and made love to Maddock?"

His face dropped in amazement. "Don't be ridiculous!"

"What's ridiculous about it?" she asked coolly. "You lay with the maid, didn't you? Lily wasn't even a butler, just a maid!"

"Sarah wouldn't dream of such a thing; she isn't a trollop. It's extraordinary and degrading of you to have said it, even in fun."

"The last thing I intended was to be funny! Why are you insulted that I should speak of it hypothetically for Sarah, and yet you can admit it of yourself without any shame at all? You're not ashamed, are you!"

The colour came back again to his face, and for the first time he looked away from her.

"I'm not very proud of it."

"Because of Sarah, or because Lily's dead?" Why was she suddenly seeing him with such clarity? It was painful, like morning light on the skin, showing all the flaws.

"You don't understand," he said exasperatedly. "When you're married, you will."

"Understand what?"

"That. . . ." He stood up. "That men—men sometimes go—" He stopped, unable to finish it delicately.

She finished it for him.

"That you have one set of rules for yourselves, and another for us," she said tartly. Her throat hurt, as if she wanted to cry. "You demand perfect loyalty from us, but feel free to give your own love wherever you like—"

"It's not love!" he exploded. "For God's sake, Charlotte—"

"What? It's appetite? License?"

"You don't understand!"

"Then explain it to me."

"Don't be naive. You are not a man. If you were married you would perhaps understand that men are different. You can't apply women's feelings, women's rules to a man."

"I can apply rules of loyalty and honour to anybody."

He was angry now. "This has nothing to do with loyalty or honour! I love Sarah; at least, God help me, I did until she"—suddenly his face was white—"until she started to think I could be the hangman." He was staring at her and she could see helplessness and pain in his eyes.

She stood up also, and without thinking she put her hand out to touch him, catching his hand. He clung to it.

"Charlotte, she does! She clearly said so!"

"She believed Emily," she said quietly. "And perhaps she knew about Lily as well."

"But for God's sake! That's hardly the same as murdering four helpless girls and leaving their bodies in the street!"

"If she knew about Lily, and believes something about me, then you have hurt her. Perhaps she merely wanted to hurt you back?"

"But that's preposterous! She can't be so hurt—that—" He stared at her.

She looked back gravely. "I would be. If I'd given you all my love, my heart and body, and been loyal to you and thought of no one else, I would be hurt beyond anything I could imagine if I knew you had slept with my maid, and if I thought you had courted my sister. I might hurt you as deeply as I could. If you could betray me that way, murder might not seem so very much worse."

"Charlotte!" his voice cracked a little and went higher.

"Charlotte, you can't think that? Oh, please heaven! I mean, I didn't—I never hurt anyone!" He grabbed at her hand again, holding it so tightly he crushed her fingers.

She did not pull away.

"Except Sarah, and perhaps Lily? Did she love you, too, or are maids allowed to have appetites, like men?"

"Charlotte, for God's sake don't be sarcastic! Help me!"

"I don't know how to!" She gave him, for a moment, an answering pressure of her own hand. "I can't make Sarah feel differently; I can't take back whatever she said, or make you forget she said it."

He stood still for a long time, close to her, looking at her eyes, her face.

"No," he said at last. He closed his eyes. "And dear God," he said very softly, "you can't make me absolutely sure I didn't do it. That damnable policeman of yours said this man could be unaware himself of what he's doing. That means it could be me. I could be doing this, and not know it. I saw your father in the street; no one else seems to have realized yet that that means I was also there. And I knew all four of the girls—and was out when each one of them was killed."

She could think of only one thing to say that would be of any comfort, and still be true. "If Pitt thought you could have done it, he would have been back here, questioning you. He wouldn't exclude you just because you're a gentleman."

"Do you think he really has any idea?" he said eagerly. It was painfully clear how much he wanted to believe her, and how hard it was for him.

"I know you don't like him, but do you think you could deceive him for long?"

His mouth turned down in self-mockery. "I don't think I really dislike him. I think I'm afraid of him."

"Because you think he's clever?"

"Yes." He sighed. "Thank you, Charlotte. Yes, I suppose Pitt has looked at us closely enough. Perhaps, if it were one of us, he would be closing in now. You don't think he is, do you?" The sharp fear was back again.

This time she lied, as if to protect a child.

"No."

He let out his breath again, and sat down. "How can Sarah think I could have done it? Surely anyone who knew me at all...? You said she loves me, how could you love anyone and think that of him?"

"Because being in love with someone is not the same as knowing them," she said, hearing her words harshly and clearly in her head. Would they mean as much to him as they did now to her?

"She doesn't really love me," he said slowly, "or she would not have thought it."

"You thought it of yourself!"

"That's different. I know myself. But I never thought ill of her, not in any way."

"Then you don't know her, any more than she knows you." Charlotte meant it, although she was discovering her thoughts even as she spoke them.

"What do you mean?"

"We all have faults—Sarah, too. If you expect her to be perfect that is a wrong you're doing her that is as great as the wrong she is doing you."

"I don't understand you, Charlotte." He frowned. "Sometimes I think you don't know what you're saying."

"No," she agreed. It hurt, because she realized he really did not understand. "No, I thought you might not." She made up her mind quickly, from a deep feeling. "I'm going up to see if Sarah is all right."

"Sarah?" He was surprised.

She went to the door and turned.

"Yes."

He was looking at her with a pucker between his brows. She ached inside, all down her throat and in her stomach. She wanted to put her arms round him, to comfort away the fear she knew was in him, but her love for him was quite different. It was no longer mysterious, romantic, blood-quickening. She felt older than he, and stronger.

"Charlotte—"

She knew what he wanted to say, he wanted to say "Help me," and he did not know how.

She smiled. "I'm not going to tell her anything. And every man near Cater Street who has thought at all, must have the same fears as you do."

He let out his breath and tried to smile. "Thank you, Charlotte. Good night."

"Good night."

Upstairs she found Sarah sitting in her bed, staring at the wall, a book lying open, face down on the covers.

"How are you?" Charlotte asked.

"What do you want?" Sarah looked at her coolly.

"Can I get anything for you? A hot drink?"

"No, thank you. What's the matter? Won't Dominic talk to you?" There was a bitter edge to Sarah's voice, and Charlotte thought she was near tears.

She sat down on the edge of the bed. "Yes, he talked to me for quite a while."

"Oh," Sarah affected disinterest. "About what?"

"The hangman."

"How gruesome. It will make you dream."

Charlotte put out her hand and took Sarah's. "Sarah, you shouldn't let him think you suspect him—"

"Has he been complaining to you, crying on your shoulder?"

"It's easy to see what you're thinking! Sarah!" She held onto her more tightly as Sarah tried to pull away. "Even if you think so, can't you have the kindness, or the sense, not to let him know it? If he were guilty, there would be time enough to know it when it couldn't be denied. If he's innocent and you suspect him wrongly, you'll have built a gap between you that will be difficult to bridge later."

The tears brimmed over Sarah's eyes. "I don't suspect him," she said gulping. "Not really. It just crossed my mind for a moment. Is that so hard to understand? I couldn't help it! He's been out so much lately. He hardly takes notice of

223

me anymore. Is he in love with you, Charlotte; tell me honestly? I think I would rather know now."

"No," Charlotte shook her head with a smile. "I used to be in love with him, which is what Emily meant. But he never even saw me."

The tears were running down Sarah's face. "Oh, Charlotte, I'm sorry. I didn't know."

"I didn't want you to." Charlotte made herself smile. Her own feelings were suddenly very clear. She was desperately, painfully sorry for Sarah because Sarah had wounded Dominic and irreparably hurt herself; and even now Sarah did not understand how, or seem able to undo it.

Sarah was staring at her, pity showing through the tears.

"Oh, it's all right," Charlotte said easily. "I'm not in love with him anymore. I like him very much, but I'm not in love."

Sarah smiled and sniffed. "Your wretched policeman?"

Charlotte was shocked. "Good heavens, no!"

Sarah's smile widened.

Charlotte leaned forward a little. More than anything on earth she wanted to help and protect Sarah, to take things back to the way they used to be.

"Sarah, tell Dominic you don't suspect him really, that it was just a momentary thought of how awful it would be. Even lie, if you have to. But don't let him go on thinking—"

"He won't come to me."

"Then go to him!"

"No." Sarah shook her head.

"Sarah!"

"I can't."

There was nothing else Charlotte could say. Silently she touched Sarah's hair, pushing a strand out of her eyes, then stood up and walked away slowly. She was too tired, too shaken with the upheaval in her life, to feel anything more tonight. Tomorrow the fear and the pity would all come back.

Chapter
Eleven

Sarah thought about the things that Charlotte had said, but she could not bring herself to go to Dominic. He had been so cold lately, so unapproachable, she was afraid of another rebuff. And if he really were hurt, he could so easily come to her.

Or was there something more than hurt? Could it be quite a different guilt he felt? She remembered small, smug looks on Lily's face, and laughter. At the time she had refused to understand, although half her mind knew women too well for complete ignorance. She had thought it was all over, and for her own peace of mind had learned to forget it. Now it was resurrected in all its ugly embarrassment. Was it Lily's death that had reminded him?

But if he were to ask, even once, she would immediately tell him in such a way that he could not help believing her, that she had not really thought him capable of murder. It had been only a passing, absurd fear, which reason had dismissed as soon as she recognized it.

But he did not come, and she did not speak of it to him.

One thing it had altered was the way Sarah felt about Charlotte. Her admission explained so many things. Now she understood why Charlotte had had so little interest in all the eligible young men Mama had contrived to introduce to her. In the new light of knowledge she remembered odd little incidents, words, looks, tempers, and unexplained tears. She could not comprehend how Charlotte had kept it from her—for her complete insensitivity, if not merely for marrying Dominic. How could she have been so blind? She had taken her own happiness for granted, and never stopped to think of Charlotte. Emily had seen it and in a moment of anger betrayed it. That was hard to forgive.

At least that part was over now. Charlotte had fallen out of love again. Could she possibly be attracted to that fearful policeman? Surely not! But if anyone were capable of such a social lunacy, it would be Charlotte!

Well, time to worry about that if it actually happened. No doubt Papa would sort it out quickly enough, although he did not seem to be doing much about Emily and that dandy Ashworth. She would have to remind him, or Emily might not only be hurt, but ruined as well. At the moment Sarah was tempted to think it would serve Emily right for her betrayal of Charlotte, but perhaps fortune would hurt her quite enough without any hand from her family.

It was two days later, when she was visiting Martha Prebble on some parish business, that Mrs. Attwood, the invalid woman whom Papa had been visiting on the night Lily was killed, was mentioned.

"Poor soul," Martha said with a slight sigh. "She really is a trial."

Sarah recalled what Papa had said. "I hear she is prone to exaggerating rather a lot, and gets memory confused with imagination. A little wishful thinking, perhaps?"

Martha raised her eyebrows. "I didn't know that. When

I saw her she just talked unceasingly, and always of past glories, although I must confess I didn't trouble to listen closely enough to judge whether they were true or not. I imagine the poor creature is merely lonely."

"Does no one visit her?" Sarah asked, feeling a quick pang of pity, and at the same time a reluctance to do it herself.

"Not many people, I'm afraid. As I said, she is more than a little trying."

"I believe she is an invalid, restricted to the house?" Sarah felt obliged to pursue it. She would feel guilty if the woman were in need, and she had ignored her—especially if in the past her husband had really done Papa some favour.

"Oh no," Martha was quite firm. "She suffers nothing more than the usual small ailments of age."

"Not bedridden?" Sarah frowned. Could she have misunderstood Papa? She tried to remember exactly what he had said, and could not.

"Oh no, not at all. But I'm sure she would be most grateful if you visited her, just to talk a little while."

"Is she in any need, I mean financially?" Sarah would rather have given practical help than her time.

"My dear Sarah, how very generous you are. It is so like you to want to help, not to spare yourself but to think only of others' needs. But she is not poor, I assure you, except in spirit. She needs friends," she said hesitatingly, her hands tightening on Sarah's shoulders, "and a little warmth." Her voice was suddenly husky, as though she were labouring under some strong emotion. For an instant Sarah was embarrassed, then she recalled the icy righteousness of the vicar, and tried to put herself in Martha's place. Oddly enough, Dominic's recent coldness helped her. She answered Martha's grip by reaching out and touching her in return.

"Of course," she said quietly. "We all do. I shall call on her this afternoon. I cannot take her anything this time; I will just visit socially, while I have the opportunity of using the carriage. But I will call another time, perhaps with Charlotte or Mama, and take her something, just as a token."

Martha was staring at her, her eyes fixed.

"Do you not think that is a good idea?" Sarah asked, looking back at the pale face. "Should I not go until I have been introduced, do you think?"

Martha's eyes cleared. "Of course," she said, catching her breath. "You should go, yes, go today."

"Mrs. Prebble, are you all right?" Sarah now felt anxious for her; she looked very strained, a little overwrought. Had Sarah said something to distress her? Or was it the sudden recollection of her own emotionally barren life?

Sarah put her hands over Martha's and gripped them hard, then as she felt the older woman's muscles tense, she leaned forward and kissed her gently on the cheek, and moved to the door.

"I shall tell you asked kindly after her. I'm sure she will appreciate it. You do so much for so many people, there can hardly be a house in the parish that doesn't think of you with kindness." And before Martha could fumble for a reply to this, she excused herself and took her departure.

Sarah did not know precisely what she had expected, but the woman who finally opened the door to her was such a surprise to her she could only stand and stare.

"Yes?" the woman raised her eyebrows enquiringly.

Sarah swallowed and recollected herself.

"My name is Sarah Corde. I have not had the pleasure of meeting you before, but Mrs. Prebble spoke so well of you, I decided, if it would not be inconvenient to you, I would like to make your acquaintance?"

The woman's face lightened immediately. She was a handsome creature, and perhaps twenty-five years ago she might well have been beautiful. The remnants of beauty were still there in the bones and the elegant sweep of hair, faded, but not yet thinning. There seemed nothing even remotely pathetic about her, and if she was lonely, it was not obvious.

"Please come in," she invited, standing back so Sarah could accept the invitation.

The sitting room was small, and furnished with unusual simplicity, but Sarah had the impression that it was a matter of taste rather than poverty. She found the effect surprisingly pleasing. It was more restful than the usually crowded rooms she was accustomed to with dozens of photographs and paintings, stuffed birds, dried flower arrangements, embroidery samplers and ornaments, and furniture in almost every available space. This seemed much lighter, much less oppressive.

"Thank you." She sat down in the offered chair. She was profoundly glad now that she had brought no gift of food; it would have seemed redundant here, perhaps even offensive.

"It was kind of Mrs. Prebble to speak well of me," the woman said. "I'm afraid I don't know her as well as I might. I find church functions—." She stopped, obviously recollecting that Sarah probably attended them, and revising what she had been going to say.

Sarah found herself smiling. "Tedious," she filled in for her.

The woman's face relaxed. "Thank you so much for your frankness. Yes, I'm afraid so. She does a great deal of good work, but she must be a saint to persevere through all those endless idle conversations, and the gossip. And my dear, it isn't even interesting gossip!"

"Is gossip ever interesting, except to those who are spreading it?"

"Of course! Some gossip has great wit, and of course some carries the burden of genuine scandal. Or it used to. I haven't heard a good scandal for years. But then hardly anyone ever comes to see me these days. I have grown respectable. What a fearful epitaph."

Sarah's curiosity was mounting. Who, precisely, was this woman? So far she appeared nothing at all like the pathetic and wandering creature Papa had described. On the contrary, she was entertaining, and very much in command of herself.

"Isn't an epitaph a little premature?" Sarah asked with a smile. "You are not dead yet."

"I might as well be, sitting here in a room in Cater Street

watching the world pass by outside. And I've no one to listen to me, even if I were able to make witty remarks! It's a terrible thing, my dear, to have wit, and no one on whom to exercise it. May I offer you some refreshment, a dish of tea, perhaps? I have no maid, as you will have observed, but I can easily enough prepare it myself, if you will excuse me."

"Oh no, please," Sarah put out a hand as if to restrain her. "I have just taken tea with Mrs. Prebble." That was a lie, but she did not want to disturb her. "Unless, of course, you wish it for yourself? In which case let me make it, and bring it to you?"

"Good heavens, child, you are anxious for good works! Very well, it would be most charming to be waited upon. You will find everything in the kitchen. If there is anything you cannot put your hand on, pray ask me."

Fifteen minutes later Sarah returned with a large tray and tea set for two. She poured it herself, and they resumed their conversation.

"How long have you lived in Cater Street?" she asked.

The woman smiled. "Ever since my husband died, and dear Edward found me this place," she answered.

"Edward? Is he your son?"

The woman's graceful eyebrows arched in amused surprise. "Good heavens no! He was my lover. A long time ago now, over twenty-five years. I was forty then, and he was in his thirties."

"You didn't marry him?"

She gave a rich laugh. "Of course I didn't marry him. He was already married, with a very handsome wife, so I heard, and one daughter. My dear, what's the matter? You look pale. Did you swallow something amiss?"

Sarah was stunned. An unspeakable thought had entered her mind. She stared at the woman's face, trying to see her as she must have been twenty-five years ago. Was that why Papa had really been here? Was that why he had lied at first, saying he had been at his club all evening, until Dominic had given him away? Was that why he had refused to give Pitt either the woman's name or her address?

The more she sought to evade the conclusion, the more inescapably it entrenched itself in her mind. She heard her voice asking, as if willed from outside herself:

"I suppose it was a sort of parting gift, to make sure you were all right?"

"How very romantic," the woman smiled. "A grand good-bye, all hidden tears and momentoes to be kept forever, in tissue and ribbons? He isn't dead, my dear, nor did he emigrate. In fact he's perfectly well, and we remain moderately good friends, as far as discretion and the alterations of time will allow. Nothing as romantic as you imagine, merely an affair that became a friendship, and then little more than an acquaintance with pleasant memories."

"Then he must live near here?" Sarah was compelled to continue, hoping that even now something would disprove her fear. Every new fact was a chance to discover one that would not fit Papa.

The woman smiled, her eyes bright with humour.

"Indeed," she agreed. "So perhaps it would be indiscreet of me to tell you anything more about him. He could be someone you know!"

"Yes, I suppose," Sarah was answering mechanically. Her conversation became stilted, but her mind was in chaos, trying to find a way through the fragments of all sorts of beliefs, about Papa, about Dominic. Did Mama know? Had she always known, and been prepared to turn a blind eye to it? Did she even mind? Or was it one of the things she had been brought up to expect, to accept as part of the nature of man? But men in general were quite different from one's own Papa—or husband!

Sarah did not, and could not, accept it. She had never even entertained thoughts of any man other than Dominic, and her concept of love did not permit that she might. Love incorporated fidelity. One gave promises, and one kept them. One might occasionally be selfish, unreasonable, or ill-tempered; one might be untidy or extravagant. But one did not lie either in word or deed.

She stayed a little longer, talking with the woman, although she had no idea what she said—polite nonsense, stock phrases that everyone said and no one listened to. Then she took her leave and stepped into the carriage to return home.

Caroline sat alone in her bedroom. Sarah had just left and closed the door behind her.

She felt numb, her mind refusing to move, stuck fast on the one thought, repeating it over and over as if use would make it easier to bear. Edward had been having an affair with another woman, and for twenty-five years he had retained her acquaintance, still visiting her even now. Was it love? The embers of past romance? Or some kind of debt that could not be shaken off? Even pity?

Poor Sarah.

Sarah had come to her for guidance, assurance that she was not alone, and peculiarly betrayed; and Caroline had been able to give her none. Sarah had been confused, too shocked herself to understand what she was doing and to realize that Caroline had known nothing about it. Sarah had broken a thirty-year peace in thirty minutes.

Caroline stared at herself in the mirror. It was not even a matter of growing old. This other woman was older! What had Edward seen in her that Caroline had lacked? Beauty, warmth, wit, sophistication? Or was it just love, love without reason?

Why had he left his mistress? To avoid scandal? The children? Could it even have been anything as mundane as finance? She would never know, because she would never know whether whatever he said was the truth.

And that raised the other question. Was she going to tell him she knew? There could be little purpose now; on the other hand, could she conceal it? She could not possibly feel the same way about him. The years had brought familiarity, a certain contempt for patterns of life, the habit of overlooking small failings and weaknesses; but there had always been a trust, a knowledge that the bad things were superficial.

Her mind kept going back to the woman. What kind of a woman was she? Had she loved Edward, committed any lasting part of herself to him; or was it an affair, something to be set against profit and loss, so much social prestige, so much money or security, so much fun? What was it she gave him that Caroline could not?

She tried to think back to the way she had felt in those first years. Sarah must have been a small child, Charlotte newly born, Emily not yet thought of. Was that it? Had she been too involved with the children? Had she ignored him? Surely not. She thought she could remember many hours spent together, long evenings at home, nights out at dinners, parties, even concerts. Or were they later? Time was confused, telescoping.

Had he loved that other woman, or was she a diversion, something to fill a need, an appetite? Was all the past a lie?

The thought that he had loved Mrs. Attwood was appalling, something that hurt profoundly, altering years of feelings, shattering peace, destroying anything of tenderness or trust. Even if it had been appetite, was that any better?

She shivered. Suddenly she felt unclean, as if something soiled had entered her and she could not wash it out. The memory of his touch, of their familiarity, became offensive, something she wanted to forget, because she could not undo it.

She stood up, tidying her hair automatically, and pulling her dress straight. She must go downstairs and present a face to the family that masked at least some of the misery and the confusion inside her.

Grandmama knew there was something wrong with both Sarah and Caroline. At first she presumed they had had a quarrel of some sort, and naturally she wanted to know what it was about. Sarah was in the rear sitting room the following morning, and Grandmama went in, ostensibly to enquire about the arrangements for afternoon tea and what visitors they might expect, but actually to learn the facts of the quarrel.

"Good morning, Sarah, my dear," she said purposefully.

"Good morning, Grandmama," Sarah replied, not looking up from the letter she was writing.

"You look a little pale. Didn't you sleep?" Grandmama pursued, sitting down on the sofa.

"Yes, thank you."

"Are you sure? You seem a little agitated to me."

"I'm perfectly all right, thank you. Don't distress yourself on my account."

Grandmama seized on the suggestion immediately.

"But I am distressed, my dear; I cannot help worrying about you when I see both you and your Mama looking tired and upset. If you have had some sort of disagreement, perhaps I can help to see that it is sorted out?"

If Sarah had been Charlotte, she would have said bluntly that Grandmama was more likely to add fuel to it than sort it out, but being Sarah she remained at least nominally polite.

"There is no quarrel, Grandmama; we are very close." She smiled with unconcealed bitterness. "In fact we are fellows in misfortune."

"Misfortune? What misfortune is that? I didn't know anything had happened?"

"You wouldn't. It happened twenty-five years ago."

"What on earth do you mean?" Grandmama demanded. "What happened twenty-five years ago?"

Sarah retreated. "Nothing that need concern you. It is all over now."

"If it still distresses you and your mother, it is not all over!" Grandmama said sharply. "What has happened, Sarah?"

"Men," Sarah replied. "Life. Perhaps it even happened to you once." She gave a tight little smile. "I shouldn't be surprised. I shouldn't be surprised at all!"

"What are you talking about? What about men?"

234

"They are shallow, disloyal and hypocritical!" Sarah said furiously. "They preach one thing and practice quite another. They have one set of rules for us and another for themselves."

"Some men do, of course. That has always been the case. But not all. There are upright and decent men as well. Your father is one of them. I'm sorry if your husband is not."

"Papa!" Sarah spat. "You old fool! He's the worst of them all. Dominic may have cast his eyes where he shouldn't, but he never set up a mistress and kept her for twenty-five years!"

The words had no meaning for Grandmama. They were a preposterous lie. Sarah must be out of her mind, temporarily deranged by the shock of discovering Dominic had behaved badly. Of course, marrying a man as handsome as that was bound to lead to disaster. She knew it from the beginning. She had said as much to Caroline. But of course Caroline never would be told.

"Nonsense!" she said crossly. "That is a childish thing to say, and quite ridiculous. I will excuse you this once, on account of the obvious disturbance you have suffered in your mind on discovering things about your husband which I could have told you in the beginning. Indeed, I did tell your mother. But if you repeat such a wicked calumny about your father outside this room, or in the presence of others, I shall..." She hesitated, not quite sure what might be sufficiently awful to threaten Sarah with.

"You will do what?" Sarah said harshly. "Prove it untrue? You can't! If you have a spare afternoon I shall take you to meet her! She's old, older than Papa, but still very handsome. She must have been quite a beauty."

"Sarah! This is not in the least amusing. I order you to control yourself immediately. If you cannot, then go upstairs and lie down until you can. Take some smelling salts, and wash your face in cold water."

"Cold water! Papa is keeping a mistress, and you suggest I cure that by washing my face in cold water!" Sarah's voice rose in vicious ridicule. "Did you offer smelling salts to Mama as well? And is that what *you* did? Did Grandpapa keep a mistress somewhere?"

Old distasteful memories returned.

"Sarah, you are becoming hysterical!" Grandmama snapped. "Leave the room. You are behaving like a servant. Pull yourself together and remember your dignity. You had better lie down until you have come to your senses." As Sarah did not move she became angrier. "Immediately!" she raised her voice. "I shall explain to your mother that you are unwell. I have no wish for you to make an exhibition of yourself, and I am sure you haven't either. What if one of the servants were to come in? Do you wish to become the talk of the servants' hall? And no doubt the servants' halls of the entire street?"

With a look of deep malevolence, Sarah departed.

Grandmama sat down hard. What an appalling morning! Whatever could have overcome Sarah to make such a shocking allegation? She must have completely lost control of herself.

Edward had no doubt committed the usual indiscretions, but nothing could warrant an accusation of dishonesty! To expect a man to behave without fault for thirty years of marriage was asking too much; any woman knew that. One accepted such things, and bore them with fortitude and, above all, with dignity.

But to keep a mistress, to set up an establishment and provide regular financial assistance was quite a different matter. It was unpardonable. How dare Sarah suggest such a thing! Whatever she had discovered about Dominic, to blacken her father's name in such a way was inexcusable. It could not possibly have any foundation.

Could it?

Grandmama was considering the impossibility of Edward's behaving in such a manner, when Charlotte came in. She also looked grim and decidedly strained. Still, she was a peculiar girl, most impractical and given to unreliable moods. Possibly she was also disappointed in Dominic. Very foolish, her infatuation with Dominic. She really should have grown out of such childish romances by now.

"What's the matter with you, Charlotte?" she demanded. "Surely you haven't been listening to Sarah's foolish vapourings?" Charlotte turned round sharply. Grandmama took another breath. "She is naturally somewhat upset to discover Dominic is fallible, but she will get over it, if you help instead of wilting around like something out of a tragic poem. Pull yourself together, girl, and stop being selfish."

"And Mama?" Charlotte said bitterly. "Will she pull herself together and get over it as well?"

"There is nothing to get over!" Grandmama snapped. "I'm surprised that you should be so foolish, and so gullible as to believe Sarah. Can't you see she is upset?"

"Of course she's upset! So am I. If you are not upset by it, I can only presume that your moral standards are different from mine!"

That was really too much! Grandmama felt outrage rise inside her till she found it hard to catch her breath. Charlotte's insolence was beyond any bounds she could tolerate.

"Certainly my standards are different from yours!" she said acidly. "I did not fall in love with my sister's husband!"

"I'm perfectly sure you never fell in love at all," Charlotte said icily.

"I never lost control of myself," Grandmama said viciously, "if that is what you mean by 'falling in love.' I do not consider an emotional excess any excuse for immoral behaviour. And if you had been properly brought up, neither would you!"

That was the chance Charlotte had been waiting for. Her face lit with fierce triumph. "You are hoist with your own petard, Grandmama. If upbringing is to blame, what happened to Papa? How is it that you did not explain to him that one does not betray one's wife and children by keeping a mistress for twenty-five years!"

Grandmama felt the blood rush to her face. She was dizzy

with outrage, fear—and the fact that her stays were extremely tight.

"How dare you repeat such malicious and irresponsible lies! Go to your room! If it would not be both embarrassing and hurtful to your father, I should demand that you apologize to him."

"I'm sure it would be embarrassing, to both of you," Charlotte said with a cynical smile. "You would see from his face that he is guilty, and then you would be obliged to retract your words, and a good many of your ideas."

"Nonsense!" Grandmama said icily. She would not have Edward criticized by this insolent child. How dare Sarah have spread this slander everywhere? It was unforgivable. "I dare say your father may have indulged in certain tastes—gentlemen do—but nothing dishonest, or dishonourable, as you suggest. To talk of betrayal is ridiculous!"

Charlotte's lip curled with disgust. "I admired Dominic, although I never did anything about it, never even spoke, and I am immoral; yet Papa keeps a mistress for twenty-five years, buys her a house and supports her, and he is only behaving as gentlemen do; there is nothing dishonourable in it! You hyprocrite! I know there is one standard for men and another for women, but even you cannot stretch it as far as that! Why should it be unpardonable sin for a woman to betray a man, but a mere peccadillo, nothing to raise the eyebrows, if a man betrays a woman? Surely a sin is a sin, whoever commits it; only some may be extended forgiveness because of ignorance or greater weakness? Is that man's plea, greater weakness? They are always saying it is we who are the weaker ones, or is that only physical? Are we supposed to be morally stronger?"

"Don't talk nonsense, Charlotte!" But the sting had gone out of her reply. She was remembering Caroline's face at breakfast. Unless she was very much mistaken, there had been the marks of tears, carefully powdered over, but Grandmama's eyes were still perfectly good enough to see through that.

Caroline believed it.

Was it possible? Had Edward kept another woman all these years? And what kind of a woman was she?

She looked at Charlotte's hard, hurt face.

Charlotte saw her waver, saw the doubt. Contempt flickered in her eyes.

Grandmama felt the chill of disillusion trickle through her mind, leaving her with the bleak acceptance that there must be at least some truth in this story. She had always loved Edward, clung to the image of his father in him, and in some way her own youth and the things that had been good in it. She had seen in Edward the epitome of all that is fine and admirable in a man: the best of his father, without the worst.

Now she was obliged to face the fact that she saw him this way because she saw him from a distance. Had she looked more closely, as Caroline must, she would have seen the flaws. Then this would not have been such a blow. It was not only beliefs about him, but beliefs about herself that suffered. Old values were soiled, and there was nothing new to put in their place. She felt old, and bitterly lonely. The world she belonged to had died, and the remnant of it in Edward had betrayed her.

She hated Charlotte for having exposed her to the truth. "You are not strong, Charlotte," she said viciously in answer to the question. "You are hard. That is why Dominic chose Sarah, and not you!" She searched for something that would hurt even more. "No man will ever love you. You are totally unfeminine. Even that wretched policeman only admires you because he is vulgar and doesn't know the qualities of a lady. He imagines that he could better himself through you. And, of course, even if you accepted him—it might well be the only offer you get—you would not raise him to your social station. He was born common and he will remain common. You would sink to his station. Which may very well be where you belong!"

Charlotte's face was white. "You're a vicious and ugly old

woman," she said quietly. "I shouldn't be surprised if Grand-papa kept a mistress as well, to get away from you. Perhaps she was someone gentle. Perhaps that's where Papa learnt it. He may not be so very much to blame. That's something I've learned from your vulgar policeman; how much our parents make us what we are, how they influence not only our education, our wealth or poverty, our social standing, but our beliefs as well. When I look at you, I realize maybe Papa is not as much at fault as I thought."

And with that she turned and went out the door, leaving Grandmama gasping for breath, her throat tight, her stays digging into her like knives. She cried out for help, hoping instinctively to elicit pity, but Charlotte had closed the door.

Luncheon was awful. It was eaten in almost total silence, and afterwards everyone made separate excuses to leave as soon as possible. Emily said she was going out to the dress-maker's and would Mama accompany her, to prevent her being in the streets alone? Grandmama gave a vicious look to Charlotte and said she was retiring upstairs, as she felt profoundly unwell. Sarah expressed a desire to visit Martha Prebble, a sympathetic and virtuous woman. The vicar's house might be a little self-consciously righteous, but free-dom from carnal thoughts and the sins of the flesh were coming to appeal to her more and more.

"Sarah, you should not go alone," Charlotte said quickly. "Do you wish me to come with you?" It was the last thing she wanted to do, but recently she had felt closer to Sarah than at any time since Dominic had first come to the house and she had been barely more than a child. She ached for Sarah's sense of loss, her disappointment and shock. She felt some of it herself, because she too had loved Dominic. But for her the commitment was different, and she was amazed at herself for finding it so easy to recover. She feared her love had been a great deal shallower than she had imagined, a love based not on any knowledge but on her fancy. For

Sarah it was different; hers was the loss of intimacy, of things shared, of fact, not dreams.

Sarah was looking at her. "No, thank you," she said with the best smile she could manage. "I know how you dislike the vicar, and he may well be home. And if he is not, I would rather like to talk to Martha alone."

"I'll come and leave you at the door, if you like?" Charlotte pressed.

"Don't be ridiculous! Then you would have to walk back alone. I shall be perfectly safe. I think perhaps this madman has gone anyway. Nothing has happened for ages. We were probably wrong. Probably he did come from the slums, and has now gone back to them."

"Inspector Pitt didn't think so." Charlotte half stood up.

"Are you as taken with him as he is with you?" Emily raised her eyebrows. "He is not infallible, you know!"

"I shall go straight to the vicar's, then from door to door on parish work," Sarah said firmly. "And I dare say Martha will even accompany me. I shall be perfectly safe! Don't fuss. I shall see you all this evening. Good-bye."

The others departed also and Charlotte was left alone with nothing in particular to do. She searched quickly for a job to prevent her from allowing her mind to dwell on Papa or Dominic, the hurt that disillusion caused, the foolishness of building dreams around people—and behind it all the dark fear of the hangman, because in spite of what Sarah and Emily had implied, she did not think for a moment that he had returned to whatever slum one might delude oneself he came from. He was local, from Cater Street or its immediate proximity; she knew it in her heart.

It was twenty minutes to three, and she was busy writing a list of letters to distant relations to whom she had owed correspondence for some time and had put off as a chore, when Maddock came to say that Inspector Pitt was at the door, and wished to see her.

She felt a quite unreasonable pleasure, almost a sense of relief, as if he could somehow ameliorate her sense of disillusion; and yet she was also afraid of him. Everyone in the house knew about Papa's behaviour, even though no one spoke of it to more than one other person at a time. It was never discussed except as a confidence, yet it seemed as if the house itself knew, and Pitt would only have to come into its walls to know also. And if Papa were capable of one such betrayal, one deceit of twenty-five years, what else might he not have kept from them? This other life that they knew nothing of might incorporate all sorts of things. Perhaps even he himself was not fully aware of it? That was the monstrous thought that had been at the back of her mind for hours. It was out now. Was it possible for a man to behave in such a way? Could he have had other mistresses? Perhaps have made some advances towards the murdered girls, and then, rather than be exposed, have killed them? Surely not! Papa? What on earth was she thinking? She had known Papa all her life. He had held her on his knee, played with her when she was a child. She could remember birthdays, Christmases, toys he had given her.

But all that time he had been intimate with that other woman less than a couple of miles away! And poor Mama had never known it!

"Miss Charlotte?" Maddock brought her back to the present again.

"Oh yes, Maddock, you had better ask him to come in, I suppose."

"Do you wish me to bring any refreshment, Miss?"

"Certainly not," she said, a little sharply. "I doubt he will be here more than a half hour at the most."

"Yes, ma'am." Maddock withdrew, and a moment later Pitt came in. He was as untidy as always, and with the usual broad smile.

"Good afternoon, Charlotte," he said cheerfully.

She gave him a frown to indicate she resented the familiarity, but it seemed to be entirely wasted on him.

"Good afternoon, Mr. Pitt. Is there some further way we

can assist you in your enquiries? Do you feel any nearer success?"

"Oh yes, we have excluded many more that we believed to be possibilities." He was still smiling. Did nothing penetrate the thickness of his skin?

"I'm glad to hear it. Tell me, do you have a large population to go through?"

He raised his eyebrows. "Something has upset you." It was a statement, although touched with a note of enquiry.

"Several things have upset me, but none of them is in any way your concern," she replied coolly. "They are not to do with the hangman."

"If they upset you, then it concerns me."

She turned round to find him looking at her with an expression in his eyes that was unmistakably gentle, and something that was more than gentleness. She had never seen such a look in any man's face before, and it disturbed her profoundly. She felt the blood coming to her face and a totally unaccustomed warmth inside her. She looked away quickly, confused.

"That is courteous of you," she said awkwardly, "but they are family matters, and no doubt will sort themselves out in due course."

"Are you still worried about Emily and George Ashworth?"

She had entirely forgotten them, but it seemed an obvious escape from the truth, and he had offered it to her.

"Yes," she lied. "I am concerned that he will hurt her. She is not of his social position, and he will tire of her presently; then she will find her reputation damaged, and have nothing to show for it but a deep hurt to her feelings."

"You believe that because his social position is higher than hers he will not consider marrying her?" he asked.

It seemed a foolish question. She was a little annoyed with him for having asked.

"Of course he won't!" she said tartly. "Men of his situation either marry for family reasons, or for money. Emily has neither."

"Do you admire that?"

She turned round sharply. "Of course not! It is weak, contemptible. But that is the way it is." Then she saw the smile on his face, and something else. Could it conceivably be hope? She felt her skin flame. It was ridiculous! She drew a deep breath and tried hard to control herself.

He was still staring at her, but there was self-mockery in his face now. Very gently he helped her out of her embarrassment.

"I think you worry about Emily too much," he observed. "She is far more practical than you credit. Ashworth may imagine he is calling the pace, but I think it will be Emily who will decide whether he marries her or not. A wife like Emily could be an advantage to a man in his position. She is far cleverer than he is, for a start, and wise enough to hide it sufficiently so that he may suspect it, but never be sure enough for it to make him feel in any way less superior. She will be right, but she will convince him that it was his idea."

"You make her sound extremely—conniving."

"She is." He smiled. "She is in every way opposite from you. Where you charge headlong, Emily will outflank and come up behind."

"And you make *me* sound stupid!"

His smile broadened into a grin. "Not at all. You could not win Ashworth, but then you also have the sense not to want him!"

She relaxed in spite of herself. "Indeed I do not. What have you come for, Mr. Pitt? Surely not to talk about Ashworth and Emily again? Are you really no nearer the hangman?"

"I'm not sure," he said honestly. "Once or twice I've thought we were almost onto him, but then we were proved wrong. If only we knew why! If we just knew why he did it, why those girls? Why not any of a hundred others? Was it no more than chance?"

"But surely—" she faltered, "if it were no more than that—how will you ever find him? He could be anyone at all!"

"I know." He held out no false hope, no comfort, and for that she both praised and blamed him. She wanted comfort, and yet she wanted honesty as well. It seemed she could not have both.

"Is there no connecting link, no person they all knew who might have...?"

"We are still looking. That is why I've come today. I would like to speak to Dora, if I may, and also to Mrs. Dunphy. I've heard that Dora was friendly with the Hiltons' maid, more friendly than she has told us. Possibly she denied it out of fear. A lot of people hide information because they feel murder is scandalous, and even to know anything somehow rubs the scandal onto them. Guilt by association." His mouth turned down at the corners.

"And Mrs. Dunphy? She might have held something back; she hates scandal."

"I'm sure. All good servants do, even more than their masters, if such a thing were possible. But actually I only want her confirmation. It might serve to prevent Dora from being evasive again. Dora might lie to me, but if she is anything like most housemaids, she will not dare lie to the cook."

Charlotte smiled. It was perfectly true.

Then another thought occurred to her. Was that all he wanted to ask? And even if it was, would Dora or Mrs. Dunphy accidentally betray the anguish in the house at the moment? It was a fallacy of self-preservation, of dignity, to suppose that the servants did not know the private quarrels and tears above the stairs. They had eyes and ears, and curiosity. Someone would have overheard. Gossip would be discreet, even sympathetic, but it would be there. Of course it would never go outside the house. Loyalty and pride of establishment were fierce, but they would know.

"Do you wish me to call her in here?" she asked, thinking she would be able to control the situation if she were there to prevent any slips of the tongue. "She won't lie to me either."

Anne Perry

Pitt looked at her, eyes narrowed very slightly.

"Please don't trouble yourself. Besides, I think she might well be reticent in front of you. I don't wish to question her in Mrs. Dunphy's presence either, only to confirm with Mrs. Dunphy first, and then use the information to press Dora. If she did something you would not approve of, she won't say so in front of you, but she might tell me, alone."

She wanted to argue, to find some reason to be present, but she could think of nothing that sounded honest. Yet she must prevent his learning of Papa and the woman. She believed he would feel, as she did, that it was a betrayal, a moral dishonesty that one might try to pardon with one's mind, but could never forget. Respect was gone; one could not trust again.

That was foolish. Pitt was a man, and would no doubt feel as other men did that such things were quite ordinary and to be accepted—as long as women did not do the same, of course. Perhaps she was afraid unnecessarily. Murder was quite a different thing from adultery, to men.

"How is your sergeant?" she asked, in an attempt to delay him until she could think of a reason to prevent him from seeing Dora alone.

"Getting better, thank you." If he was surprised he did not show it.

"Do you have to have another sergeant now?" she went on.

"Yes." He smiled. "You would like him; he's quite an entertaining character. A little like Willie."

"Oh?" The interest she expressed was quite genuine. And it was a few minutes' respite. "I see Willie as a very uneasy policeman."

"Oh, Dickon was uneasy to begin with, but he was obliged to find work very early, and naturally found dishonest employment easier to come by. He gained an excellent knowledge of the underworld, and then, after an extremely narrow squeak, decided it might be safer to profit from his expertise on the side of the law rather than against it." He grinned

246

broadly. "Actually he fell rather seriously in love with a girl socially above him. He promised her he would become respectable if she would marry him. So far he's kept at it."

"Why did he have to go out to work so young?" she was interested to know, as well as still wishing to keep him from the kitchen. The memory of Willie's wry face was clear, and in her mind she saw this Dickon with the same features.

"His father died at a hanging, in 'forty-seven or 'forty-eight, and his mother was left with five children of which he was the youngest; and the other four were girls."

"Oh no! However did she manage? How irresponsible of him to commit a crime that got him hanged!" She could think only of the poor woman with five children to feed.

"He wasn't hanged," Pitt corrected her. "He was killed at a hanging. They used to have public hangings then, and they were considered quite a sporting event."

She did not believe him. "Hanging? Don't be ridiculous. What kind of a person would wish to see some wretched creature taken out to a gibbet and hanged?" She swallowed hard, flaring her nose in disgust.

"Many kinds," he answered seriously. "It used to be quite a spectacle; hundreds of people came to watch, and others came to pick their pockets, to gamble, to sell their muffins and winkles and hot chestnuts in winter. And, of course, the odd dogfight to warm them up.

"The poor crowded into the square, while the quality, the gentlemen, booked rooms in nearby houses with front windows—"

"That's obscene!" she said fiercely. "It's disgusting!"

"They let them for very high rents," he continued as if she had not spoken. "Unfortunately the excitement of the actual hanging often spilled over into the crowd, and fights broke out. Dickon's father was beaten to death in one of these."

He smiled bleakly at her horror. "They don't have public hangings anymore. Now let me speak to Dora. I don't know whether I shall discover whatever it is you are so afraid of, but I must try."

She swallowed hard again.

"I don't know what you mean! Ask Dora anything you wish. There's nothing I am afraid of, except the hangman himself, and we are all afraid of him."

"But you are afraid that he is someone you know, aren't you, Charlotte?"

"Isn't he? Isn't he someone we all know?" she demanded. There was no point in lying anymore. "At least I'm not afraid it's me, in some black, terrible other side of myself I don't know about. But any man who has any imagination at all must have feared just that at least once in the dark hours of the night."

"And you've thought of it for them," he finished softly. "Your father, Dominic, George Ashworth, Maddock, probably the vicar and the sexton too. Which one are you afraid for now, Charlotte?"

She opened her mouth to deny it, then realized it was futile. Instead she simply refused to commit herself.

Pitt touched her hand lightly, and went out of the door into the hallway and the kitchen to find Dora.

Chapter
Twelve

Charlotte went back to her letters since Pitt would not question Dora in her presence. She did not know whether he intended to speak to her again before leaving, or whether he would tell her what Dora had told him if it were of any value. For the first fifteen minutes she could only think of what might be said in the kitchen—whether Pitt would ask about anything other than the Hiltons' maid, or whether, even by accident, he might stumble on the knowledge of Papa and the woman in Cater Street.

When she finally settled to writing, the letters were scrappy, and she feared full of repetition and irrelevancies but, even so, better than letting her mind dwell on the kitchen.

By four o'clock it was darkening outside with fog swirling up from the river and already hanging in haze 'round the gas lamps in the street.

Mama and Emily returned a few minutes later, cold and

dissatisfied with the dress. They requested tea immediately and asked if Sarah were home yet.

"No." Charlotte replied with a slight frown. "Inspector Pitt was here earlier. I'm not even sure if he has gone now."

Mama looked up agitatedly.

"Why was he here?" she asked with an edge to her voice. Was she harbouring the same fear as Charlotte: that somehow he would find out about Papa and the woman? Charlotte did not wish to ask, in case her mother had not even thought of it.

"Something to do with Dora knowing the Hiltons' maid, and not having said so before," she replied.

"Why should Dora lie?" Emily enquired, putting down her cup, still untouched, too hot to drink. "There could be nothing wrong in it if she had."

"Fear, I suppose," Charlotte answered her. "Scandal, and all that. Didn't want to be mixed up with the police. Easier just to deny it."

"Perhaps she didn't know her, and Pitt is wrong?" Emily suggested. "It hardly matters anyway. You know it's quite dark outside. Surely Sarah can't still be trailing around with Martha Prebble on parish work at this hour?"

Caroline stood up and went to the window. There was nothing to see but opaque fog and darkness.

"If she is I shall speak to her very sharply when she returns. Unless someone has been taken ill, there is no need whatsoever to be out as late as this, and on such a wretched night. We shall have to send Maddock to bring her back. She cannot possibly travel alone in this."

"I dare say the vicar will accompany her," Emily observed calmly. "I don't care for him, any more than Charlotte does," she looked sideways at her sister, "but he is not so completely without manners or breeding as to let Sarah walk home alone after dark."

"No, of course not," Caroline came away from the window and sat down, making a determined effort to control herself. "I am just being foolish. I don't know why I should be afraid.

We know where she is, and no doubt she is doing excellent work. Neither death nor birth, unfortunately, restricts itself to convenient weather or times of the day. And illness certainly doesn't. I heard old Mrs. Petheridge was very unwell. Perhaps Sarah is sitting with her?"

"Yes, possibly," Charlotte agreed quickly. She tried to think of some other topic of conversation sufficiently interesting to hold their attention. "Do you think Sir Nigel will marry Miss Decker? She has certainly tried hard enough."

"Probably," Emily said drily. "He is a very silly creature."

They managed to keep the conversation alive for another hour, interspersed with small jobs till Edward returned a few moments after five.

"Where's Sarah?" he asked immediately.

"With the vicar and Mrs. Prebble," Caroline replied, glancing instinctively towards the window.

"At this hour?" Edward raised his eyebrows. "Has there been some emergency? They can hardly be doing ordinary parish work in the dark. Have you any idea what kind of an evening it is?"

"Of course I have!" Caroline said sharply. "I have been out in it myself, and I have eyes to look at it even from here."

"Yes, my dear, I'm sorry," Edward said gently. "It was a foolish question. I am a little concerned about Sarah. She is putting far too much time into this work. I am all for charity, but it is requiring too much of her at the moment. She will wear herself out, and on a night like this she could very well catch a chill."

He had said nothing about the hangman, only about a chill from the fog, and Charlotte felt a sudden rush of warmth towards him for it. Perhaps the woman was an indiscretion he regretted and had been unable to cast off. She stood up and kissed him quickly on the cheek and he was too surprised to respond. She turned at the door and caught his eye. Could it even be gratitude she saw there? She was going to the kitchen to find out what Dora had told Pitt.

"I'm going to see if dinner is progressing satisfactorily,"

she announced. "I don't imagine Dora is upset, but I had as well make sure."

"Why would Dora be upset?" she heard Edward ask as she closed the door.

It appeared the questioning of Dora had elicited very little other than the details of her friendship with the Hiltons' maid, and she returned to the withdrawing room perfectly satisfied.

It was twenty minutes to six when the door from the hall opened and Pitt stood gray-faced on the threshold. Maddock was nowhere to be seen.

Edward turned and then, when he saw who it was, half rose. He was about to require some explanation for Pitt's coming unannounced when he saw the man's face more closely. It was always a mirror of his feelings, and now it showed shock and distress beyond anything they had seen before. His eyes flickered just once to Charlotte, and then back to Edward again.

"For God's sake, man, what is it?" Edward stood up. "Are you ill?" He must be, to look so dreadful.

Pitt struggled forwards, and seemed unable to find them.

Charlotte felt a bitter coldness inside her. "Sarah," she said quietly. "It's Sarah, isn't it?"

Pitt nodded. He shut his eyes. "I'm sorry."

Edward did not seem to understand. "What about Sarah? What's wrong with her? Has there been an accident?" He teetered a little on his feet.

Charlotte stood up and went to him, putting her arm in his and holding on to him hard. She faced Pitt, her heart choking in her throat, pins and needles already numbing her fingers and creeping up her arms. She knew before she spoke what the answer must be.

"The hangman?" she asked. She did not want to know if Sarah too had been molested. It was unbearable.

"Yes," his face was wracked with misery and guilt.

"It can't be!" Edward said, shaking his head a little, uncomprehending, unable to believe. "Why Sarah? Why should anyone want to hurt Sarah?" His voice wavered and he struggled to continue. "She was so. . . ." He stopped, tears running down his face.

Behind them Emily moved to sit with Caroline, putting her arms round her, clinging, hiding her face. Caroline wept deeply and agonizingly, shaking with her grief.

"I don't know," Pitt answered. "God, I don't know."

"Is there anything to do?" Charlotte asked huskily. The pins and needles were up to her elbows, and Pitt's face seemed to swim far away.

"No," he shook his head.

"Where's Maddock?"

"I'm afraid he—wasn't well. He took it very hard. I sent him to fetch some brandy and smelling salts, in case—" he trailed off, not knowing what else to say.

Charlotte gripped her father even harder. "Papa, you had better sit down. There isn't anything to do. There will be things, tomorrow, but tonight it's all finished."

Edward backed obediently towards his chair and his legs seemed to buckle underneath him.

A moment later Maddock came in with a tray, the brandy decanter and glasses. He looked at the ground without speaking. Emily and Caroline did not see him, and he put the smelling salts on the table awkwardly. He was leaving again when Charlotte spoke.

"Maddock, you had better cancel dinner, and ask Mrs. Dunphy to prepare something cold for about eight o'clock, if you please."

He gave her a look of incredulity, and she knew he found her inexplicably cold, as if she did not care. She could not explain to him that she cared abominably, so much that she could not bear to think of it, that doing something practical, concerning herself with the grief of others, was more bearable than thinking of her own. She turned from Maddock to Pitt, and saw again in him the tenderness that had so embarrassed her before, but this time it was like warmth and sweetness enveloping her. She knew he understood what she was doing, and why. She looked away quickly, tears choking her. It was far harder to bear than misunderstanding; there was nothing to fight against.

"Thank you, Inspector Pitt." She tried to keep the wavering in her voice from obliterating her words. "Perhaps if you would ask whatever questions you have tomorrow? There is little we can tell you tonight, except that Sarah left in the early afternoon to visit Mrs. Prebble, and we presumed to do some parish visiting afterwards. If you ask Mrs. Prebble, no doubt she will be able to tell you...what time...." She found herself unable to finish. Suddenly they were not talking about facts, but about Sarah. She could see her clearly in her mind. She forced the picture out. She wanted him to leave before she lost control. "Tomorrow we shall be better able to answer any other questions."

"Of course," he agreed quickly. "It would be better for me to speak to the vicar and Mrs. Prebble now anyway." He turned to Edward again. He seemed unable to look at Caroline. "I'm—I'm sorry," he stammered.

Edward rose to the occasion. "Of course," he said. "I'm sure you have done everything anyone could. Sane men are at a loss in the face of madness. Thank you for coming in person to tell us. Good night, Inspector."

There was nothing to say in the silence after Pitt left. There were no questions, except the one that could not be answered: why Sarah?

It was a long time before anyone moved, and then it was Edward who went to the kitchen to tell the servants formally. Emily took Caroline upstairs. Supper was a cold plate served in the withdrawing room. All except Caroline forced themselves to eat something. At nine o'clock Edward sent Charlotte and Emily upstairs to bed, and waited alone to tell Dominic whenever he might return.

Charlotte went gratefully. Her control was slipping away from her quickly as the evening dragged on. She was suddenly very tired and the effort of stopping the tears was becoming too much.

In her room she undressed, hung up her clothes, washed her face in hot water, then cold, took her hair down and brushed it, then climbed into bed and at last cried with all her heart until she had no more strength left.

The following morning was bleak and cold. Charlotte woke up and for a few minutes everything was as always, but then memory returned. Sarah was dead. She had to say it over several times. It was a little like the morning after Sarah's marriage; then, too, a lifelong relationship had gone. Sarah was no longer her sister, but Dominic's wife. She could look back on all the years of her childhood. It was Sarah who had first showed her how to button her own shoes, Sarah with whom she had played at dolls, Sarah's clothes she had grown into, Sarah who had taught her to read, Sarah in whom she had confided her first admirations and heartaches. Something had gone from her life when Sarah had married and was no longer especially hers. But that was a natural part of growing up; she had always known it would happen one day. This was different. It was not natural. It was monstrous. And this time there was no envy in it, only wrenching, unbearable loss.

Had Sarah known, had she seen the face of her murderer? Had she felt the choking, heart-tearing fear? Please, God, let it have been quick!

There was no point in lying here thinking. Better to get up, find something practical to do. It would be worse for Mama. There was something terrible beyond understanding to lose a child, a person to whom you have given life from your own body.

Downstairs everyone else was also up and dressed, searching for something to do.

Breakfast was almost silent. Dominic looked white and his eyes did not meet anyone else's. Charlotte watched him for a little while. Then, afraid that he would notice, she looked down at her toast. The mere mechanics of eating became exaggerated, something to do to occupy one's mind.

Where had Dominic been last night? Was it fair to wonder if Sarah would not have gone out if he had been at home, or if she had expected him? Or had the hangman wanted her, and, if not yesterday, then some other time?

Was he some lunatic from the fogbound slums driven mad by filth and poverty till all he could think of was to kill? Or was he someone from Cater Street who knew them all, who watched and waited for his chance, who followed, perhaps even spoke to them, walked with them, and then suddenly drew out the wire, and—

She must not think about Sarah. It was past now; whatever pain there had been, whatever terror or knowledge, was finished.

Had she known him?

What did he feel this morning? Was he sitting somewhere at breakfast? Was he hungry? Was he alone in some dirty room, eating bread, or was he sitting at a polished dining room table with a family round him, eating eggs and kidneys and toast? Perhaps talking to others, even children? What would he talk about? Had his family even the faintest idea of what he was, where he had been? Were they afraid as she had been afraid? Had they been through all the same suspicions—the first idea, the self-disgust and guilt for having thought of such things, then the examination of little things remembered from the past, fitting them in with the facts and at last having the phantom of fear take definite shape?

And what was he thinking himself? Or did he not know? Was he sitting somewhere wondering as much as she was, perhaps even thinking the same things, looking at others, his father, his brother, fearing for them?

She looked across at Dominic again. Where had he been last night? Did he know—exactly? Pitt would ask him.

Breakfast was cleared away and everyone sought something to do until the police would arrive and begin the questions which had to come.

Mercifully they did not have long to wait. Pitt and his new sergeant arrived before nine. Pitt looked tired—as if he had been up long into the night—and unusually tidy. Oddly enough, it made him look uncomfortable, prepared for some ordeal.

"Good morning," he said formally. "I'm sorry, but this is necessary."

Everyone acknowledged that. It was easier to get it over with. They all sat down except Dominic, who remained standing, and waited for Pitt to begin.

He did not temper his approach. "You were out last night, Mr. Corde?"

"Yes," Dominic coloured painfully. Watching him, Charlotte felt that he also wondered whether, if he had been at home, Sarah would not have gone out.

"Where?"

"What?" Dominic seemed to be lost.

"Where were you?" Pitt repeated.

"At my club."

"Again? Was anyone with you?"

The blood drained from Dominic's face as he realized the possibilities in Pitt's mind. Even though it was Sarah who was dead, he was not excluded as a suspect.

"Yes...yes," he stammered. "Several people. I can't remember all their names. D-do you need them?"

"I'd better have them, Mr. Corde, before you forget—or they do."

Dominic opened his mouth, perhaps to protest, and gave up. He reeled off half a dozen names. "I—I think those are correct. I think they were all there last night. I didn't spend all evening with any one of them, you understand."

"No doubt we shall be able to piece things together. Why were you at your club last night, Mr. Corde? Was there some particular function?"

Dominic looked surprised, then confused as he understood Pitt's meaning. Why was he not at home?

"Er—no, nothing special."

Pitt did not pursue it further. He turned instead to Caroline, decided against it, and spoke to Charlotte.

"Mrs. Corde left in the early afternoon to visit the vicar's wife?"

"Yes, a little after luncheon."

"Alone?"

"Yes." Charlotte looked down. She remembered with pain, and now guilt, the scene of such a short time ago. It was impossible to understand how the whole of one's life could change so quickly.

"Why?"

She looked back at him. "I offered to go with her, but she preferred to go alone. She wanted to speak to Martha Prebble in private, and then perhaps to go on and do some parish visiting." She found it hard to speak; her throat ached and she had to stop.

"She did a lot of parish work," Emily said quietly.

"Parish work? You mean she visits the poor, the sick?" Unconsciously he used the present tense.

"Yes."

"Do you know whom she intended to visit yesterday?"

"No. What did Martha say? Mrs. Prebble."

"That Sarah mentioned several people to her, but that she left the vicar's house quite late, and she did not say precisely whom she meant to visit, or in which order. Mrs. Prebble herself was feeling unwell, and said she advised her against going alone, but Sarah would not listen. Apparently there were several sick...." His voice trailed off.

"Do you think..." she began, "...just chance?"

"I don't know. Perhaps. Possibly he was just waiting for someone—anyone—"

"Then how in God's name will you ever find him?" Edward shouted. "You can hardly fill the streets with policemen till he strikes again. He'll merely wait until you leave. He could walk past you, speak to you, tip his hat, and you wouldn't even know him from—from the vicar, or one of your own!"

No one answered him.

"You said she did a great deal of parish work lately?" Pitt

began again. "Did she do it at regular times, and always with the same people?"

Dominic stared at him. "You think he wanted...Sarah? I mean Sarah, in particular?"

"I don't know, Mr. Corde. Do you know anyone who loved or hated her enough to do that?"

"Loved!" Dominic said incredulously. "God! Do you mean me?"

It was the first time anyone had said it aloud. Charlotte looked at their faces, trying to see who had thought of it before. It looked as if only Papa had not. She looked back at Pitt, waiting.

"I don't know who I mean, Mr. Corde, or the hunt would be over."

"But it could be me!" Dominic's voice rose in hysteria. "Even though it was Sarah this time, you still think it could be me!"

"Are you sure it isn't?"

Dominic looked at him in silence for several moments. "Unless I'm completely insane, capable of becoming another person I know nothing of, I couldn't have hurt Sarah. I'm not really sure how much I loved her, how much I love anyone, but far too much to have hurt her deliberately. Accidentally— I know—and through stubbornness, both of us—but not, not anything like that."

Charlotte could not keep the tears back. If only Sarah could have known that much for certain. Why is it that one does not tell people things while there is time? One lets such trivial things matter.

Now she must not upset all the others by weeping in front of them. She stood up.

"Excuse me," she said quickly and walked out; to run would betray her need and its urgency.

It was not Dominic Emily was afraid for, but her father. She had never considered the existence of a darker side to her sister's husband. He was no more than he seemed to be;

handsome, pleasant-natured if a little spoiled, witty when he chose, and quite often kind—but also without great imagination. It was funny that Charlotte should have fallen in love with him. He was utterly wrong for her and would have made her dreadfully unhappy. He would never have matched her depth of feeling and she would have spent her whole life seeking for something that was not there.

But Papa was quite different. There were obviously hungers in him that none of them had recognized before. And he had been either unwilling or unable to prevent himself from satisfying them.

Was the woman in Cater Street the only one? She was an old woman now, according to Sarah. When Papa had finished with her, who had replaced her? That was something that she thought had not occurred to the others.

But it occurred to Emily as she sat sewing in the afternoon, and she wondered if it would occur to Pitt when he found out, which he undoubtedly would, either from some gossip in the neighbourhood about Sarah's visit, or from some slip of the tongue by one of the servants, or possibly even from Charlotte. She was about as transparent as water! Or perhaps he had even been to speak to the woman himself. He might be inelegant, and of very ordinary birth, but he was far from stupid.

Anyway, Emily thought, she had better accustom herself to thinking well of him, because no doubt he would have the courage to make an offer for Charlotte, and she might well take him if she had the courage and the sense. Papa would hum and haw, and Grandmama would have a fit, but that did not matter.

Unless of course Papa really had done something more serious than keep a mistress, or even a series of mistresses? In which case they would all be ruined and the question of marriage to anyone would be moot. Surely he could not have? She could not really believe it, but neither could she dismiss the fear from the back of her mind until she had done something about it. She knew that he was alone in the library.

The abominable vicar would be duty-bound to call some time today or tomorrow, now that the police had gone, for the time being at least. Better to get this over with.

Edward looked up with surprise when she went into the library. "Emily? Are you seeking something to read?"

"No," she sat down in the other big leather chair opposite him.

"What then? You find it hard to be alone? I confess, I'm glad of your company also."

She smiled very slightly. This was going to be harder than she had anticipated.

"Papa?"

"Yes, my dear?" How very tired he looked. She had forgot how old he was.

"Papa, the woman in Cater Street—how long is it since she was your mistress?" Better to be direct. She could be devious with most people, but she had never been able to deceive him with any success.

"How very like Charlotte you are at times," he smiled with profound regret, and she knew instinctively he was thinking neither of her nor of Charlotte, but of Sarah.

"How long?" she repeated. It had to be got over now; to have to try again would only extend the pain.

He looked at her. Was he weighing up how much she knew? Whether even now he could lie, evade?

"We know about her," she said cruelly. "Sarah went to visit her, as a charity. She discovered the truth. Please Papa, don't make it worse?" Her voice wavered. She hated doing this, but the doubt hurt even more. The suspense was a cancer deeper than the clean wound of knowing. She must not let him lie now, degrade himself.

He was still looking at her. She wanted to shut her eyes, to withdraw the question, but she knew it was too late.

He gave in. "A long time," he answered with a little sigh. "It was all very brief, that part of it. It was all over a year or two after you were born. But I still liked her. Your mother was often busy—with you. You didn't know her then, but she

Anne Perry

was not unlike Sarah; a little stubborn, always thinking she knew best." Suddenly his eyes filled with tears and Emily looked away, to save him embarrassment. She stood up and walked to the window, to give him time to regain his control.

"Was there anyone after her?" she asked. Better to get it all over in one attempt.

"No," he sounded surprised. "Of course not! Why do you ask, Emily?"

She wanted to think of a lie quickly, so that he should not ever know what she had suspected. Idiotically, now she wanted to protect him. She had thought she would never forgive him for having hurt Mama, but instead here she was wanting to shield him as if he had been the injured one. She did not understand herself, which was a new experience, but not an entirely unpleasant one.

"For Mama, of course," she answered. "One can overlook one mistake, especially if it happened a long time ago. One cannot forget something that has been repeated over and over again."

"Do you think your mother will feel the same way?" His voice sounded pathetically hopeful. She was a little embarrassed by it.

"I should ask her," she said quickly. "I believe she is lying down upstairs. She is grieving very much for Sarah, you know."

He stood up. "Yes, I know. I don't think I realized how much she meant to me either." He put his arm round her and kissed her gently, on the brow. She found herself suddenly clinging to him, crying for Sarah, for herself, for everybody, because it was all too much to bear.

In the late afternoon George Ashworth called to express his condolences. Naturally these were extended to the entire family, and therefore he was seen formally in the withdrawing room by Edward. It was necessary that afternoon tea should be offered, and equally necessary that it be refused. Afterwards Ashworth asked if he might speak with Emily.

She received him in the library, as somewhere where they might be sure not to risk interruption.

He closed the door behind him. "Emily, I'm so sorry. Perhaps I should not have come so soon, but I could not bear to let you think I was unaffected, that I was not concerned for your grief. I suppose it is foolish to ask if there is anything I can do?"

Emily was touched and surprised that he should have feelings deeper than those required by good manners. She had desired, indeed planned, to marry him for some time; indeed she quite genuinely liked him, but had not perceived in him such sensitivity. It was a pleasant revelation, and curiously robbed her of some of the control she had just recently managed to acquire.

"Thank you," she said carefully. "It is kind of you to offer, but there really isn't anything to be done; except endure it, until we can feel it is time to take up our lives again."

"I suppose they still have no idea who?"

"I don't think so. I'm beginning to wonder if they ever will. In fact I heard some silly servant the other day suggest that it was not a human being at all, but some creature of the supernatural, a vampire or a demon of some sort." She made a little choking sound, which was intended as a laugh of scorn, but died away.

"You haven't entertained the idea?" he asked awkwardly, "have you?"

"Of course not!" she said with disgust. "He is someone from Cater Street or nearby, someone who is afflicted with a terrible madness that drives him to kill. I don't know whether he kills people for any reason, or just because they happen to be there when his madness strikes. But he's perfectly human, of that I'm sure."

"Why are you so sure, Emily?" He sat down on the side of one of the armchairs.

She looked at him curiously. This was the man she intended to marry, to spend the rest of her life dependent upon. He was uncommonly handsome and, far more importantly,

263

he pleased her—the more today because of his unexpected concern for her.

"Because I don't believe in monsters," she said frankly. "Evil men, certainly, and madness, but not monsters. I daresay he would like us to believe he is such, for then we could cease to look for him among ourselves. Perhaps we would even cease to look for him at all."

"What a practical creature you are, Emily," he said with a smile. "Do you ever do anything foolish?"

"Not often," she said frankly, then smiled also. "Would you prefer me to?"

"Great heavens, no! You are the ideal combination. You look feminine and fragile, you know when to speak and when to remain silent; and yet you behave with all the excellent sense of the best of men."

"Thank you," she said with a flush of genuine pleasure.

"In fact," he looked down at the floor, then up at her again, "if I had any sense I should marry you."

She took in her breath, held it for a second, then let it out.

"And have you?" she said very carefully.

His smile widened into a grin. "Not usually. But I think on this occasion I shall make an exception."

"Are you making me a proposal, George?" She turned to look at him.

"Don't you know?"

"I would like to be quite sure. It would be uncommonly silly to make an error in a matter of such importance."

"Yes, I am?" He made it a question by the expression in his eyes. He looked vulnerable, as if it mattered to him.

She found herself liking him even more than she had thought.

"I should be most honoured," she said honestly. "And I accept. You had better speak to Papa in a few weeks' time, when it is more suitable."

"Indeed I shall," he stood up. "And I shall make perfectly sure he finds my offer acceptable. Now I had better take my leave, before I have outstayed propriety. Good afternoon, Emily, my dear."

Chapter
Thirteen

That evening Edward decided that he would no longer
require Caroline to attempt to soothe Grandmama or to put
up with her criticism and bad humour. He sent Maddock with
a message to Susannah that as soon as possible Grandmama
would be dispatched with her necessary clothes and toiletries,
and that they did not look to see her return until such time
as they should feel themselves recovered from their bereavement. It would be no pleasure for Susannah, but that was
one of the burdens of family life, and she would have to make
the best of it.

Grandmama complained with bitter self-pity and at least
one dizzy spell, but no one paid her the least attention. Emily
was in a world of her own. Edward and Caroline seemed at
last to have come to terms with the whole subject of Mrs.
Attwood. The previous evening they had talked for a long
time, and Caroline had learned many things, not only about
Edward, but about loneliness, about the feeling of being out-

side a close circle of dependence, and about herself. Now there was a new perception between them, and they seemed to have much to say to each other.

Dominic for once exercised none of his usual diplomacy, and Charlotte was even less than ordinarily inclined to mince her words. Accordingly, the following morning Caroline and Emily assisted Grandmama with her packing, and at ten o'clock accompanied her in the carriage to Susannah's.

Charlotte was thus alone when the vicar and Martha Prebble came to formally convey their sympathy and deep shock at the loss of Sarah. Dora showed them in.

"My dear Miss Ellison," the vicar began solemnly, "I can hardly find words to express our grief to you."

Charlotte could not help hoping he would continue to fail to find them, but such was far from the case.

"What a monstrous evil walks among us," he went on, taking her hand, "that could strike down a woman like your sister, in the prime of her life, and leave her husband and her family bereft. I assure you all the righteous men and women of the parish join me in extending all our deepest condolences to you, and your poor mother."

"Thank you," Charlotte withdrew her hand. "I am quite sure of the best wishes of you all, and I shall inform my parents and my sister, and of course my brother-in-law, of your kindness."

"It is our duty," the vicar replied, apparently unaware that his remark would rob the visit of any value in Charlotte's eyes.

"Is there anything we can do?" Martha offered.

Charlotte turned to her in relief, but it was short-lived. Martha's face was more haggard than she had ever seen it before. Her eyes were bedded in dark hollows, her hair hanging like string in loops over her ears.

"Your sympathy is the greatest help," Charlotte said gently, moved to a profound pity for the woman. Surely to live with such a duty-suffocated creature as the vicar must be almost more than any human, caring woman could stand?

"When will it be convenient for me to consult with your father about the—er—arrangements?" the vicar went on without looking at Martha. "These things must be done, you know; a proper order preserved. We return to the dust from which we came, and our souls to the judgement of God."

There was no answer to that, so Charlotte returned to the first question.

"I have no idea, but I would have thought it appropriate to speak with my brother-in-law, at least to begin with." She was delighted to find some point of propriety on which to correct him. "If he feels unable to do so, then, of course, I'm sure Papa will deal with the matter."

The vicar endeavoured to hide his annoyance. He smiled, showing his teeth, but his cheeks coloured faintly and his eyes were hard.

"Of course," he agreed. "I had thought, perhaps—an older man—the grief—"

"It may quite possibly be so," Charlotte was not about to give him the slightest victory. She smiled also, equally coldly. "But it would be an added unkindness not to consult him, an unnecessary rudeness, I feel?"

The muscles along the vicar's face tightened.

"Have the police made even the slightest progress towards discovering the perpetrator of these horrendous crimes? I understand you are—somewhat close—to one of the—policemen." He invested the last word with the same tone he might have used for rat catchers or those who remove the kitchen waste. There was a gleam of pleasure in his eyes.

"I don't know whom you can have been listening to, Vicar, to gather such an impression." Charlotte looked him straight in the face. "Have the servants been talking?"

The colour washed up his face in a wave of anger.

"I do not listen to servants, Miss Ellison! And I take it unkindly that you should suggest such a thing. I am not some gossiping woman!"

"It was not intended as an insult, Vicar," Charlotte lied without the slightest qualm. "Since I am a woman myself,

I would not have chosen that phrase in order to be derogatory."

"Indeed, of course not," he said tartly. "God made woman, as He made man—the weaker vessel, of course, but still the creation of the Almighty."

"I understood everything was the creation of God," Charlotte was going to push every prick home. "But it is indeed comforting to be reminded that we are. To answer your question, I am not aware that the police have made any further discoveries in the course of their investigations, but of course it is not incumbent on them to advise me if they have."

"I see the whole matter has preyed upon your mind." The vicar altered his tone to one of sententiousness. "Quite natural. It is far too great a burden for one of your tender birth and years to bear. You must lean upon the church, and put your trust in the Lord Almighty to help you through this crisis. Read your Bible every day; you will find great comfort in it. Observe its commandments diligently, and it will bring joy to your soul even through the darkest vicissitudes of this vale of tears."

"Thank you," Charlotte said drily. She had hitherto enjoyed her Bible, but this was quite enough to sour it for her. "I will pass on your advice. I am sure we shall all benefit from it."

"And never fear that the wicked shall escape punishment. If they do not meet the justice of this world, then God's vengeance will catch up with them in the eternities, and they shall perish in hell fire! The wages of sin is death. The lusts of the flesh consume in everlasting fire the souls of the wicked and no man shall escape. No, not the least thought that pursues the pleasures of the flesh shall go unknown in the great judgement!"

Charlotte shivered. She found the idea of comfort in such a philosophy appalling. She had thoughts she was ashamed of, hungers and dreams she would far rather were not known, and as she needed her own forgiven, she would forgive another's.

"Surely thoughts that are controlled," she said hesitantly, "and not acted upon—"

Martha looked up suddenly, her face white, the muscles in her jaw clenching. Her voice was rough when she spoke, as if it would not entirely obey her.

"All sin is sin, my dear. The thought is father to the wish, and the wish father to the deed. Therefore the thought itself is evil, and must be plucked out, eradicated like a poisonous weed that will rise and choke the seeds of the Lord's word in you. If thy right eye offend thee, pluck it out! Better a limb should be chopped off, than the whole body should become infected and perish!"

"I . . . I hadn't thought of it like that," Charlotte stammered. She was embarrassed by Martha's intensity, by the passion she felt just beneath the surface of these words. She was almost tangibly conscious of some deep pain in the room with her, something beyond all her previous experience. It frightened her, because she did not know how to comfort Martha.

"You must," Martha said urgently. "That is how it is. Sin is ever-present, deep in our hearts and minds, the devil striving to claim us for his own, seeking the weaknesses of the flesh, seeking to govern us. He is cleverer than we are, and he never sleeps. Remember that, Charlotte! Always be on your guard. Pray continually for the saving grace of Our Redeemer to show you the Evil One in his true light, that you may recognize him, and tear him out of your bosom, destroy his influence, and remain clean." She suddenly stopped and stared down at her hands in her lap. "I have the great blessing of a man of God in my house to guide me. God has been extremely good to me, to save me from all my weaknesses, and show me the way. I am not sure I can ever be worthy of such a blessing."

"There, there, my dear," the vicar put his hand on her shoulder. "I am sure we all receive blessings appropriate to our deserts, ultimately. You have no need to chastise yourself. God made women to be the handmaids of His servants, and you have acquitted yourself excellently in your calling. You never cease to labour for the poor and the fallen. I'm sure it does not go unseen in heaven."

"It does not go unseen on earth either," Charlotte said quickly. "Sarah was always saying what wonderful work you do." She found herself embarrassingly near to tears again at the mention of Sarah's name. Above all things she did not wish to weep in front of the vicar.

"Sarah." An indescribable look came over Martha's face. She seemed to struggle with some inner torment, a mighty effort to control herself which lasted visibly, and to Charlotte's unbearable pity, for several moments.

"I'm sure she rests in peace now." Charlotte put her hand over Martha's, forgetting her own grief and attempting to ease the other woman's. "If all we are told of heaven is true, we should not grieve for her, but only for ourselves because we miss her."

"Heaven?" Martha repeated. "May God be merciful to forgive her all her sins, and remember only her virtues, and wash her clean in the blood of Christ."

"Amen," the vicar said sonorously. "Now, my dear Miss Ellison, we must leave you to your deliberations and such privacy as you may require. Please advise your brother-in-law that I shall be available to him at whatever hour is convenient. Come, Martha, my dear, we have other duties to perform. Good morning, Miss Ellison."

"Good morning, Vicar." Charlotte held out her hand to Martha. "Good morning, Mrs. Prebble. I am sure Mama will be most touched by your sympathy."

The vicar and Martha departed and Charlotte sat down hard on the overstuffed chair in the withdrawing room feeling suddenly cold and painfully unhappy.

Naturally Charlotte reported the substance of the vicar's call when Mama and Emily returned for luncheon. No comment was passed, except the acknowledgement required by courtesy.

272

Mama returned to her room to spend the afternoon writing the necessary letters to inform other members of the family, godparents, cousins, of Sarah's death. Emily found something to do in the kitchen. Charlotte busied herself with mending. It was really Millie's job, but Charlotte wished for something to keep her from idleness; Millie would have to find another task, perhaps even doing the ironing again.

It was nearly three when Pitt came again. For the first time she admitted freely that she was pleased to see him.

"Charlotte," he took one of her hands gently. His touch was warm, and she did not wish to withdraw; indeed her mind went ahead of her wishes to think of more.

"Good afternoon, Inspector," she said formally. She must keep control. "What can we do this time? Have you thought of some further questions?"

"No," he smiled ruefully. "I can think of nothing else. I came merely to see you. I hope I do not need an excuse."

She found herself embarrassed and unable to answer. It was ridiculous. No man had embarrassed her in this fashion except Dominic, and with Dominic it had been an empty confusion, without any end she could see. This time she hoped profoundly, with shaking heart, what the end might be.

She withdrew her hand. "Still, I should like to know if you have any further...information? Some beliefs perhaps?"

"Some," he looked at the chair, questioning if he might sit down. She nodded and he relaxed into it, still watching her. "But it is only the faintest idea as yet. I cannot see it clearly, and perhaps when I do there will be nothing there."

She wanted to tell him about the distress she felt for Martha Prebble, the sense of her deep pain that had filled the room, her own helplessness in the face of something she thought she had seen, but not understood.

"Charlotte? What is troubling you? Has something happened since I was here last?"

She turned to look at him. For once she was not quite sure how to put her thoughts into words, a failing she was not accustomed to. It was difficult to express the sense of oppres-

sion that had weighed on her during and after the Prebbles'
visit without sounding foolish, over-imaginative. Yet she
wished to tell him, it would comfort her profoundly if he
understood. Perhaps he would even be able to dismiss it,
show her it was a fancy.

He was still waiting, apparently knowing she was seeking
words.

"The vicar and Mrs. Prebble were here this morning," she
began.

"Natural enough," he was listening. "He was bound to
call." He shifted his weight. "I know you dislike him. I must
say I have the greatest trouble being civil to him myself."
He smiled wryly. "I imagine it is even harder for you."

She glanced at him, not sure for a moment if he were
mocking her. He was, but there was tenderness in his face
as well as amusement. For a moment the warmth of it, the
sweetness of pleasure it brought her drove Martha Prebble
from her mind.

"Why should that have upset you?" he brought her back
to the present.

She turned away, so his look should not disturb her. "I've
always felt ambivalent about Martha." She was seriously
trying now to tell him what was still struggling for form in
her mind. "Her talk about sin is so depressing. She sounds
like the vicar, seeing evil where I believe there is only perhaps a little foolishness which passes anyway with time and
responsibility. People like the vicar always seem bent on
spoiling pleasure, as if pleasure itself were against God. I
can see that some pleasures are, or that they beguile one
from the things one ought to do; but—"

"Perhaps he sees that as his duty?" Pitt suggested. "It's
clear-cut, easier than preaching charity, and certainly easier
than practicing it."

"I suppose so. And if I lived with someone like him for a
long time I should learn to feel the same way as Martha
Prebble does. Perhaps her father was a vicar, too. I never
thought of that before."

"And what is your other feeling?" he asked. "You said you were ambivalent."

"Oh, pity, of course. And I think some admiration, too. You know, she really does try to live up to all that that wretched man teaches. And more. She is always visiting, caring for the sick and the lonely. I sometimes wonder how much she believes what she says about sin, or if she just adds it out of habit, and because she thinks she ought to, because she knows he would."

"I dare say she doesn't know herself. But that is not all, Charlotte. Why did they disturb you especially today? They have always been like this; you could not have expected anything else."

What was the unease she had felt? She wanted to tell him, indeed she needed to. "She was talking about the need for punishment, even things like 'if thine eye offend thee, pluck it out,' and cutting off hands and things. It seemed so...so extreme, as if she were frightened of it—I mean really panicked. She talked about washing in the blood of Christ, and things." She looked at him. "And she spoke about Sarah as if there were evil in her, I mean not just general weakness, as there is in all of us, but as if she knew of something. I suppose that's what upset me—she spoke as if she knew something I didn't."

He frowned. "Charlotte," he began slowly, "please don't be angry with me, but do you think Sarah confided in her something that she did not tell you? Is it possible?"

Charlotte was repelled by the thought, yet she remembered that Sarah had wanted to see Martha alone; she had trusted Martha. Sometimes it was easier to speak to someone outside the family.

"Perhaps," she admitted reluctantly. "I don't think so. I don't know what Sarah could have done, but it could be—"

He stood up and came closer to her. She could feel his presence as if it were a warmth. She did not wish to move away. Indeed, she wished it were not immodest, improper to touch him.

"It could be something very slight," he said gently. "Something that was of little importance, but to Martha Prebble, in the vicar's eyes, a sin needing forgiveness. And for heaven's sake don't confuse the vicar with God. I'm sure God is nothing like as self-righteous—"

In spite of herself she smiled. "Don't be ridiculous. God is love. I'm sure the vicar never loved anyone in his life." She was touched by a bleak knowledge. "Including Martha." She took a deep breath. "No wonder poor Martha is desperate, underneath all her good works, and her condemnation of sin. Not to be loved, not to love—"

He touched her arm very lightly. "And you, Charlotte? Do you still love Dominic?"

She felt herself colour with shame that she should have been so obvious.

"What made you believe—that I—?"

"Of course, I knew." There was regret in his voice, a memory of pain. "I love you. How could I remain unaware that you loved someone else?"

"Oh."

"You haven't answered me. Do you still love him?"

"Don't you know that I don't? Or does it not matter to you now?" She was almost sure of what the answer would be, and yet she needed to have it spoken.

He turned her arm firmly till she was facing him.

"It matters to me. I don't want to be second best?" There was a lift in his voice making it a question.

Very slowly she looked up at him. At first she was a little afraid, embarrassed by the power of feeling in his face, and by the depth and the sweetness of her own feeling. Then she stopped hiding, let go of pretence.

"You are not second best," she said clearly. She put up her fingers and touched his cheek, at first shyly. "Dominic was only a dream. I'm awake now, and you are the first best."

He reached up and took hold of her hand, keeping it to his face, his lips.

"And you have the courage to marry an ordinary police-man, Charlotte?"

"Do you doubt my courage, Mr. Pitt? Surely at least you cannot doubt my self-will?"

Slowly he smiled, more and more widely until it was a grin.

"Then I shall prepare for battle with your father." His face became sober again, "but I'll wait until this business is settled, and a suitable time has passed."

"You can settle it?" she asked doubtfully.

"I think so. I have a feeling the answer is just beyond us, only just. I have caught a glimpse of something grotesque, something we have not even dreamed before. I cannot grasp it yet, but it is there. I have felt its darkness and its pain touch me."

She shivered. "Be careful. He has not killed a man yet, but if his own life is in danger—"

"I shall. Now I must go. There are a few more questions, things that may help to make it plain, to put a face to the shadow. It is so close, a little thought...."

She moved away slowly, the shadow of the hangman out-side her, and a white, singing happiness inside. She showed him to the door herself.

The following day arrangements were being made for Sarah's funeral and everyone was busy when Millie came in with a note to say that Martha Prebble had been taken ill, and been confined to her bed.

"Oh dear, that really is too much!" Caroline said in ex-asperation. "She was going to deal with so many of the de-tails, especially at the church. And I don't even know what she has done so far!" She sat down hard in the wooden chair behind her. "I suppose I shall have to write a list of questions and send one of the servants 'round to her. It seems heartless, if the poor creature is ill, but what else can I do? And it's raining!"

"We can't send a servant, Mama," Charlotte said wearily.

"The least we can do is go ourselves. She visits all the sick in the parish, takes them things, even sits up with them all night if they are alone. It would be unpardonable if now, when she is ill, all we can do is send a servant with a message to know how far she has got in making arrangements on our behalf. One of us must go, and take her something."

"She will have plenty of things," Emily pointed out. "We cannot be the only people to know. It will be all 'round the parish. You know what gossips they are."

"And quite possibly they will all think as you do, that someone else will call," Charlotte argued. "Anyway, that isn't the point."

"What is the point?"

"The point is that we should take her something, even if her house is bulging at the walls with things, to show that we care."

Emily raised her eyebrows. "I didn't think you did care! In fact I thought you were indifferent to Martha, and positively disliked the vicar."

"I do. That is especially when one should take something! She cannot help being unlikeable. So would you be, I daresay, if you had lived all your life married to the vicar!"

"I should be worse than unlikeable," Emily said tartly. "I should be quite mad by now. I think he is an appalling man!"

"Emily, please!" Caroline was almost to the point of tears. "I cannot spare both of you. Emily, will you make sure we have informed everyone we should have, go over my list again, and check those we can be sure will attend, then go over the catering arrangements with Mrs. Dunphy. Charlotte, you had better go to the kitchen and find something to take to Martha, if you insist. And for goodness' sake, find out as tactfully as you can how far she has got with the arrangements at the church. And you had better not forget to find out precisely what is the matter, if it is tactful. It may not be. I must know, or I shall appear to be callous."

"Yes, Mama. What shall I take her?"

"Since we don't know what is the nature of her illness, it is a little difficult to say. See if Mrs. Dunphy has some egg custard. She is very good at it, and I know Martha's cook has a heavy hand."

Mrs. Dunphy had no egg custard ready, and it was the middle of the afternoon before she had prepared one and sent a message upstairs to Charlotte to tell her it was ready.

Charlotte put on her cloak and hat, then went down to the kitchen to collect it.

"There you are, Miss Charlotte." Mrs. Dunphy gave her a basket, neatly packed with a folded napkin on the top.

"Egg custard in a dish there, and I put in a small jar of preserves and a little beef tea as well. The poor soul. I hope she feels better soon. Too much for her, all this tragedy, I expect. She knew all of those poor girls. And she does so much, for the poor and the like. Never stops. Time someone showed her a little kindness, I say."

"Yes, Mrs. Dunphy, thank you." Charlotte took the basket. "I'm sure she'll be very grateful."

"Take her my best wishes, will you, Miss Charlotte?"

"Of course." She turned round to leave, and felt a sudden icy fear as she saw on the side table a long, thin wire with a handle on one end. The coldness rippled through her as if someone were holding the thing, as if only lately it had been pulled tight into the flesh of someone's throat.

"Mrs. Dunphy," she stammered. "Wh—what in heaven's name—"

Mrs. Dunphy followed her eyes. "Oh, Miss Charlotte," she said with a laugh. "Why, that's only an ordinary cheese cutter. Bless my soul! If you were a little fonder of cooking, you'd have known that. What did you think—oh my, saints alive! Did you think that was a garotting wire! Oh my!" she sat down hard. "Oh my. Why, just about every kitchen has one of those. Cuts the cheese nice and clean, better than a knife; knife sticks to it. Miss Charlotte, should you be going out alone? It'll be dark in an hour or two, and I shouldn't be surprised if the rain stops and there's not a fog."

"I have to go, Mrs. Dunphy. Mrs. Prebble is ill, and apart from that, we need to know about the arrangements for Miss Sarah's funeral."

Mrs. Dunphy's face dropped and Charlotte was afraid she was going to dissolve in tears. She patted her on the arm and made her escape quickly.

It was cold and clammy outside, and she walked as rapidly as possible, keeping her cloak wrapped tightly round her and drawn up round her neck. It stopped raining just as she turned the corner into Cater Street; the sky was dry but heavy when she reached the Prebbles'.

The maid let her in and she was led straight to Martha's bedroom. It was very dark, full of furniture and surprisingly comfortless, so unlike her own with its pictures and ornaments and books with pictures in them, relics of childhood.

Martha was sitting propped up in bed with a treatise on the sermons of John Knox. Her face was haggard and she looked as if she had woken from a nightmare, its figures still shadowing her. She smiled as soon as she saw Charlotte, but it was an effort.

Charlotte sat down on the bed and put the basket between them.

"I'm so sorry to hear you are ill," she said genuinely. "I've brought a few things. I hope they will comfort you." She took the napkin off the basket to show her what was inside. "Mama and Emily send their regards, and Mrs. Dunphy, our cook you know, wished to be remembered to you, spoke of how much you do for everyone."

"That was most kind of her," Martha tried to smile. "Please thank her for me, and of course your mother and Emily."

"Is there anything I can do for you?" Charlotte offered. "Is there anything you wish? Do you need any letters written, any small duties that I can help with?"

"I cannot think of anything."

"Has the doctor called? You look exceedingly pale to me."

"No, I don't think I have any need to trouble him."

"You should. I'm sure he would not regard it as a trouble, but rather his duty and his calling."

"I promise you I shall send for him, if I do not recover soon."

Charlotte put the basket down on the floor.

"I dislike having to mention such a subject when you are ill, and have already done so much for us, but Mama would like to know what arrangements are yet to be made for Sarah's funeral, with regard to the church?"

An indescribable look passed over Martha's face and again Charlotte had the uneasy feeling she had touched some deep nerve of pain.

"You don't need to be concerned. Please tell your Mama it is all taken care of. Fortunately I was not overcome before I had finished everything."

"Are you sure? It seems too much for you to have done. I do hope it was not work on our behalf that hastened your illness?"

"I doubt it, but it was the least I could do. It behooves us well—to—" her voice became strained and she licked her lips, "to do what we can for the dead. They are no longer of this world. They will put off the corruption of the flesh, rise to a just judgement, and, washed in the blood of Christ, the elect will sit at the feet of God forever. Sin will be done away with."

Charlotte was embarrassed. She could think of no answer, but it seemed as if Martha were talking more to herself than to Charlotte anyway.

"It is our duty to clear away the dross that is left behind," Martha went on, her hollow eyes staring somewhere over Charlotte's shoulder at the wall. "All that corrupts and decays must be cleaned away, buried in the earth, and the words of cleansing said over them. That is our duty, our duty to the dead, and to the living."

"Yes, of course." Charlotte stood up. "Perhaps you should rest? You look feverish to me." She leaned forward and put her hand onto Martha's brow. It was hot and damp. She

281

pushed the stray hair away gently. "You are a little hot. May I fetch you something to drink? A little beef tea perhaps? Or would you prefer water?"

"No, no, thank you," Martha's voice rose and she moved from side to side, pulling the bedclothes.

Charlotte looked at the bed; it was untidy and must be uncomfortable. The pillows had not been rearranged and were dented almost flat in the centre.

"Here," she offered, "let me remake your bed? It must be most difficult to rest with it like that." And without waiting for a reply, because she was anxious to do something positive, and then excuse herself and leave, she leaned forward again and began to make the bed around Martha. She eased her up to tidy the sheet under her, and to puff up the pillows, then put her arms round her and laid her gently back again. Next she moved round the bed quickly and straightened the covers and tucked them in.

"I hope that will be better," she said surveying the bed critically. Martha looked a little flushed now. There were two spots of colour in her cheeks and her eyes were feverish. Charlotte was concerned for her.

"You don't look at all well," she said, screwing up her own face unconsciously. Again she put her hand on Martha's forehead, leaning forward. "Have you any eau de cologne?" she said and looked for it as she spoke. It was on a small table by the window. She crossed to get it, and brought it back, with a handkerchief in the other hand. "Here, let me brush your hair for a little, and then perhaps you will be able to sleep. I always find if I am unwell that sleep is the most effective cure."

Martha said nothing, and Charlotte avoided her eyes, because she could think of no conversation.

Fifteen minutes later Charlotte was in the street again, having left Martha propped up in bed, eyes cavernous, face spotted with colour and beads of sweat on her face. If she were not better tomorrow it was to be hoped the vicar would send for the doctor first thing in the morning.

It was colder outside, and the fog had already gathered quite alarmingly. Her footsteps were muffled on the wet stones and the gaslights were blurred like so many yellow moons. She shivered and drew her cloak more closely round her.

It was a wretched night. Cater Street seemed a mile long. Better to think of something happy, make the distance seem less, and the evening warmer. She smiled immediately as yesterday—and Pitt—returned to her mind. Of course, Papa would not be very pleased at the prospect of her marrying socially beneath her. But then on the other hand, he ought to be somewhat relieved that she had the offer of marrying at all! Especially if she were anything like as awkward as Grandmama believed. Anyway, whatever Papa said, she would marry Mr. Pitt; she had never been surer of anything in her life. The very thought of him lit a warmth inside her enough to dispel the fog and chill of the November dusk.

Could that be footsteps behind her?

Nonsense! And what if it were? It was early yet. There must be other people in Cater Street. She would not be the only one abroad.

Nevertheless, she hurried. It was foolish, and quite irrational to imagine the footsteps had anything to do with her. They were still a little distance behind her, and sounded more like another woman than a man.

She walked a little faster.

And what if it were a man? She knew almost every man who lived in this area; it could only be some friend or acquaintance. Perhaps they would even accompany her home.

The fog was really quite thick now, like wreaths and garlands. Now why should she think of wreaths? Natural enough; Sarah was to be buried in a few days' time. Poor Sarah.

Oh God! Had Sarah been hurrying along the street, like this, with footsteps in the mist behind her, when suddenly—?

Don't be foolish. There was no point in thinking like that!

Would she make a fool of herself if she were to run? And what did it matter if she was a fool?

She quickened her pace yet again. The footsteps were very close now. She still had the basket in her hand. Was there anything in it she could use as a weapon? Glass, a weight? No. Hadn't someone used a heavy pickle jar? Her hands were empty.

At least she would face him—if it *were* him! She would see his face and she would scream, scream as loudly as she could, scream his name so that every house in Cater Street would hear it.

House! Of course, she would go up to the very next house, past this length of garden wall, and bang on the door till someone let her in. What did it matter if they thought she was a hysterical fool? Someone would take her home. Everyone would say she was foolish, but what did that matter?

The footsteps were right behind her. She would not be taken by surprise. She swung round to face him.

He was there in front of her, her own height, no more, but broader, far broader. The gaslight shone on his head as he moved.

Don't be idiotic. It was Martha, only Martha Prebble.

"Martha!" she said in an ecstasy of relief. "What on earth are you doing out of bed? You are ill! Do you need help? Here, let me—"

But Martha's face was twisted into an unrecognizable distortion, her eyes blazing, her lips drawn back. She raised her powerful arms and the gaslight caught on the thin silver of a cheese cutting wire in her hands.

Charlotte was paralyzed.

"You filth!" Martha said between her clenched teeth. There was saliva on her lips and she was shivering. "You creature of the devil! You tempted me with your white arms, and your flesh, but you shan't win! The Lord said, better you should not have been born than that you should have tempted and brought to destruction one of these, my little ones, and brought them to sin. Better you should have a millstone tied round your neck and be put into the sea. I shall destroy you, however many times you keep coming, with your soft words and your touch of sin. I shall not fall! I know how your body burns, I know your secret lusts, but I shall destroy you all, till you leave me alone in peace. Satan shall never win!"

Charlotte only barely understood—some tortured haze of love and loneliness, of twisted hungers, suppressed for long years till they broke loose in violence that could no longer deny itself.

"Oh no! Martha." Her own fear was consumed in pity. "Oh, Martha, you misunderstood, you poor creature—"

But Martha had raised the wire, stretched taut between her hands, and was coming towards her, less than a yard away.

The spell was broken.

Charlotte screamed as loudly as her lungs would permit. She screamed Martha's name over and over again. She swung the basket at her, at her face, hoping to scare her, to blind her temporarily, even to knock her over.

It seemed like eternity, and Martha's hands were already on her arms, gripping her like steel, when the enormous figure of Pitt came out of the fog, and a second later, two constables. They grasped Martha, hauling her off, forcing her arms behind her back.

Charlotte collapsed against the street wall; her knees seemed to have no strength to support her and her hands were tingling with pins and needles.

Pitt bent down to her, taking her face in his hands very gently. "You blazing idiot!" he choked. "What in God's name were you doing going to see her alone? Do you realize if I hadn't gone to see you again today, and they had not told me where you'd come, you'd be lying on this very stone, dead like Sarah and all the others?"

She nodded and gulped, tears beginning to run down her face.

"Yes."

"You—you—" He was lost for a word fierce enough.

Before he could struggle any further there were more heavy feet on the pavement, and a moment later the vicar's solid form materialized out of the fog.

"What's going on?" he demanded. "What's happened? Who's hurt?"

Pitt turned to him, bitter dislike in his face. "No one is hurt, Mr. Prebble—in the way you mean. The injury is a lifelong one, I think."

"I don't know what you mean. Explain yourself! Martha! What on earth are those policemen doing with Martha? She should be at home in bed. She is ill. I found her missing; that's why I came out. You can let her go now. I shall take her home."

"No, Mr. Prebble, you won't. I'm afraid Mrs. Prebble is under arrest, and will remain with us."

"Under arrest!" The vicar's face twitched. "Are you insane? Martha could have done nothing wrong. She is a good woman. If she has been foolish—" His voice hardened a little in irritation, as if he had been trespassed against. "She is not well—"

Pitt stopped him. "No, Mr. Prebble, she is not. She is so ill, she has murdered and disfigured five women."

The vicar stared at him, his face working as he struggled between disbelief and rage. He swivelled to stare at Martha, sagging, eyes wild, saliva on her lips and chin, policemen holding her up. He swung back to Pitt.

"Possessed!" he said furiously. "Sin!" His voice rose. "Oh frailty, thy name is woman."

Pitt's face was frozen with his own anger. "Frail?" he demanded. "Because she cares, and you don't? Because she is capable of love, and you are not? Because she has weaknesses, hungers, and compassion, and you know none of these? Go away, Mr. Prebble, and pray, if you know how!"

The fog swirled in, and he was lost.

"I was sorry for her," Charlotte said softly. She sniffed. "I still am. I didn't even know women could feel like that— about other women. Please don't be angry with me?"

"Oh, Charlotte—I—" He gave up. "Stand up. You'll get cold sitting on the stone. It's wet." He pulled her to her feet, looked at the tears running down her face, then put his arms round her and held onto her as tightly as he could, not bothering to push the hair out of her eyes or to pick up the basket, just clinging to her.

"I know you're sorry for her," he whispered. "Dear God, so am I."

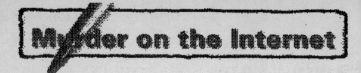